Everybody is talking about *Going Too Far*!

"A brave and powerful story, searingly romantic and daring, yet also full of hilarious moments. Meg's voice will stay in your head long after the intense conclusion."

—R. A. Nelson, author of *Teach Me* and *Breathe My Name*

"Naughty in all the best ways . . . the perfect blend of romance, wit, and rebelliousness. I loved it!"

—Niki Burnham, author of *Royally Jacked* and *Sticky Fingers*

"A thoroughly engrossing look into two people's personal stories of loss and strength, this atypical romance is a powerful one. The two characters grow and change together, and it is mesmerizing to read, whether you're a teenager or adult."

—*Parkersburg News and Sentinel*

"None of us in the office could put the advance copy down."

—*Lipstick*

"Echols is a tremendously talented writer with a real gift for developing relationships between her characters."

—*Romantic Times*

"Powerful without being over-the-top, and reveals universal truths while still being a very personal story. The past haunts us all, and this book addresses wonderfully the hold that it has over us."

—Teen Book Review

"An amazing book that either had me laughing out loud or sitting on the edge of my seat wondering what was going to happen next. . . . *Going Too Far* is a book you will still be thinking about days after you have read it."

—Flamingnet

"What a powerful read. . . ."

—Coffee Time Romance

"The book was definitely a big roller coaster ride . . . a torrent of different emotions. . . ."

—YA Book Realm

"Fast paced, detailed, and addicting. . . ."

—Lauren's Crammed Bookshelf

"*Going Too Far* has everything a teen love story should have."

—Book Loons

"An amazing writer. I can't wait to read more of her books!"

—The Book Girl

"An absolute pleasure to read. I couldn't get enough of it."

—Pop Culture Junkie

"A compelling novel about the choices teens make, the consequences, and uncontrollable things that happen. . . ."

—Ms. Yingling Reads

"I stayed up late and most likely failed two tests simply because I could not physically put this book down. It was way worth it though."

—Addicted to Books

"Deeply rich characters with many layers that need to be peeled back before the reader is exposed to the real Meg, the real John After."

—YA Reads

"Edgy, tense, and seductive, with a very tough-tender, wounded heroine who is trying to figure out who she is, and an intelligent, thoughtful hero who thought he had that all figured out. It mixes humor and sarcastic wit (my favorite) alternating with terribly tender and sneakily seductive scenes."

—Smart Bitches Trashy Books

Don't miss Jennifer Echols's first tale of romantic drama...

GOING TOO FAR

forget you

JENNIFER ECHOLS

GALLERY BOOKS   MTV BOOKS
NEW YORK   LONDON   TORONTO   SYDNEY

Gallery Books
A Division of Simon & Schuster, Inc.
1230 Avenue of the Americas
New York, NY 10020

MTV Music Television and all related titles, logos, and characters are trademarks of
MTV Networks, a division of Viacom International Inc.

First MTV Books/Gallery Books trade paperback edition July 2010

GALLERY BOOKS and colophon are trademarks of Simon & Schuster, Inc.

For information about special discounts for bulk purchases, please contact Simon &
Schuster Special Sales at 1-866-506-1949 or business@simonandschuster.com.

The Simon & Schuster Speakers Bureau can bring authors to your live event. For more
information or to book an event contact the Simon & Schuster Speakers Bureau at
1-866-248-3049 or visit our website at www.simonspeakers.com.

Manufactured in the United States of America

10   9   8

Library of Congress Cataloging-in-Publication Data is available.

ISBN 978-1-4391-7823-2

ISBN 978-1-4391-8047-1 (ebook)

This book is for readers of *Going Too Far* who enjoyed it and told a friend. I appreciate you.

Acknowledgments

Thanks to my editor, Jennifer Heddle; my literary agent, Nicole Kenealy; my friends and family who supported me in writing this book, Marley Gibson, Leanne Cianfrini, and Alan and Tammy Stimson; and as always, my critique partners, Victoria Dahl and Catherine Chant, who will not let me drown.

forget you

1

Every strong swimmer has a story about nearly drowning. This is mine:

Late one June afternoon I was driving home from my summer job at my dad's water park, Slide with Clyde, when my phone rang and Brandon's name flashed on the screen. He knew I never answered my phone while driving. And everybody working at Slide with Clyde today had heard that my dad had gotten Ashley, the twenty-four-year-old human resources manager, pregnant. That meant all my friends knew, because I'd found Brandon a job there and my entire swim team jobs as lifeguards, all seventeen of us—everybody but Doug Fox.

My dad had left work a little early—to tell my mom before she found out from another source, I guessed. So if Brandon wanted to talk to me *now*, it must be important. Maybe it had something to do with my parents.

I parked my vintage Volkswagon Bug in the courtyard outside my house, between my dad's Benz and my mom's eco-friendly hybrid, and cut the engine. The Bug had no air-conditioning. The Florida heat had been bearable while I was damp from swimming and the car was moving. But my bikini had dried underneath my T-shirt and gym shorts. The sun beat down. The heat crept through the open windows like a dangerous animal unafraid of humans and settled on my chest.

I picked up my phone and pushed the button to call Brandon back.

"Zoey," he said.

"Hey, baby. Is something wrong?"

"Everything!" he exclaimed. "You're going to kill me. You know how I was telling you at lunch about Clarissa?"

"Who?" I'd been distracted when I talked to him at lunch. I'd just learned the latest about Ashley.

"Clarissa? The brunette who works at the top of the Tropical Terror Plunge? She's in college. You told me I should ask her out anyway."

"Right." I couldn't believe he'd called me about this. We'd become friends because I was a good listener, and I gave him advice on his girl troubles—but surely he knew this was not the time.

"Well, I asked her out, and she said yes. But then her big sister came to pick her up from work, and *Zoey.* This chick was on *fire.* I don't know how much older she is than me. She might have graduated from college already. That's kind of a reach, even for me. But I could go out with Clarissa this once, give it a few weeks to cool off, then try her sister. What do you think?"

"I think you're jailbait."

He laughed shortly.

In the silence that followed, I heard how mean my comment had sounded. True but mean. I could not have a friendly conversation right now.

"Brandon, can we talk about this later?" I asked. "I'm sitting outside my house, and I think my dad is inside telling my mom about Ashley."

"Oh," Brandon said. He sounded like he'd really forgotten about the rumors at work today. "Are you scared?"

"I'm . . ." I stared at the front door. "No, I'm used to the idea. Everybody's been talking about my dad and Ashley since the park opened in May. I'm more relieved that I don't have to be the one to tell my mom." I held up my hand and admired how perfect and smooth my manicure looked against the ancient steering wheel. "That's awful of me, isn't it?"

"Zoey, you could never be awful."

With that one sentence, Brandon melted my heart all over again. He was a player, but he meant well. Deep down he was truly a sweet person and a good friend, and he knew how to make me feel better.

I ended the call with him and stood up in the courtyard. Sure enough, my parents' voices reached me even here. I'd hurried home so I could support my mom through this. Now I wished I could unhear them screaming betrayal and divorce at each other. I'd sat on the edge of my seat up to the climax of this movie, but now that I knew it wouldn't have a happy ending, I didn't want to see.

Instead of going inside, I scooted around the side of the house, ripping off the T-shirt and shorts over my bikini as I went, kicking off my flip-flops, pulling the ponytail holder out of my hair. I hit the beach running.

A dark storm gathered on the horizon. Usually my beach here along the Florida Panhandle was gentle, only soft white sand underfoot, protected from sharp shells by the sandbars in deeper waters. Today the wind was full of sand, stinging my legs. Way down the beach I could just make out the red flags flying in front of the hotels, warning about strong surf and undertow. The flags were for tourists. They didn't mean me.

I splashed into the ocean. The water was warmer than the air. It soothed me, flowing under my suit and across my limbs. The waves were high with the coming storm, but I was stronger than they were. I swam straight out over them, into deep water, purposefully tiring myself out. If only I could sleep tonight. A long way from the beach, I performed a flip-turn against an imaginary wall and swam back toward shore.

A wave crashed over my head, taking me by surprise, forcing salt water into my mouth, pushing me down. Cold jets curled around my ankles and towed me along. My knee skidded across the bare sandy bottom of the ocean.

I kicked toward the surface—a few massive kicks that took all my strength. If I reached the surface and stayed there, I could skim along the tops of the waves, stroking parallel to the beach until I escaped the current that wanted to drag me under and out.

I popped into the cold air. Just as I sucked in a breath, another wave plunged me under. In the roar I coughed water and strained against the urge to breathe more in. I tumbled along the bottom.

With strength I didn't know I had left, I pushed off the bottom, propelling myself to the surface. I would glide through the water, pop into the air again, take that breath I'd missed.

The surface wasn't where I thought it would be. I couldn't fight the urge to breathe the ocean. That was when I realized I was going to die.

The ocean tossed me into the air like trash.

I breathed deep and long, already paddling before I hit the water. I knew the current would take me again soon. I didn't waste my breath screaming. The beach was empty. No lifeguards patrolled this private section. Signs warned SWIM AT OWN RISK. Even if someone had come to my rescue, it would have been another foolish swimmer without a float. Both of us would have gone under, and it would have been my fault. I was the lifeguard.

I swam until I couldn't swim anymore. Then I kept swimming.

Finally I escaped the current, stood upright on the bottom, waded to the shore, collapsed on the beach just as the storm broke over me. The rain beat me into the sand and seaweed.

I lay there for a long time, eyes squeezed shut against the raindrops, breathing. It was over. I thought only of myself, so thankful to be alive. I walked home in the cold rain.

But three months later, when my mom attempted suicide, I would look back on that afternoon as a warning. On coming home from work and hearing my parents argue, instead of escaping into the water like a troubled teen, I should have stayed and supported my mom. If I'd taken better care of her when she needed me, I could have prevented everything.

A TINY CHIP HAD APPEARED IN the pink polish at the tip of my pointer fingernail, where it was most noticeable. I rubbed the pad of my thumb across it, hoping no one would see it before I could fix it. My mom had always stressed to me that outward appearances were important. Strong personalities would challenge you no matter what, but you could repel the weaker people who might take a swipe at you by presenting yourself as moneyed, stylish, organized, together.

From across the emergency room waiting area, I heard a familiar voice, though muffled—a voice from school. I looked up from my fingernail. Doug Fox stood in the vestibule, framed by the black night outside.

Doug was hot, with black hair that never streaked in the chlorine and salt and sun, and eyes the strangest light green-blue, exactly the color of the ocean here. They were mesmerizing, framed by long black lashes in his tanned face. I could see why his eyes were famous among the girls at my high school. A boy with an ego as big as Doug's didn't deserve eyes like that.

I had a lot of classes with him this year. He was on the

varsity swim team with me. And he hated me. He was the last person I wanted to see right now, when the doctors had told me my mom would live, but I didn't know what would happen next.

Instinctively I ducked my head—which would do me no good if he looked in my direction. My hair wouldn't drape forward to cover my face. It was still pulled back in the ponytail I'd worn home from work a few hours ago, when I'd walked into the eerily quiet apartment I shared with my mom and found her. Anyway, Doug and I had known each other forever. He would recognize me instantly. My hair in my face would not save me.

But he wasn't looking at me. He talked with the policeman who'd responded first to my 911 call, who'd stood awkwardly in the apartment while I sat on my mom's bed and held my mom's hand until the ambulance came, and who had not abandoned me. My dad had been half an hour away in Destin, shopping the Labor Day sales for baby furniture with Ashley. He'd arrived only fifteen minutes ago and had burst through the hospital doors in front of me, into mysterious corridors that were off-limits to a minor like me. All this time, the policeman had sat with me in the empty waiting room. Or, not *with* me, but across from me. Not close enough to converse with me or comfort me like a friend, but in the vicinity like a protector. Around.

Now he stood in the vestibule with Doug. Doug handed him a bag printed with the name of a local seafood restaurant:

Jamaica Joe's. And I realized in a rush that the policeman was Doug's older brother, Officer Fox, equally celebrated by the girls in my school for his appropriate name. Doug had brought his brother dinner because his brother had stayed with me long enough to miss a meal.

They spoke with their heads together, and now Doug *did* look up at me. His brother was telling him what my mom had done.

I looked away again. The doors into the emergency room were white. The walls of the waiting area were white. The floor was square white tiles with gray specks.

I couldn't stand it. I looked over at the vestibule. The night was black, Officer Fox was dark in his uniform, and Doug shook his black hair out of his green eyes, piercing even at this distance. He said something to his brother and took a step toward me.

Oh God, weren't things bad enough without Doug here? I'd thought the shock of finding my mom had drained the life out of me for years to come. But my heart still worked, pounding painfully in my chest in anticipation of what Doug would say to make things worse.

The emergency room doors flew open and banged against the walls before folding shut again. My dad stalked toward me, muscular and fit at forty-seven, his handsome features set in fury. I shrank back into the vinyl seat, afraid he was angry at me.

But maybe he was furious at the world for allowing his ex-wife to sink to this low—or better yet, furious with himself. He had realized on the drive here from the baby superstore that he had failed us. Now he would come to our rescue. Yes, there was the matter of Ashley being four months' pregnant with his baby, but our family would get past that and he would come back to my mom.

He lowered himself into the seat next to mine. His brow was furrowed in anger, but as he opened his thin lips, I was sure he would utter everything I'd longed all summer to hear.

"You keep this to yourself," he snarled.

I blinked at him. My brain rushed through scenarios, painting him as the hero, and finally gave up. There was no way he could be our hero when his first words to me were a command to keep things quiet. I stammered, "Keep . . . How . . . ?"

"They're taking her to the loony bin in Fort Walton," he interrupted me. "With any luck they'll dope her up, and she'll be back at work in six weeks. You want to spread it around town that she's nuts and ruin her career, go right ahead."

I tried to hear pain in his voice, sorrow at what my mom had done, remorse for the hand he'd had in driving her to this point. Emotions like these must be behind his unsympathetic words.

But all I heard was anger. Embarrassment that his friends and business partners and employees might dish about him and his tabloid-worthy private life. Fear that my mom would lose her job and he'd have to share the proceeds of his water park with two families instead of one.

"Don't even tell those little twins, you understand me?" He leaned forward and looked straight into my eyes as he said this. It was the closest his body had come to my body since he arrived. He would not hug me. He would only invade my personal space to emphasize that I'd better not spill this secret to my best friends.

Without waiting for my answer, he stood. "Don't move," he barked, not looking at me. I assumed he meant me because I was the only other person in the room. He was already walking toward the vestibule.

Oh God, oh God. He might threaten Officer Fox into promising silence, but he had no idea who Doug was, or how little Doug cared about anybody. There was no threat my dad could make to Doug that would shut Doug up if he thought spreading the news about my mother would hurt me. Doug would think he was ruining my life, but really he would be ruining my mother's—because even if she started to recover from her mental illness, she wouldn't recover much if she lost her job and the community's respect.

I saw all this unfolding in front of me as my dad swung open the glass door to the vestibule and leaned into Officer Fox's personal space, and there wasn't a thing I could do to stop it from happening. Doug's green eyes widened as my dad growled at Officer Fox. I couldn't make out all of what my dad was saying, but when *you can kiss your job good-bye* floated to me through the glass, I turned away from the black rectangle of night. I stared at the white doors to the emergency room.

My thumb found the chip in my fingernail polish and rubbed back and forth across it. I didn't need to see it to know it was there.

The vestibule door squealed open. "Zoey," my dad called. "Let's go." He stood alone at the threshold to the darkness. He must have chased Doug and Officer Fox away.

I gestured toward the emergency room doors. I thought he would know what I meant by this. When he raised his eyebrows in expectation, I realized I would have to explain even this to him: that I didn't want to leave her. I opened my mouth and had no words for any of it.

"They won't let you see her anyway," he said. "The loony bin won't let you see her either. They say it's to protect you from her, and to protect her from you. To remove her from the environment. They'll let her call you when she's ready to see you."

He was saying what I'd been thinking. I'd been blaming myself and hoping that self-blame was natural in these circumstances but ultimately silly. He was telling me it was not silly. Even the mental hospital thought it was my fault that my mother had done this. I still didn't want to believe any of it, but I felt myself falling down that slope without anything to grab to save myself, except this:

I whispered, "When I first got here, they told me maybe I could talk to the hospital psychologist about what happened?"

"They don't need you to diagnose your mother," my dad grumbled.

"I mean"—I swallowed—"for me? To talk about me?"

He huffed out a sigh and leaned one shoulder against the glass wall of the vestibule. "So now you're crazy too? You're not going to a psycho-anything. You see how much good it did your mother. They'll just give you the drugs that you can OD on later. There's a reason we call them *shrinks*. Let's go."

I stood, only then realizing how sore my back was and how long I must have been sitting in that seat, staring at the closed emergency room doors. I followed my dad through the vestibule and into the night.

We didn't have far to walk. He had parked his Benz in a handicapped space just outside the door. The backseat was filled with large boxes with laughing babies on the labels. A high chair, a bouncing swing. I slid into the passenger seat and lost myself in an argument inside my own head.

I did not want to believe my dad was right. My mom had not OD'd on medicine a shrink had given her. She had OD'd on sleeping pills her regular doctor had given her. She had never gone to a shrink, probably because of my dad's opinion of them. I had overheard him saying something like this to her during one of their fights last spring.

I could have pointed this out to him, but he would not have listened to me, any more than he had listened to her. And though normally I might have obsessed about this point of contention and reviewed it over and over, trying to find a way to present it to him that he would understand and accept, tonight it slipped away from me as if captured by the undertow.

In my mind I was back in my mother's bedroom at our

apartment, trying to fix everything. I was the lifeguard, but I couldn't give her mouth-to-mouth because she was still breathing, and I couldn't give her CPR because her heart was still beating, faintly. What could I do to help? When the paramedics arrived, I could tell them exactly what she'd taken. Holding my cell phone to my ear with one hand because the 911 dispatcher had ordered me not to hang up, I walked to the bathroom and found her prescription bottle in the trash. Empty.

"Aren't you going in?" my dad asked.

I looked over at him in the driver's seat. He thumbed through the messages on his phone. He'd parked the Benz in front of the apartment, between my mother's hybrid and my battered Bug. He'd just bought Ashley a convertible Beamer. I drove this ancient Bug because he made me use my own money from working at Slide with Clyde for my car, insurance, and gas. He'd told me before that growing up a spoiled brat was what was wrong with my mom.

"Come to think of it," he said, still scrolling, "I'll have to help you. You need to get everything. Even after she's released, the judge won't let you live with her. You might not be back here for a while." Behind us, the trunk popped open to receive all my belongings. He stepped out of the Benz.

I followed him into the parking lot. The apartment building was the nicest one in town, which wasn't saying a lot. Everyone who could afford a house lived in one, which left the apartments for the transients. Mature palms and palmettos softened the lines of the weathered wooden building, but a huge air-conditioning unit filled the late summer night with its drone, and the scent of the community garbage Dumpster wafted from behind a high fence.

My dad noticed the smell too, nostrils flared in distaste as he stood waiting for me at the front of the car. I wondered why he didn't go ahead to the apartment. Then I remembered he didn't have a key. I pulled my key chain from my pocket. Still, he didn't move. He didn't know which apartment was mine, after I'd lived here for three months.

An instant of anger at him propelled me forward, onto the sidewalk. I inserted the key into my lock. But now I had to turn the key. Now I had to go in.

My dad was watching me. I couldn't let him see me hesitate. That would make things worse on my mom, to admit to my dad that what she'd done made her less of a person and worthy of his disdain. I shoved inside and flicked on the light.

At least the apartment was extremely clean, the way I'd left it. It didn't *look* like an insane person lived here. But viewing it through my dad's eyes, the apartment building's standard-issue furniture made it look like she had sunk low. I didn't want him venturing farther inside, judging.

I faced him. "Why don't you watch TV while you wait? I won't be long. Can I get you something to drink?"

He grunted and stepped outside, reaching into his pocket for his cigarettes—a strange habit he'd taken up last May when the water park opened for the season and he hired Ashley.

I watched him until the door closed behind him, then

dashed through the apartment, double-checking that it was neat. As I passed back and forth in front of my mother's desk in the living room, her suicide note stared up at me, the most obvious crazy item: *Zoey, I just couldn't see doing it all another day. I love you. Mom.* If I put it in the desk drawer, I would be putting my mom away. I settled for squaring the notepaper perfectly against the corner of the desk. Again.

In the kitchen I peered into the refrigerator. I would take anything perishable to the Dumpster so my mom wouldn't have a mess to clean up when she came back. I was surprised to find no fruit, no milk. My mom had cleaned it out already.

In the bathroom I selected all my toiletries, leaving my mom's. In my bedroom I grabbed armfuls of clothing from my closet and my dresser and shoved them into my suitcases. At first I went for the summer clothes only. Then I pulled out a light jacket in case I was still living with my dad when the nights got cool. As I reached the sweater box under my bed, I stared at the cotton and cashmere, heartbeat accelerating into panic, wondering just how long my mom would be gone, and what she would do in the loony bin all that time, and what they would do to her, and whether they would ever let her out, and whether a judge really would keep me from living with her my entire last year of high school.

The smell of smoke startled me. I hoped my dad wasn't smoking in the apartment, because my mom was allergic. I shoved the sweater box back under my bed, zipped my suitcases, and hauled them into the den.

The apartment door was wide open, letting the air-conditioning out, making room for the warm night air my dad had just smoked. He stood over my mom's desk, reading her note with his nostrils flared again.

"I'm ready." I left one suitcase for him and wheeled the other past him and out the door, hoping to distract him from what he'd already seen. He followed me. I pulled the door shut behind me and locked it. When I turned around, he held his hand out.

I looked up at him, puzzled. "The key? Why?"

"Because you're a teenager," he said, "and I'm your father."

I didn't like the finality of it, or the implication that I was a wild child who couldn't be trusted with the key to an empty apartment. But a part of me was grateful my dad was taking charge. I wiggled the key off the ring and held it out to him. He didn't notice. He was looking at the screen on his phone.

"Dad."

He pocketed my key but kept his phone in his hand as he wheeled my suitcase around to the open trunk of the Benz. After hefting both suitcases inside and slamming the trunk, he opened the driver's door. He nodded toward my Bug. "You're bringing your car, right? I'll see you at home."

Home. He meant the house on the beach. I hadn't been back there since my mom and I had left. He had joint custody of me, but I figured we saw enough of each other every day at work. Besides, Ashley had gleefully warned me that if I ever did want to visit, the house was a mess. She was having the kitchen remodeled.

I did not want to follow my dad back there right now. I pictured myself in my old bedroom, staring out the window at the ocean I couldn't see in the black night, wondering what was happening to my mom. I had stared at white emergency room doors for hours tonight. Panic at what she had done rushed through me like pain to my numb fingertips when I warmed them inside on a rare cold winter day. I could not sit in that bedroom tonight, wincing at my heavy heartbeat. There was just so much I could take.

"Actually," I said, "if you don't want anyone in town to know about Mom, there's a beach party I need to go to tonight, the last blowout of the year. If I'm not there, my friends will want to know why." The Slide with Clyde employees had thrown beach parties all summer. Tonight's party was special because today, Labor Day, had been our last day of work. Slide with Clyde had closed for the season. This much was true.

It was not true that my friends expected me at the party. They expected me to stay home with my mom. Some days when I came home from work, she seemed energetic as ever. Better, even. But most days she hardly ate dinner, and she went to bed early. In the last couple of weeks she'd complained that she couldn't sleep. I'd suggested that she didn't need twelve hours. Her response was to ask for those sleeping pills from her doctor. Now I wondered whether she'd had suicide in mind all along. I had worried about her all summer, so I'd stayed home from my friends' parties, not that it had done any good.

Tonight I would go.

My dad nodded absently, sinking into the driver's seat of the Benz.

"I may be out late," I warned him. "Is that okay? I know I have school tomorrow—"

He closed the door of the Benz and started the engine, already thinking of someone else.

2

My friends' beach parties were as starlit and romantic as the ones on TV and in movies, except there was no bonfire. Fires and bright lights weren't allowed on the beach because they disoriented the endangered sea turtles. Dozens of teenagers invaded the city beach park, guzzling beer in the sand and heavy-petting in the parking lot, but as long as they didn't mess with the turtles, nobody seemed to care.

I'd popped in and out of a few of these with my friends Keke and Lila when we were younger and didn't dare stay long at a party full of seniors. Now we were the seniors. I parked the Bug in the crowded lot near Keke and Lila's rusty Datsun and Brandon's laughably large 1980s Buick. I was curious, but I tried not to peer through a few steamed-up windows in familiar cars. Then I crossed the wooden bridge over the scrub and sand dunes to the beach.

Ours was not the only party. Circles of teenagers stood in the sand or sat on towels in the darkness, sipping beer. I recognized the Slide with Clyde party by Keke and Lila's laughter cackling above the roar of the ocean and the wails of a boy band on a radio. I kicked off my flip-flops at the foot of the wooden stairs, crossed the sand glowing white in the starlight, waded into the surf, and put one hand on each of their backs.

They turned around with wide eyes. "Zoey!" they both squealed at once as they rushed me, splashing water up on my shorts. They both jumped up and down and hugged me too but Lila stopped soon and gave me some air, whereas Keke did not let go until I said, "Okay," and pressed her shoulders to stop the bouncing. It was clear to me which one was drinking tonight and which was the designated driver. They were twins—not identical, but they might as well have been, the way they finished each other's sentences. They did look similar, both petite with bright red hair, but from there they diverged.

Keke put on the first clothes she found on the bedroom floor, whether they were hers or Lila's, dirty or clean. I had seen her do it. Lila handled the personal upkeep better, though she obsessed about it until she looked like a parody of a girl. Tonight her hair was hot-rolled and pinned and overfixed for a windy beach party. I had told them they both looked so extreme because they were trying to differentiate themselves from each other. If they'd relaxed and settled for the happy medium, even if that meant looking alike, boys would have asked them out more. They did not listen to me. If there had been one of them, they might have taken me seriously, but it was hard to give unsolicited advice to two people at once, because they could drown you out with protests. They told me they could never be as pretty as me, so my advice meant nothing. I started to explain that looking like I did took work, and my mother had taught me this in turn—but they shut me down.

Tonight it was impossible to tell there had ever been any tension or unwanted advice between us. "I can't believe you're here!" Keke squealed. "It took the whole summer, but for once the whole swim team is at the Slide with Clyde party!"

She gestured to the circle standing behind her—Stephanie Wetzel and the other three junior girls on the team, plus lots of boys. They all waved at me and called, "Zoey's here!"

"Wait," Keke said. "We gained you, but we lost—"

A distant boat horn cut her off. The lights of a fishing boat and their reflections skimmed parallel to each other across the blackness of the ocean and the sky.

"Dooooooug!" the other swim team boys cheered and clapped from the darkness.

"Awww," Lila said, "Doug's with us in spirit."

"Is that really Doug?" I asked. Lost in thoughts of my mom, I'd almost forgotten seeing him an hour and a half ago at the emergency room. Now that anxiety came swirling back. At least if he was stuck on his dad's fishing boat, he wouldn't be showing up here tonight.

"Yep," Lila said. "He honks every time he misses a party for one of his dad's night charters."

"He was here earlier, though," Keke said, "searching for you,

Zoey." She poked me on the breastbone. "Why does Doug hate you so much?"

I took a sharp sniff of ocean air. I'd known Doug wouldn't miss an opportunity for revenge on me.

"Doug doesn't hate her," Lila reprimanded Keke. "Don't freak her out." She turned to me. "Nobody hates you, Zoey. Who could hate you? You're so beautiful."

"And blond," Keke offered.

"And so sweet to all of us." Lila pursed her lips and reached up to pinch my cheek like I was a baby. "Besides, Doug hates everybody." Lila was trying to smooth over what Keke had stirred up.

Keke, as the tipsy one, was also the one who pressed the issue. "No, he stormed in here all dramatic and upset," Keke insisted. "There must be something up between the two of you. What is it?"

"Doug storms everywhere," Lila told Keke, "and he's always dramatic and upset."

I hoped Lila's explanation would satisfy Keke. Maybe I could change the subject to our chances at the swim meet next Saturday.

Then Gabriel splashed past us on his way to the beer stash against the dunes. "Zoooey!" He wrapped me in an alcoholic bear hug. "Doug was here looking for you earlier. What's up between you two?"

"Nothing!" we three girls said simultaneously.

"Ooooookay." Gabriel gave each of us a look that said he

did not believe us, but he was so drunk that he would not re-member this conversation in the morning. Then he let me go and splashed away.

The way the twins were watching me, I knew I wasn't get-ting out of this now without a better explanation.

In my mind I was back in my mother's bedroom, trying to fix everything. With two fingers I brushed her blond hair away from her closed eyes so she'd look better to the paramedics when they arrived.

I struggled out of those dark thoughts and back to the real-ity of the starlit beach, the sound of the ocean, and a shadowy Keke and Lila expecting answers. Of course I had told them my mom was having trouble dealing with the divorce, and I didn't want to leave her alone during the summer nights to come to the Slide with Clyde parties. I couldn't divulge more than this to them. My dad had warned me at the emergency room not to tell "those little twins" what my mother had done, and his instincts had been right. I loved Keke and Lila, but they were not discreet.

Luckily I had secrets to divulge that wouldn't touch on Doug seeing me at the emergency room. Doug had a lot of rea-sons to hate me. I had not wanted to admit this, even to them, because employee matters at Slide with Clyde were supposed to be private. But they were forcing my hand here, and keeping my mother's secret was more important than keeping Doug's. "He sent in an application for Slide with Clyde along with the rest of the swim team last May, and I told Ashley not to call him in because he's been to juvie. Those records are sealed, so she would have had no way of knowing without me telling her. He probably figured that out when everybody got hired but him."

Doug had spent part of ninth grade in juvie. People in our town did not go to juvie. I'd never heard of anyone else who'd been there. I didn't even know where juvie was. I would have suspected it didn't exist except I remembered when Doug missed two weeks of school to go there. Ever since, he was as likely to be in the principal's office as he was to be in class.

"What did you rat him out to Ashley for?" Lila asked. "He could have saved that three-hundred-pound man drowning in the wave pool instead of me."

Keke nodded. "And we could have stared at him shirtless all summer. God, those abs!"

I did not want to think about staring at Doug all summer. And I did not want to talk about this anymore. I turned toward the horizon, the black sky barely discernible from the black ocean, where Doug's fishing boat had disappeared.

But I could see out the corner of my eye that Keke and Lila both watched me, waiting for my answer as to why I had not wanted to give all of us the opportunity to stare at Doug's taut, tanned swimmer's chest all day every day for three summer months. Finally I stated the obvious, which logically should have overridden even teenage girl-lust: "He went to juvie. He's a criminal. I thought I should warn my family's business against employing a criminal."

"What did you think he was going to do," Keke asked, "embezzle funds? Did he go to juvie for embezzlement?"

"What *did* he go to juvie for?" Lila asked. "He was only in the ninth grade. What could he possibly have done?"

They were making me feel more and more sheepish. I wished I hadn't told them this after all. I wished I hadn't come to the party. "Look," I defended myself, "it wasn't the only job in town. I didn't go all over town and prevent him from getting a job anywhere."

"Yeah, but the job at Slide with Clyde was his only chance to get away from his dad this summer," Lila said, waving toward the spot we all gazed at now, where Doug was helping gung-ho tourists hold the line on big game fish beyond the horizon.

"I heard that from the guys on the swim team," she said. "Lifeguard jobs were the only jobs a teenager could get that paid more than his dad's fishing biz, and the pools around town were hiring college kids as lifeguards. It was Slide with Clyde or nothing for Doug."

"What was so bad about working with his dad?" I asked.

We all looked at each other, feet sinking in the sand underwater. A wave knocked Keke off balance and she braced herself against Lila, and still we were quiet. Possibly they were thinking what I was thinking: could Doug's situation with his dad be worse than mine?

I broke the silence. "Okay. For years there has been this weird tension between Doug and me because he asked me to homecoming in ninth grade, right before he went to juvie."

"He *did?*" Keke gasped.

"And you broke up with him because of that?" Lila asked, outraged.

"Of course not," I said. "He was just gone." I flicked my fingers in the air to show that he'd disappeared. "One day he was in junior varsity swim practice with me, hanging on to the side of the pool and asking if I'd go to homecoming with him. The next Monday he was gone. Around the middle of the week somebody had heard he was in juvie. By the time he came back to school a couple of weeks later, homecoming was over."

"He couldn't get a furlough to go to homecoming with you?" Keke asked.

"Not funny!" Lila told her.

"He never even mentioned it to me again," I said. "I went to homecoming with somebody else, and Doug came back from juvie angry at me. Or maybe he was angry at the world, but it felt like me. Y'all don't remember this, but before juvie, Doug wasn't prickly like he is now. Juvie made him prickly."

"I always thought his mother dying made him prickly," Lila said.

I had not forgotten Doug's mother had died in a car accident when we were in eighth grade. It was part of what kept girls staring at him longingly after he snapped at them. With tragedy in his past, they thought he must be vulnerable.

And come to think of it . . . maybe despite all the reasons Doug had to dislike me, he would honor my father's demand that he keep to himself what my mother had done, because he empathized with me. Perhaps I'd misread him at the emergency room—not surprising, considering my state of mind. When he'd started toward me, he hadn't intended to make a snide comment. He'd understood. This interpretation didn't jive with the way Doug had been acting for the past few years. But it did make sense when I thought of him in ninth grade, hanging onto the cement wall in the lane next to me during junior varsity swim practice, making a joke about our awful uniform bathing suits emblazoned with the ugliest dog mascot either of us had ever seen, and asking me to homecoming. His voice was soft and his smile was kind.

"No," I told Keke, "he wasn't prickly before juvie."

"There's something to this," Keke told Lila. "Doug rolls his eyes at everybody, but he has a special eye-roll whenever Zoey opens her mouth. Like this."

Her imitation was shockingly accurate. I laughed and slapped my hand over my mouth in horror at the same time.

"That is so true!" Lila exclaimed. "But I thought he did that because Zoey is cute." She turned to me. "Doug doesn't do cute."

Lila was right. Doug sympathizing with me rather than taking the opportunity to bring the rich girl down—that was wishful thinking, and no genie had granted me any wishes. I would have used them on something else.

"I wonder why he came looking for me here," I mused. "If he's come to these parties all summer, he knows I haven't been to one."

"He definitely thought you would be here." Lila shrugged. "Why *are* you here? How's your mom?"

"My mom," I said slowly, "is good for the rest of the night." In my mind I was back in her bedroom again. I straightened the covers on her bed and tucked her in more tightly, because she looked cold.

I'd come to the party to escape thoughts like this. Now that they'd chased me here, I might as well be home with my dad and Ashley. I felt like I was about to jump out of my skin, and I couldn't *stand* it.

"Zoey."

We jerked our heads toward the beach at the sound of a boy's voice, and all three of us relaxed our shoulders when we saw it wasn't Doug.

It was Brandon. One of the Slide with Clyde employees who wasn't on the swim team, he was the star of our school's football team and looked it, big, blond, and clean-cut like a cartoon superhero. He wasn't a lifeguard either. He sold ice cream and lifted things that were heavy. I'd asked him about this a few times because lifeguards got paid more than the workers at the concession stands. I could have gotten him promoted. He always brushed me off with a joke about staying out of the sun and preserving his complexion.

His lungs were another story. He cupped both hands around his cigarette to take a puff and keep it lit in the wind off the surf. Exhaling smoke, he said, "I heard you were here. I have to talk to you."

"Come into the water." Playfully I kicked a little splash at him.

"Come out of the water," he called. "I have to talk to you alone."

Lila leaned in and whispered, "Do you want us to distract him? He's had a lot of beer, and he's dangerous with that cigarette. He might light you on fire."

"Thanks, but it's okay," I whispered back. I was sure he needed solace about his latest conquest gone sour—and if I could help him, at least I had helped *someone* tonight.

I waded out of the ocean with my arms out for him. "Sure," I told him as I hugged him in greeting. "We can talk alone. Let's go to . . ."

I glanced toward the water. I felt better just touching it. Keke, Lila, and the rest of the swim team had headed up the beach, toward the beer. Brandon and I could talk in the water now and have the ocean to ourselves.

His muscled arm curved around my waist.

I looked up at him. He gazed down at me earnestly, his too-handsome comic-book hero features softened by the starlight.

His hand stroked my back. I did not think he was touching me in a flirtatious way. I thought he was having a balance problem and teetering a bit.

But I *wanted* him to flirt with me. He was a muscle-bound football player and a playboy, but I knew him to be a softie, and in that dark moment I wanted more. This was crazy. I felt tingles of attraction for Brandon all the time. Who wouldn't? But I never acted on them. This time the thoughts of my mother and the pressure from Doug seemed to push me out of the surf and against Brandon's broad chest. I had come to this party desperately needing something I couldn't name. Now I knew what it was.

I stroked my hand across his. "Could we go to your Buick?"

I HAD DATED A LOT OF nice boys in the past few years. I'd never gotten serious with anyone, and that had been okay with me. I was only seventeen. I was willing to wait for the good stuff.

But something happened to me in June when my dad told my mom about Ashley. I couldn't stop thinking about sex, my dad having sex, Ashley having sex, everyone at Slide with Clyde having sex, everyone having sex except my mom and me.

You might think my job as a lifeguard was sexy. But I spent most of my time on a platform with sunglasses on and a whistle in my mouth, poised to prevent tragedy. The tourists accepted me as part of the scenery, like the cement mountains spewing waterfalls piped in from hoses, or the stacked crates with labels I'd stenciled another summer: BANANAS BY THE BUNCH and DANGER: ANACONDA!

The tourists didn't notice me, so I observed them unabashedly. While the little kids splashed in the fountains and peed in the pools, their parents eyed each other and spread each other with oil. No question what they did in the hotel room after Junior went to sleep.

The teenage tourists didn't have a place to do it. Unlike the locals, they didn't know about the city beach for parking. But it was clear what they wanted. The dance clubs in Panama City looked like Sunday school compared to what Slide with Clyde brought out in people. A few piña coladas bought by college kids and slipped to underage teenagers for fun. Cool rushing water. Hot bare skin and lots of it. Whether you got any or not, Slide with Clyde sold sex.

The employees felt it. And to hear them talk, most of them got it at their beach parties every weekend, the ones I missed because I stayed home with my mom. I was concerned for my friends. Or feeling left out. Or very angry at my dad for impregnating the human resources manager while my mom slept longer and longer every day and slowly ground to a halt. The next time my dad sent me to the wholesale club for paper towels and soda straws for Slide with Clyde, I also bought the world's largest box of condoms. My dad never checked the receipt anyway. He just wanted me to show up with the toilet paper and the pickle relish. I gave condoms out to anyone who asked. I also gave condoms to people who didn't ask. If I heard rumors about them, I slipped condoms through the vents in their lockers in the break room.

Brandon found me poking a packet into his locker one afternoon. I was mortified. We were friends at school and I'd gotten him the job, but I didn't know him well enough to stuff his locker with condoms. He was really nice about it, though. He asked me for advice about the chick he was doing. I wanted to help him. And that's how we became buddies.

For the rest of the summer, chicks winked at me and said, "*Yeah*, you and Brandon are just *friends*," meaning, *How could you be just friends with a piece of meat like that?* But we honestly were. He came to me for advice about a new girlfriend every week.

Girls fell all over Brandon. Threw themselves at him. It rained girls through the sunroof of his Buick. A lot of his complaints had to do with girls he went out with getting mad at him about the other girls he went out with. I didn't want a boyfriend like that. And he didn't want a girlfriend like me. All the boys at school knew I was just Zoey, everybody's friend, and I didn't put out.

Until now. "Just a sec," I said as we passed my Bug on our stroll through the parking lot. "Let me get something out of my car." While he finished another cigarette, I unlocked my trunk and leaned into it for the king-size box of condoms. I pulled one out and poked it into my pocket, hoping Brandon wouldn't notice. Not yet. I turned around.

He stared at my pocket. Then he looked straight at me with blue eyes I would have sworn were innocent as a baby's if I hadn't known him so well. He seemed to see me with perfect clarity.

He didn't say a word about it, though. He just turned toward his Buick again and asked as we walked, "You know that girl Phoebe who does the airbrush tattoos at Slide with Clyde?" He unlocked the passenger door of the Buick and pushed it open a little for me. We couldn't open it wide because it was huge and would ding the car in the next space. Carefully I squeezed inside and closed the door behind me.

Brandon sat in the driver's side, still talking. I suspected he'd been talking outside the car too, and hadn't noticed I wasn't there to listen. "—down at the beach right now with her cousin from Destin who is *hot*, Zoey, and somehow I have to find a way into that without scaring both of them off." He put his elbow on the steering wheel and his chin in his hand, staring into space with his brow down, perplexed.

When I'd first discussed such matters with Brandon, I'd thought he was kidding. No real person could take problems like this seriously. But Brandon did, and once you realized this about him, it was easy to like him. He had no malice. He just loved girls, and sex.

I leaned back against the door and pointed my knees toward him. "Can I ask you something?"

"I know, I know," he said. "Why can't I hit on Phoebe and be satisfied with that, instead of chasing her cousin? Why do I always want the one I can't have? I don't know, Zoey. If I knew, I wouldn't need you."

"You wouldn't?" I slid my hand onto his bare thigh—the hand without the chip in the fingernail polish.

A lot of boys would have asked me what I thought I was doing. Brandon did not. Either he knew exactly what I was doing, or he was easy. That's why he got as many girls as he did. I wanted to be easy for once.

"That's not what I was going to ask you." I smoothed my hand down the crisp blond hairs on his tanned leg. "Why haven't we hooked up?"

He laughed. "Because I want to keep my job?"

"My dad doesn't care." It hurt to say this. I kept smiling.

Brandon shrugged. "I only see you at work. You've hardly come out with us a single time all summer."

"I'm here now," I said.

His brow furrowed. I was busted. He knew there was something wrong with me, and he would refuse to help me make it worse, some line like that.

But no. Rising from the steering wheel and scooting closer across the wide seat, he reached behind my head and pulled his fingers along the length of a lock of my hair. "I don't know, Zoey. I guess I figured you'd say no. You're such a nice girl." He leaned in and kissed me.

My body was there in the car with him, making out with him. My mind raced through a lifetime of warnings about sex. Before this night I'd assumed I wouldn't be doing it for a while. I had too much to look forward to—graduation, college, a job, travel. I couldn't risk losing it all to satisfy my raging hormones.

But as he pulled my shorts down, these lessons didn't make sense to me anymore. Where was the risk? We were only doing it. It was amazingly easy. His fingers found the condom in my pocket and pulled it out. I kept kissing his neck as plastic crinkled, and then he scooted me down until I lay on the long seat.

He paused at the edge of me, not pushing in but maintaining pressure there, threatening. I was putting up barriers, even now, that were hard for him to get past. I tried to relax for him. I visualized opening for him, letting him into me.

Something inside me screamed *Noooooo, this is crazy.* Something else inside me reached up with one hand to cover my mouth. It held me down so I couldn't escape until the damage was done. Brandon slid himself all the way inside me, the point of no return, so swiftly and so deep that I gasped. I felt a little sick to my stomach, and my arms had gone tingly and cold, like I had some strange disease.

"That's it," he whispered, pushing farther in.

I hadn't realized how far in he could go, but it was best to trust him since he'd done this before. I let him push into me, pull out, push in again, until he found a rhythm, and the sex turned into every pornographic snippet I'd ever walked in on boys viewing on the computer in the break room at Slide with Clyde. This was familiar. It wasn't comfortable, but at least I recognized it. I was doing what everybody else had already done, which made me normal. My arms still tingled, but my whole body flashed from cold to hot now, and I understood the animal nature of it, doing it to reproduce. Brandon was the biggest, best example of my species, and I felt an animal pride in having caught him.

* * *

Later, holding hands, we crossed the bridge over the sand dunes and sat on the wooden stairs, looking out over the party. This was perfect. We were part of the party but apart from it, above it, because of what we'd just shared.

Then he asked, "You want a beer?"

The question struck me as funny. I never drank. I was afraid of losing control that way. All my friends knew this about me, except the one I'd just lost my virginity to.

"Why're you laughing?" he slurred. "I take that as a yes?"

"No thanks. Not while I'm in training." I put my hand on my belly and phrased my refusal in terms Brandon would accept. As an athlete, he would understand abstaining for the sake of training, even if it would never occur to him to abstain himself.

"Mind if I get one?" he asked, already pushing up to standing, steadying himself with one hand on my shoulder. If he'd been sober, he would have known he was putting enough weight on me to hurt me.

I didn't mind. I grinned through it. "I'll be waiting." I watched him walk across the sand, into the shadows toward the beer stash against the sand dunes, staggering only a little.

A few seconds later a silhouette moved back toward me. That was fast. But the silhouette was too small to be Brandon, and as it moved closer I recognized the outline of girly curls. Lila. I felt like I hadn't seen her in a year. She dashed up the stairs and scattered sand over me as she plunked down next to me. Over the noise of crashing waves, she stage-whispered, "I just heard you hooked up with Brandon Moore!"

"We did," I said.

"No, I mean I heard you *did it* with Brandon Moore."

I suppressed the urge to glance suspiciously at the parking lot behind me, beyond the bridge. I'd noticed fogged-up windows in cars when I first arrived. People could have seen Brandon and me too. I asked carefully, "Where did you hear that?"

"From Brandon Moore!"

"Oh." I wasn't sure what to make of this. I hadn't counted on Brandon kissing and telling. But he was drunk, and I forgave him. He must be happy about what we'd done, or he wouldn't announce it. "We did," I said again.

Lila persisted, "Wasn't that your first time? Ever?"

"Yes. He was really sweet."

Lila frowned at me and bit her lip. I was beginning to get a little annoyed with her. I felt good about what Brandon and I had done, but Lila's response gave me second thoughts. I did not want second thoughts. I reminded her, "Brandon and I are good friends."

"Yeah," she said.

"Everybody at Slide with Clyde told me all summer we should hook up."

"Yeah." She nodded slowly. "That is great, Zoey."

"I'm happy." I wrapped my arms around my knees and hugged myself. The breeze off the ocean remained steady, but suddenly it seemed colder. "Where's Keke?"

"Embarrassing me," Lila said bitterly. "I will never get laid at this rate."

I unwrapped one arm from my knees and fingered her springy red curls. "Give it time. It will happen."

"Oh, like you're the expert on this suddenly in the last five minutes."

My hand stopped in her hair. Not that it mattered in the dark, but I could feel the blood rushing to my face with anger at what she'd said to me, and embarrassment at what I'd said to her. I *did* sound like a sex ed film from middle school PE class.

"I'm sorry," she said quickly. "That was ugly. I didn't mean it that way."

"I know what you meant." I tugged at her curls for a few more strokes, even though I didn't want to, to show her everything was okay. We were quiet at first, but eventually we talked about the swim meet next Saturday and pretended nothing had happened. I yawned, terribly tired now, done with this party. I could probably sleep, even after the day I'd had, even at my dad's house. I wished Brandon would come back with his beer. I would offer to take him home, and we would have a sweet parting of ways at the end of our first night together.

He did not come back. After a few minutes I would go looking for him, worried. My brief search would begin to feel hysterical, thinking something had happened to him, only at the very end. Then my friends would tell me Brandon had pitched over in the sand, and the guys had helped him across the next bridge down the beach, to the parking lot. Stephanie Wetzel lived in his neighborhood, and she had taken him home.

But chatting with Lila and watching the silhouettes dotting the beach, I didn't know this yet, and I couldn't have predicted it. I still hugged my knees to my chest, almost as if I needed comfort. I felt okay, though. In the opposite direction Brandon had headed, an unseen boy asked in an incredulous tone, "Brandon Moore and Zoey Commander?" and a girl shushed him. That was okay too. They would get used to it. So would I.

FOR THAT SHORT SCHOOL WEEK, I was almost glad Ashley was pregnant with my father's baby. It kept me busy. Late Labor Day night when I came in from the party, I found a note from Ashley saying she had moved my bedroom. It used to be upstairs next to my parents' room. Ashley had put me on the first floor, in what used to be the guest room. She said she wanted the baby's room upstairs with her. She had made up the guest room bed for me with my old comforter.

I spent the rest of the week unpacking stuff I'd wanted from my mom's apartment and arranging it perfectly. Then I volunteered to put together the high chair and baby swing Ashley and my dad had bought in Destin. All this was complicated by the bustle of workmen in the house. Ashley insisted that they finish the kitchen remodel before she and my dad left Saturday for their trip to Hawaii to get married. And my dad was having cameras installed.

They'd planned their elopement weeks ago. They hadn't planned on a dependent minor in the house. My dad's solution was to have cameras record everything that went on while he was gone, and he could view the video on the internet. We used to have a cat, and when we went on vacation, my mom always wanted to board her at the vet. My dad wanted to fill lots of bowls with cat food, shut her up in the house, and leave her. She'd be okay, he'd say. What could happen? I was a cat, and the vet was closed for repairs.

I hardly minded. I didn't want to go with them to Hawaii, and I didn't want them to miss their trip and resent me. And I appreciated all the activity in preparation. Now I understood why people went to so much trouble over funerals, with wakes and food and flowers and caskets and choices. It gave them something to do besides mourn unbearably. In my mind I hardly ever slipped back to my mother's bedroom and tried to fix everything, until I lay in bed at night, praying for sleep.

Brandon was another bright spot in my week. It wasn't his fault we didn't see each other. His football practice lasted even longer in the afternoons than my swim team practice. Our classes and our lunch periods were different. Everybody had break at the same time between second and third periods, but I was hurrying between history and calculus then, and he was probably on the other end of the school. I'd never asked around or gone searching for him because that's the kind of thing his chicks did before me, back in the summer when it was raining girls through his sunroof. My relationship with him was different because we had been dear friends first. I didn't need to be reassured constantly that he wanted to be with me.

Besides, my friends brought him up all the time, amazed and vaguely amused that we were together, so it was almost like he sat next to me in every class. He texted me a message with cute misspellings at least once a day, which I actually found annoying because whenever I saw the light on my phone blinking, for a split second I always hoped my mother had called me. And on Thursday night when my phone rang and I threw down my fork in the middle of the nice spaghetti dinner Ashley had made with my dad's help and scrambled into the guest room to find my phone, that was also Brandon, not my mom. He'd called to tell me he couldn't go out with me Friday night after his game because the football team was throwing their own beach party, boys only. That was fine. I understood.

The only bad thing that happened all week was that Doug started pressing my buttons about my mother. At least, I thought so. The first two weeks of school, he'd come to swim practice on time like everybody else. Since we practiced the last period of school, he had no reason to be late. All he had to do was cross the courtyard from the liberal arts wing. But every day this week, he had been tardy. We were supposed to arrive on time, change into our swimsuits, get in the water, and warm up while Coach wrapped things up with the junior varsity team that practiced before us. As varsity team captain, I was in charge of turning in anyone who didn't comply.

This terrified me. I hadn't heard any rumors about my mom, so I assumed Doug was keeping mum. He hadn't tried to talk to me about it. Whatever he'd been so desperate to yell at me at the party on Monday night, he'd decided it could wait. But I didn't want to press my luck by turning him in and angering him. Each day I gently reprimanded him about being late. He snapped back at me and was late again the next day.

The swim team forced my hand. Keke and Lila asked why I showed favoritism to Doug. The boys called Doug a diva and demanded that I turn his ass in. In the end I hoped Doug would realize I had no choice, and he would not retaliate in kind.

That's when my luck ran out.

3

"Thanks a lot, Zoey."

I was shocked to hear Doug's voice. I looked up at him before I could stop myself. I'd been afraid he'd have words with me tonight, after I turned him in and Coach talked with him behind closed doors in the office. That would never have prevented me from coming to the football game to cheer Brandon on and hang with the rest of the swim team in the crowded stadium. Still, I'd felt relieved when Doug didn't show up quarter after quarter. And now here he was in the fourth, typically late, typically wandering in for free after the booster club abandoned taking tickets at the gate.

"Coach didn't kick you off the team, did he?" I hoped I sounded surprised Doug was upset. He was the best swimmer we had, too good for Coach to kick off for minor infractions. He wasn't in any real trouble, and I hoped by pointing this out, I would take the edge off his anger at me.

Avoiding his gaze, I turned back to the game far below us on the spotlit field. I looked for Brandon's white 24 on his red Bulldogs jersey. He nabbed the ball and plowed his way upfield. "Go, Brandon!" I screamed. "Go, go, go—ouch!" He slammed into an enemy player even bigger than him and stopped short. Whistles blew, the refs gestured toward a penalty somewhere downfield, and the game paused. The marching band broke into "Who Let the Dogs Out?" for the third time in the fourth quarter. My excuse was gone to ignore Doug.

He stared down at me, waiting for me to give him my full attention before he answered my question with an insult. "No, Coach didn't kick me off," he sneered. "But that's what you wanted, Zoey. You can pull that sweetheart act with anyone but me."

The sneering made me uneasy. I hoped my mother's secret was still secret. And I found it hard to remember what I'd planned to say next with Doug glaring at me.

Finally I managed, "I have nothing against you, Doug. Nothing except you've been late for practice every day this week. It's my job to mark you tardy."

"And point it out to Coach? He never would have noticed I was late if you hadn't told him." Doug's voice rose as he spoke. Mike and Ian, standing on the row below us, heard him even with "Who Let the Dogs Out?" still blasting through the stadium. They turned around to look at us. Mike blushed red—which wasn't unusual for Mike, but indicated he could hear Doug clearly. Ian, with sandy brown hair, stayed sand colored, as if he were trying to blend into his beach surroundings. But his eyes met mine for the briefest moment. This argument between Doug and me was bound to stir up talk again that something had happened between us.

My heart sped up. I could feel it knocking against my chest and hear the blood pumping in my ears. I said, clearly and reasonably, so maybe he'd think twice about raising his voice to me again, "I *have* to point things out to Coach. Nothing would get done otherwise. If I didn't remind him, he'd show up late to swim practice himself."

"Exactly," Doug said just as clearly, imitating me. "And now Coach is watching me. You've got him thinking he shouldn't give me special favors—"

"But he *shouldn't* give you special favors," I protested.

"—which is not for you to decide. He was going to recommend me for a swim scholarship to Florida State. Do you understand? This is not about your stupid team."

Mike and Ian looked at each other. They were both on the stupid team too.

Doug didn't glance at them or slow down. "I'd have zero chance of getting a scholarship to FSU if I got kicked off the team and I didn't have Coach to help me. It's not like I'm coming from a long line of Olympic athletes here, Zoey. My dad is a freaking fisherman."

Oh. For the first time I realized what I'd almost done to him. A bigger town would have had a swim club that we all could have joined in elementary school and competed in ever since. When Doug started to show real potential last year, different parents might have moved to a bigger town with a swim club just so he could train with Olympic-caliber coaches. But Doug lived in this town with this father. The team was all he had, and I'd nearly taken even that away from him. I hadn't been thinking of him. I'd been thinking of the team breathing down my neck.

I put my hand on his forearm. The heat of his skin surprised me. It shouldn't have. Mid-September in Florida was still summer. Though my palm started to sweat, I kept my hand on his arm, hoping my touch would help me connect with him.

"You're not the only one trying for a scholarship to FSU," I pointed out. "If I keep my grades up and my extracurriculars loaded, I'll get an academic scholarship." Of course, no one cared about my good grades in comparison to an arrogant boy's athletic scholarship, but I was trying to call Doug off here. I nodded at the field. "And Brandon's trying for a football scholarship. The difference is, Brandon's doing what the football coach tells him. If your scholarship is so important to you, why don't you come to swim practice on time?"

Doug smiled. Maybe I should have smiled too, and laughed like I thought we'd come to an understanding. But I knew my laugh would come out nervous. So I continued to gaze earnestly up at him.

He held my gaze. I had every subject except math with him because we were both in AP, but in most classes he sat across the room. In English he sat right in front of me, so I was familiar with the deeply tanned back of his neck and the way his black hair quirked into curls. I'd never been this close to the front of him, though, without his hair tucked into a swim cap and his eyes blurry behind goggles. Funny how he could avoid me since the ninth grade, but the instant I got him in trouble, he was in my face. I could see every black hair in the day-old stubble on his chin.

His voice was so honeyed, I would have thought he was complimenting me, except for his words, and the subtlest sarcasm in his tone that I'd come to know well in the past year on the varsity team with him. "No, Zoey. The difference is that I actually *need* a scholarship, and you're a spoiled brat." He twisted his arm out of my hand and rubbed it like I'd hurt him, though I was sure I'd hardly touched him. "And I'm worried about your academic scholarship if you're dense enough to think Brandon Moore gives a shit about you."

Then I was staring at Doug's back. He bounced down the stands, stepping over the seats to join some other guys at the edge of the swim team. He said something to them and they laughed. People complained to me privately about Doug, but when he was around, he was the life of the party. Now the huddle looked so conspiratorial that Ian walked along the bench below me to join it. Even Mike, who hated Doug, edged closer. I hoped they weren't talking about me. Or if they were, I hoped they were only talking about my argument with Doug, and not about my mom.

And then in my mind I was back in my mother's bedroom

at our apartment, trying to fix everything. I held my phone to my ear with one hand, whispering to the 911 dispatcher. With the other hand, I straightened her bottles of expensive perfume on the cheap rental dresser. I rubbed imaginary dust from the glass stoppers decorated with glass jewels and glass ribbons.

I jumped and forgot the bottles as the marching band blared "Who Let the Dogs Out?" for the fourth time. In the end zone, the refs held their hands up, and Brandon's teammates slapped his helmet. My whole purpose in coming to the game was to watch Brandon play. Now Brandon had scored, and I had no idea how it had happened.

And *now* Keke and Lila trudged back up the stairs. Their hands were full of Cokes and popcorn and cotton candy, junk they shouldn't be eating with a swim meet tomorrow. If they'd stayed with me instead of going to the concession stand, Doug wouldn't have attacked me like a lion on the savanna targeting the vulnerable gazelle at the edge of the herd. Or . . . the species that bounced hysterically instead of running. I confused the deerlike animals with each other. Impala. "What?"

"I *said*, are you seeing Brandon after the game?" Keke asked through a mouthful of popcorn.

"Zoey loves Brandon. It's perfect and dreamy," Lila said in a voice from TV commercials about princess dolls. She was a princess herself, with her gauzy top flowing around her in the breeze, and her red curls pinned up and cascading into ringlets around her shoulders.

"Brandon's going to a party tonight with the football team at the city beach park," I told them. "Male bonding."

"The swim team should crash the party," Keke declared.

"Yeah!" Lila skipped a few steps down the bleachers to discuss this idea with the junior girls on the swim team.

"No!" I caught Lila by the arm and dragged her back. She and Keke both waited for an explanation. I wished everyone would stop looking at me. Had I yelled *no* too loudly and yanked Lila back too hard? They must think I was crazy. "I was planning to go to his house tomorrow night after the swim meet and take him parking," I said as calmly and sanely as I could.

"Oooh," Lila said appreciatively.

"That's ridiculous," Keke said. "He can't ban you from coming to his beach party. It's not his damn beach."

"Good point." Lila escaped toward the junior girls again before I could grab her. She whispered to them and they squealed.

It was too easy, too good to be true. I hadn't planned it. I hadn't asked for it. I wouldn't look pitiful chasing Brandon around, because crashing the party was the swim team's idea, not mine. I'd fought resentment all day that Brandon was going out with the guys tonight instead of me, when I hadn't seen him since Monday night. I'd thought it was okay, I'd told him it was okay, but the longer I considered it, the less it was okay. Now suddenly the problem was solved without me doing a thing? It felt dangerous. I didn't trust it.

As if in agreement, the forest of pines and magnolias behind the guest bleachers bent in a gust of wind. A few puffs of popcorn escaped from the top of Keke's bag. My hair whipped into my eyes. "What about the hurricane?" I murmured, smoothing my hair back and knotting it into a heavy bun.

"It veered toward Mississippi," Keke said. "We'll only get thunderstorms late tonight. Goooooooo . . ." She cheered and circled her fist in the air like everyone else in the stadium but me as the Bulldogs kicked off. The ball lobbed through the air. The line of players ran forward and collided with the enemy team. Then Brandon jogged to the sidelines with the rest of the offense. I located his red helmet with the white 24 almost immediately because he was so tall.

And my stomach twisted with anticipation because he was mine, and I was about to have him again. Part of me didn't want to have sex with him anymore—the part of me that had felt nauseated and hadn't wanted to do it with him last weekend. I liked to keep everything in its place. Brandon Moore inside me seemed hopelessly out of place. But that was just nerves. I could overrule that part of me tonight, like I had before. Since we were going to see each other less often than I'd assumed, we needed to make the most of our time together whenever we had the chance.

And if the swim team crashed the football players' party,

Doug would see me there with Brandon. Strange that I cared so much about this with everything else going on in my life, but after Doug's insult, I cared very deeply about looking desired and perfectly normal. He would see that Brandon did, in fact, give a shit about me. And as my mother had always told me, if I gave the appearance of keeping everything together, people like Doug would be less likely to attack me.

"Dee-fense! Good Lord!" Keke shouted through cupped hands, her popcorn bag in the crook of her arm. I looked past her at what Lila was up to. She'd finished with the junior girls and had moved on to the swim team boys. Then she stood on her tiptoes to see over their shoulders. She winked at me. The party was a go.

Her face lit up with laughter as a howl rose over the crowd noise. I knew from experience it was Mike singing his falsetto boy band imitation, which he'd started this season when Lila and Keke blasted their CDs in the swim team van. Normally Mike was painfully shy and turned beet red if you looked at him, which made this strange performance that much funnier to the other swim team boys. They beatboxed along with him. The girls on the team weren't as into the performance because whenever Mike howled and the other boys beatboxed in the van, we couldn't hear each other talking. We were imprisoned by Mike's falsetto until he coughed to a stop. It's hard to explain what many, many afternoons spent with the same seventeen people could do to you.

But this time, because we weren't stuck in the van with

him and it wasn't so annoying, Lila laughed and fluttered her eyelashes at Mike. Keke said, "Oh my God," and pointed, grinning. The junior girls danced to the beat Mike had built with the swim team boys. Across the aisle from us, a few drummers in the marching band took up the beat, and the trumpets echoed the falsetto tune. The dancing spread to the majorettes. The drum major looked befuddled.

Only Doug stood aloof from the swim team, stock-still in the midst of the dancing crowd, arms folded across his T-shirt. He'd been to juvie, so no girl at our school wanted to date Doug. He was that hilarious guy with the black hair and beautiful eyes and the temper. Girls kept their distance because he might turn on them and cut them down. Last year there was a rumor he dated a girl who went to high school in Destin. It was only a matter of time until she found out about juvie. Sure enough, somehow Mike spilled the beans to her—which was why Doug and Mike hated each other. I'd overheard half this story on the van last year and mentally cursed everyone for making so much noise that I couldn't hear the rest, but I did not like to pry, and I didn't want to give anyone the impression I cared about Doug's love life.

I was thinking this about Doug, but I didn't realize I was staring at him until he glanced over at me and caught me. He stared hard, expecting me to chicken out and avert my eyes. My heart sped up again and the skin on my forearms tingled.

I was that impala making a fight-or-flight decision, targeted by that lion. But I didn't look away. I stared right back at him as Mike sang hateful words about a girl who broke his heart and wasn't worth the trouble. Doug Fox didn't own this football stadium, and I would not show him weakness and open the door for him to hurt my mother. He would not ruin my carefree high school experience, my party, my night with Brandon.

And that's the last thing I remember.

"Zoey."

"I'm up!" I sat straighter on whatever I'd slumped against. It had a bottom and a high back, so it must be a sofa. Whose sofa? I hoped no one had seen me fall asleep in public. I was captain of the swim team, a school leader. I couldn't go around falling asleep just anywhere. And I wasn't drunk. I never lost control that way, ever.

"You had a wreck." It took me a second to place the smooth voice: Doug. His voice had the slightest edge, like he'd seen the wreck happen and was a little freaked out but was trying to remain calm. "You need to get out of the car."

Issuing commands was not Doug's usual style. Getting pissed when other people issued commands, yes. Issuing them himself, no. Now he was telling me what to do, and it scared me.

I was in the driver's seat. I slid toward his voice on the passenger side. He was lying on the ground and leaning through the doorway, half in and half out of the car. Headlights from outside blanked his face like an overexposed photo in shades of white. His hair hung black over his forehead, and his shadowed eyes were two black sockets. Something must be horribly wrong.

"I totaled my Bug," I wailed.

"Yes, you did," he said grimly.

"Did I total your Jeep?"

"Get out of the car." He nodded toward the empty space beside him in the doorway. "Get out of the car now, Zoey."

I slid farther toward him. When I reached the passenger side, the dashboard leaned so far forward that it blocked my way. To get by, I had to draw my legs up onto the seat. Then I slid them beside Doug on the ground and stood up.

And fell down, splatting into mud.

"That's what I was afraid of," Doug called from several feet away. "You can't stand up?"

"I can stand up," I protested. It was better to lie down, though. I just wished the headlights from the car I'd hit weren't so bright, streaming into my eyes. Long blades of grass glowed green around us, and white raindrops streaked down on us. Beyond the small circle where we lay, the night was black, and I couldn't see.

I felt him crawling beside me until his face was even with mine. He rose above me. His arm circled me, warm after the cool wet grass. He hoisted me upward and groaned.

"I am not fat," I said.

"Of course you're not fat." Now he sounded like he was talking with his teeth clenched.

"Brandon told me I look like I've gained weight since the summer." He hadn't meant it as an insult. He was just kidding around, flirting with me. I'd actually lost weight since the competitive swim season began. But since Brandon had texted that message to me on Tuesday, I'd skipped breakfast, just to make sure.

"Brandon," grunted Doug as he took a big step and slung me forward. "Can." He took another step and groaned again. "Kiss. My. Broken. Ass." He let me slip through his arms to the ground, and he collapsed beside me.

From this distance, through the bright raindrops in the dark night, I could see the two cars kissing each other with steam rising from their lips. My Bug and definitely not Doug's Jeep. "Whose car?"

"Mike's Miata."

"Mike *Abrams?*" I'd wrecked the whole swim team.

"He's not hurt, but he's stuck inside. He's calling 911. We'll get help soon. Don't worry."

I hadn't been worried. But now that he brought it up, the gravity of the situation sank in. It was night. It was raining. We'd crashed head-on. And Doug must be hurt, or he wouldn't be lying down in the grass in a rainstorm. "Doug, I'm so sorry."

"Sorry! It's not your fault. Don't you remember what happened? You and Mike both swerved to keep from hitting a deer in the road."

No, I didn't remember the deer. "Is the deer okay?"

"Fuck the deer. Hush now." Gently he drew me to him and pressed down on the back of my neck until I lay my head on his chest.

It was totally innocent. Doug was comforting me after we'd been in a wreck together. Brandon still would not approve. But I couldn't do anything about it because I felt dizzy. My hands found Doug's T-shirt, and I gripped fistfuls of fabric to keep from falling off the edge of the earth. I nuzzled his warm chest. He smelled faintly of chlorine.

He stroked my hair, which had fallen free of the bun I'd knotted. He stroked from the roots all the way past my shoulders to the ends, firmly, with both hands, in a way I hadn't even known I'd ached for Brandon to touch me. Lightning flashed, thunder rolled, and the dull roar of rain grew louder.

Doug sucked in a slow breath through his teeth and let it out just as slowly. At first I thought he was doing a deep breathing exercise we'd learned on the swim team, and I was going to joke that we didn't have nearly enough water for swimming, even with all this rain. As I opened my mouth to murmur against his chest, I heard the shudder in his exhalation. He must be dizzy like I was, trying to keep control. He needed comfort, just like I did. I put one hand in his hair. It was soaked. His hand massaged the back of my neck. His chest rose and fell under me, like waves as I swam in the ocean.

Some time must have passed, because the police couldn't have materialized from thin air. The siren shrieked in one of my ears. Doug's heart throbbed under my other ear, and his voice rumbled in his chest. He talked to a policeman somewhere above us. I didn't bother looking. The blue lights were too bright. I squeezed my eyes shut against them.

"She hit her head," I heard Doug say.

"I didn't hit my head," I corrected him. I didn't remember hitting anything.

"She hit her head," Doug repeated, "and my leg's broken."

"Oh." I tried to roll off him. I'd known he was hurt, yet I was lying on top of him like I needed coddling when I wasn't hurt at all. But his arm tightened around me, and I couldn't move. Well, fine then. I was still dizzy, and Doug was a warm blanket.

"Then how'd you get over here?" asked the policeman. I opened one eye. With the headlights shining on his back and the blue lights circling him, I couldn't see his darkened face. "Did you carry her over here with a broken leg?"

"More or less," Doug muttered. His fingers stroked my wet hair.

I jerked alert when the policeman asked, "What the hell for?" His tone and his words didn't sound official and coplike. It was Doug's brother, Officer Fox. "Jesus, Doug," he said, "you probably screwed your leg up for nothing."

"I had to get her away from the car in case it exploded," Doug snapped. "Can you shut up and go do your duty and let Mike out of the Miata before it bursts into flames? Thanks."

"You dumbass," Officer Fox said. "Cars don't explode on impact."

I giggled. "Doug, you're my hero." Then, hoping I hadn't offended him, I hugged him hard and whispered in his ear, "It's the thought that counts." I wasn't sure whether he laughed with me, but he did hug me back, and he never took his hands out of my hair. I laughed myself to sleep.

4

"Zoey."

"I'm up!" Sitting up in my bed, I blinked at the pain in my forehead and the daylight streaming through the windows.

"Your boyfriend's here," Ashley called softly. Almost *motherly*, except nothing could sound truly motherly coming from a chick only seven years older than me. "You feel okay?"

I nodded. As my brain sloshed around, the throbbing started—and I remembered the wreck. I must have hit my head after all, like Doug had said. Painkillers please! There was no prescription bottle on my nightstand. "Ashley?" I called. Too late. She was only a long, tanned leg leaving the doorway of my bedroom.

Well, painkillers could wait. Brandon was here to see me! And I needed to get all the good out of his visit before I left for this afternoon's swim meet.

I rolled off the bed, head splitting, eyes sticky. I'd worn my contacts to bed. I'd also worn my wet clothes to bed, I realized as the air-conditioning turned them from moist to clammy. Everything was still damp: jeans, underwear, bra, shirt. Of course my dad was hands-off as far as parenting went, and Ashley was a strange twenty-four-year-old living in my home. But I would have thought *someone* would figure out *some* way to prevent me from sinking into a coma while wearing my contacts and wet clothes.

I staggered into my bathroom to peel the contacts off my eyeballs and brush my teeth to spare Brandon my morning breath. I stopped with my toothbrush in midstroke when I saw the strangest bruise on my forehead. Toothbrush sticking from my foamy mouth, I fumbled in a drawer for my glasses, then leaned toward the mirror for an examination. The bruise formed three sides of the outline of a rectangle: top, side, and bottom. Green at the center of the lines, it faded through brown to purple at the edges. Like my head had taken out the rearview mirror of my Bug.

From the geometric bruise, my gaze sank to my earlobes, left and then right. I fingered the empty holes. I didn't remember removing the diamond earrings my parents had given me for my seventeenth birthday last January.

Come to think of it, I didn't remember what I'd done between the end of the football game last night and the wreck.

Or how I'd gotten from the wreck to my bed.

But Brandon was waiting for me, and he knew.

I spit toothpaste, splashed water on my face, and desperately drew my bangs over my forehead to hide the bruise. They wouldn't cooperate, cowlicking too far to one side, leaving the bruise bare. But with my panic rising about my missing night, I hardly cared about my looks. I didn't even bother to hide my glasses from Brandon. I schlepped into the living room in cold jeans and bare feet.

Doug sat on the sofa.

I stopped short and scanned the huge room of polished wood. Brandon wasn't here. Only Doug. And there was no way Ashley should have made this mistake, calling Doug my boyfriend. She'd hired Brandon to work at Slide with Clyde. When I'd told her last Tuesday that I was going out with him, she'd said she remembered him and even acknowledged his hotness. I wasn't making this up. I wasn't *that* crazy.

Doug stared up at the vaulted glass ceiling. This feature was common in the newer beachfront houses, but it probably seemed impressive to Doug if he lived a few miles inland where the houses were less expensive, like most of the people in our high school.

Then his eyes fell to me, flashing green even across the shadowy room. He leaped to his feet like a polite Southern gentleman. On crutches. With a brace on his lower leg. He lost his balance, pitched forward, and caught himself just in time on one crutch.

"Sit down!" I gasped, running toward him. My first instinct was to force him down by reaching up and pulling on his shoulders until he sat. But I hesitated. I didn't know how vulnerable his leg was inside the brace. I didn't want to hurt him. My hands fluttered around his chest.

One crutch bounced off the sofa and clattered to the hardwood floor as he leaned over to hug me. I stepped closer before he fell. Why was he so intent on hugging me that he risked life and another limb? Maybe he thought we needed to hug because we'd been in the same wreck. We'd shared a traumatic experience. Actually I didn't remember whether it was traumatic or not, but logically the wreck should have been traumatic and we should hug.

His arms were around me. My arms were down by my sides. So I brought my arms up and slipped them around his waist, trying my best to steady him as he swayed on one leg. He solved this problem by shifting his center of gravity down. He slid his hands to my butt and pressed his face to my neck.

Brandon would not like this.

My dad might not like this either. The cameras already rolled, recording everything that went on inside his house. When he logged on to the internet later, he could watch a video of what Doug and I did.

And Doug and I were about to do something. Now his warm hands slid under my shirt, pressing my back, with his fingertips just inside the waistband of my jeans. His face moved at my neck. His caress would transform into a kiss any second.

Strangest of all, I felt myself arching into him, pressing my chest into his at the same time I lifted my butt to keep his hands on my back. I tilted my head to give him better access to my neck. This was the boy who'd saved my life last night, or at least intended to.

This was also the boy who, at the football game a few hours before the wreck, had stared down at me with cold green eyes while he called me a spoiled brat and told me my boyfriend didn't care about me. Almost like he knew exactly what would hurt me worst.

Just as his lips brushed my neck and sent a zap of electricity along every inch of my skin, I pulled back from him. His hands slid around to either side of my waist where he could hold me more firmly in place. I wanted to let him hold me, to find out what he would do next to my neck. But it was too weird and made no sense. I croaked, "My dad can see us." When Doug glanced down at me, I nodded toward a camera in the corner of the ceiling.

"Let's move out of view," Doug told the camera.

Gazing up at his chin—he'd shaved since last night—I wanted to kiss *his* neck. Which would mean I was cheating on Brandon. Even as the urge to give up and make out with Doug spread across my chest, the thought of Brandon knocked like a golf ball on the inside of my skull. "Let's sit down," I said again.

"Oh, sorry." He eased onto the sofa and held out his hands to me. I collapsed beside him. He put one hand to my forehead above my glasses, brushed my bangs away, and traced his thumb around the outline of my bruise.

Maybe he thought I'd meant we should sit down to duck out of the sight line of the camera. He certainly seemed intent on touching me. God, this was so weird, and the golf ball banged inside my head. "There are cameras all over the house," I clarified, nodding toward another above the entrance to the kitchen. "This morning my dad's going to Hawaii for a week. I won't be eighteen until January, and he didn't think it was proper to leave me alone for that long until I'm a legal adult. So he had the cameras installed as babysitters."

Doug kept tracing around the very edge of too much. His fingers slid past my bangs to my ear and found the back of my hair, usually smooth and straight, now hopelessly tangled with rain and sleep. He didn't mind. Stroking there, he whispered, "How about your bedroom?"

"No cameras in my bedroom. There's just one trained on the door so my dad can see if someone goes in there besides me." My dad wasn't a perv. Well, I guess he sort of was, doing it with a twenty-four-year-old. But he wasn't a perv to *me*. And then, by degrees, I realized what Doug was getting at. He wanted to go into my bedroom with me.

I should have been outraged. I wasn't. I gaped at him, wondering where in the world this desire for him had come from, and blinking hard every time the golf ball whacked the inside of my skull.

"Damn," he said, like it was a bummer we couldn't sneak into my bedroom together. *Not* like this was a bizarre proposition for him to make in the first place. "Your sister seems pretty cool. Isn't she staying with you while your dad's gone?"

I laughed, which made my head hurt worse. "Ashley? That's my dad's girlfriend. She lives here."

"Oh." Doug's hand stopped in my hair.

"But he's making an honest woman out of her. Next Wednesday at exactly eight P.M., she'll become my stepmother. She figured out the time change from Oahu for me so I can think of them and celebrate simultaneously. I am so thrilled."

Doug raised one eyebrow at me. "Is that sarcasm? You are not sarcastic." He detangled his fingers from my hair and put his hand on the knee of my damp jeans. The warmth of his body soaked through the fabric and started me tingling again. "I woke you up coming over, didn't I? I wanted to make sure you were okay. *Are* you okay?" He looked straight into my eyes.

I wasn't sure of the answer to this question. So I asked, "How about you?"

He extended his leg with the brace and gazed ruefully at it. "It was just my fibula, the smaller bone, which they said only bears ten percent of the weight in your leg."

"That's lucky," I sighed, feeling a lot less guilty. "So you got a brace instead of a cast."

"No, the splint's on just until the swelling goes down. They'll put a cast on it in a few days. I should have it off again in six weeks."

I ticked off calendar days in my head. "Six weeks! That's

a few days before State!" Doing well at the State swim tournament was the only way for Doug to get his scholarship to FSU.

He shrugged, but I saw the tension in his shoulders. It crackled down his arm to his hand on my knee.

I asked, "Did you hurt your leg worse by pulling me out of the car?"

He shook his head no without looking at me, so I knew the answer was yes. "And Mike's okay. They didn't even take him to the hospital."

"And the deer?"

He smiled and squeezed my knee. Again I was struck by how weird it was that he touched me like this. But I got lost in his green eyes that crinkled at the edges as he grinned. "You and that damn deer. You and Mike both missed it and hit each other."

Leaning closer, he rubbed my knee. Hard. A deep-tissue massage. Sparks shot through my thigh. "We're safe from killer ruminants when we stick to the coastline," he said. "This morning we can crash together, ha ha." Here was something I'd never seen: Doug nervous. He made jokes all the time, but he never looked nervous when he did it. "Then later, if you're feeling better, we could get some dinner, go see a movie, hang out after." His eyebrows went up briefly like *hang out after* held hidden meaning, but I figured this was a tick of his that I hadn't noticed before. I'd hardly exchanged a word with him since the ninth grade except this week:

Me: You're late for swim practice.

Doug: You're not the boss of me.

And in years past, before we were on the varsity swim team together:

Me: Stop copying off my math test.

Doug: You think awfully highly of your math skills, Miss Commander.

"I can't drive until I get my cast off," he went on. "You can drive my Jeep. I feel stupid asking you to drive, but I really want to see you. Or we could stay in and watch TV if you're not up to it. Zoey?"

His tone had turned to concern because I'd closed one eye against the throbbing in my head. I was a bit slow on the up-take this morning. But I finally understood. Strange as the last twelve hours had been, they'd just gotten a lot stranger. Doug Fox was asking me out.

Something didn't add up. I fished for more information. Pressing my fingertips to my eyebrow above my glasses to keep my brain from spilling onto the upholstery, I asked, "If you can't drive, how'd you get here?"

I felt terrible about Doug essentially giving up his chance at State by saving my life (or not). I felt almost as guilty about him losing his ability to drive. Most things to do in our town were lined up along the beach where the tourists could reach them in the summer. Because the beach houses and condos were so expensive, the population of our town was centered a few miles inland where the land was cheaper, along with downtown and the high school. And though thousands of tourists swelled the population in the height of the season, now that it was September and they'd left, the town was small. Too small for public transportation. Not a bus or a subway or a taxi in sight. If Doug couldn't drive, he was stuck.

"My brother brought me," Doug said.

I leaped up, snatching my knee away from his hand. I crossed the room and heaved open the heavy front door.

Our porch looked over our garden, which my mom had hired a landscaper to design with native grasses and flowering vines that could survive the hot summers. Six other houses had similar porches and gardens sloping to a common courtyard paved with local stone. In the center of the courtyard idled a pickup I recognized from around town, with a man's bare feet sticking out the passenger window. Not the police car I'd expected, but after a long night of responding to his brother's wrecks and patrolling for rogue deer, Officer Fox must be off duty.

And suddenly, staring at that pickup, I understood all the problems that were throwing the golf ball as hard as they could at the inside of my skull. Last night Doug had rescued me from my car, feeling like a hero to my damsel in distress. I'd lain on top of him in a thunderstorm and snuggled with him and let him put his hands in my hair. And he'd taken that *seriously*, even though this had happened just a few hours after I very possibly had sex with Brandon for the second time.

Or, in an alternative scenario so awful that I hardly dared consider it, Doug's invitation for a date was some kind of blackmail. He sure was being nice to me after my dad's threat to his brother. And his brother sat in his pickup in the center of my neighborhood's courtyard. He had come to our home and stuck his feet into the ocean breeze as if to say *I know everything about your mother.*

The door banged shut behind me. Only then I realized I'd left it open. Doug and I stood in a bubble of escaped air-conditioning in the hot day. His hot finger traced a *Z* on my back, through my T-shirt. Every one of his touches had been a quirky brush against an unexpected part of my body. But this time I was determined to keep things cold.

I turned to him. As I spun, he kept his finger at the same level so it trailed around my shoulder and across my breast, making me shudder. His fingertip centered over my heart as I faced him.

This had gone too far. I had a new relationship with Brandon that I didn't want to ruin. And if Doug did have some wild blackmail scenario in mind, reminding him I was with Brandon might make him think twice.

I grabbed his hand, pulled it down to waist level, and squeezed it. "Doug, I don't want to hurt your feelings, but

Brandon is my boyfriend." Of course, in rejecting Doug, I was giving him yet another reason to hate me, and to get revenge on me by telling the whole town about my mother. I hoped against hope he would be reasonable for once. I looked down, past our clasped hands at the expensive faux-weathered wood floor of the porch.

My mom had told me it was important to look people in the eye, especially men, when you were trying to control a situation.

I was scared to see the expression on Doug's face, but I forced my eyes upward from the rubber tips of his crutches, his one tanned foot in a battered leather flip-flop, and the other splinted leg he held awkwardly a few inches off the ground. Upward to his cargo shorts, loose around his waist. Like me, he must have lost weight since competition started. The heathered gray waistband of his underwear peeked out above his shorts. His FSU SWIMMING T-shirt was so old and loved, the dark red had faded to a doubtful magenta.

Finally my gaze reached his clean-shaven jaw locked in anger, his angry eyes. He glared down at me with exactly the look he'd given me last night at the game.

Hastily I dropped his hand.

And then he took a slow breath. His chest expanded and his broad shoulders rose. He exhaled through his nose. The anger left his eyes. He gave me a small nod. "You mean you need to break up with Brandon officially? You want to tell him in person to get closure? I mean, yeah, but, you're not going *out* with him tonight, are you? You don't need to go out with him to break up with him."

"I'm not breaking up with him." The porch was shady, but even the sunlight beyond us in the courtyard was too bright and fueled the throbbing in my forehead. "Doug, Brandon is my boyfriend. I'm glad you're okay. I'm glad Mike's okay. I'm grateful to you for pulling me out of the car. But I'm with Brandon."

"I don't understand," Doug said coldly.

"I don't know how to make it more clear." The golf ball in my head grew to billiard ball size. "Last night doesn't change the fact that you've hated me since the ninth grade."

He rocked backward and shifted the pads of the crutches under his arms. "No, I haven't," he said innocently. He might have used his customary honeyed sarcasm. I couldn't tell because the billiard ball had grown to a bowling ball inside my head.

"You made fun of me to the swim team at the football game," I reminded him.

"When? No, I didn't."

He seemed so adamant, I wondered whether I could have been wrong. I hadn't actually *heard* the boy half of the swim team make fun of me. But this much I was sure of. "You told me I'm a spoiled brat!"

He gaped at me. "I already apologized for that, Zoey."

I didn't remember him apologizing. Now *brain damage* was etched across the bowling ball banging against the inside of my skull. "Look, I have a headache, for real. Thanks for checking on me." I took a step back from him, giving him room to move down the porch steps to his brother's truck.

He stared blankly at me with those beautiful eyes for a moment more. Then he said, "If I weren't still high from the drugs the hospital gave me intravenously, I think I would be very angry with you right now."

"What's new?" Saying it made me realize what was new. This misunderstanding with Doug might do more than make our relations worse. It might ruin what I had with Brandon too. "Oh God. You didn't *tell* anybody about last night, did you?"

"I haven't had time."

"Well, don't!" I shrieked. "Doug, you can't say anything to Brandon. Promise me you'll tell Mike and your brother not to say anything to *anybody*." Brandon was laid back, but I couldn't expect him to understand my behavior with Doug in the grass last night when I didn't understand it myself. I couldn't lose him just because Doug had dragged me from the wreck!

"Fine." Doug heaved himself across the porch and down the first step. Tall though he was, he was one of the most agile boys I'd ever seen. It was bizarre to watch him miss the next step with his crutch and stumble forward.

I leaped to catch him.

He caught himself with the crutch in time. My hand on his elbow was unnecessary. He was so much heavier than me, I wouldn't have been able to prevent him from tumbling into the sea oats anyway. In full sunlight now, he moved out from under my fingers, across the stone courtyard, without looking back.

I almost ran forward to help again as he struggled to open the truck door while balancing on one leg and one crutch. The bare feet disappeared from the window, and Officer Fox leaned across the seat to open the door. Doug tossed his crutches into the payload, hopped a few times, and dove into the truck, wincing as he dragged his broken leg after him. He never looked up at me. Officer Fox shook his head. He glanced behind him to back the truck in a turn, then drove forward and made a fast, sharp, un-policeman-like turn onto the road.

As soon as the gate folded shut behind the truck, I dashed back inside and ran through the house to my bathroom to double-check the counter and drawers for a prescription painkiller bottle. Nothing. And there was no way something like that would have gotten lost under the surface. I'd just moved back in, after all, and I kept my room and my bathroom neat so I never misplaced anything.

I sank onto my bed, reached for my cell phone on my bedside table, and held it facedown in my lap for a few seconds, wishing. I needed my mother right now. If I hadn't checked my phone since the football game last night, this was the longest I'd gone without making sure there was no message from her. I actually crossed my fingers and turned the phone over.

Nothing. I was still alone.

So I headed out back to the pool on a fact-finding mission. When my parents built this house a few years ago, I'd said, and my mom had agreed, that it was silly to build a pool overlooking an ocean. Wasn't the ocean good enough for us? Wasn't that why people vacationed in Florida in the first place? Building a pool at your oceanside house was like the theme restaurants in town—Jamaica Joe's, Tahiti Cuisine, California Eatin'—all evoking a different place on the ocean as if the place we already had on the ocean was somehow inferior. Jamaica and Tahiti and California probably had restaurants named Florida Foodie. It was like my dad and Ashley living in a beach house on the Emerald Coast and flying to Hawaii to get married.

But my mom had said people who'd grown up with money, like her, and me, didn't care about showing off that they had it, whereas people who'd grown up without it, like my dad, cared very much. All the other houses in the neighborhood had a pool overlooking the ocean, so my dad needed one too. He also needed a Benz, a Rolex, a flat-screen TV that took up his entire bedroom wall, a mistress, a love child, and a divorce. And now, with a wedding in Hawaii, a trophy wife.

"Good morning!" Ashley called brightly as I dragged myself out the back door. She and my dad, wearing matching robes, lay in cushioned teak lounge chairs in the shade of a potted palm. The roar of the ocean, which my dad had moved here to be near, could hardly be heard over the wall protecting the pool. My dad stubbed out his cigarette.

"Good morning!" I replied even more brightly. Normally I tried to stay out of Ashley's face. I didn't want to be the spoiled brat my dad expected me to be. However, a post–car crash greeting as enthusiastic as hers begged for such a response. Doug was right: I'd become sarcastic overnight. Or maybe it was just the headache. I sat down on the foot of the chair next to my dad's.

Still grinning at me, she reached for my dad's hand. He did her one better and massaged between her fingers with his thumb. Like I was a threat to their relationship and they needed to show solidarity.

I didn't care. My head was about to fall off. "Where are my pain pills?"

They looked at each other. At least, they turned toward each other, but I couldn't see their eyes behind their his-and-hers designer sunglasses. They turned back to me. My dad said, "The hospital didn't give you anything. You're not supposed to take anything stronger than Tylenol because it might mask symptoms if there were something really wrong with your head. They told you this four times last night!" He sounded angry with me, and then I understood why. He spat toward Ashley, "There goes Hawaii. We have to take her back to the hospital. And another hurricane's forming in the Gulf. God knows how long we'll be grounded if we miss this flight."

I found myself concentrating on how handsome he was, how manly and tall and tan, as he said to me, "You'd better be damn sure you have amnesia."

I wasn't sure what he was getting at. The pain in my head brought tears to my eyes, but through the throbbing I was beginning to realize I was in big trouble with my dad. "What?"

He let go of Ashley's hand, leaned forward with a creak of the lounge chair, and counted off the offenses to him on long, shaking fingers. "Ashley and I plan this trip," first finger, "and your mother picks that very week to crack up," second finger, "you total your car the day before we leave," third finger, "and now you have *amnesia?*" He moved his extended pinky finger close to my face. "If that's your story, I will take you back to the hospital." He made a fist. "But by God, I will make sure they lock you up in the loony bin with your mother."

5

In my mind I was back in my mother's bedroom, trying to fix everything, but I just sat there, helpless, with one hand pressed to the throbbing in my head, watching my mother die quietly.

Ashley shook her head at me and rolled her eyes as if my dad was being silly. As if what he had just said to me could be considered a silly, impatient thing to say to his daughter when he was under a lot of stress with a Hawaiian vacation planned.

Then she reached for my dad's hand and spoke in that calming, motherly tone I did not like at all. "Clyde. They said the concussion confused her and that's very common. They said she might not remember the entire night, and if she didn't, there wouldn't be anything they could do." She turned back to me. "You don't remember last night?"

"Oh, sure, I remember," I lied. My words came out gravely. I cleared my throat. "My head really hurts. I was hoping a nurse had taken mercy and slipped you some pills for me on our way out."

"Sorry," Ashley said with an exaggerated *sorry* face, bottom lip poked out. "The nurses were preoccupied with your boy-friend."

"Doug?" The gremlin in my head had given up on the balls of increasing size and was now taking whacks at the inside of my skull with a baseball bat. "You know my boyfriend, Bran-don. He worked at Slide with Clyde with us this summer? You hired him?"

"Ohhhh." She and my dad gave each other another look through their sunglasses. Ashley said, "We thought you'd got-ten together with Doug, the way the two of you were acting last night."

"Right. That was because of the wreck. We were so relieved to be alive." I hoped I sounded embarrassed instead of mor-tified. No wonder Doug had thought we were together now and I would break up with Brandon for him. *What had I done?* Had I freaking humped Doug Fox in the ER?

"Wasn't he the one there with the policeman last Monday at the emergency room?" my dad barked. "And suddenly you're in a wreck with him?"

"I have almost every class with Doug, and we're on the swim team together." I had been ready to accuse Doug with some conspiracy theory a few minutes ago, but now that my dad verbalized it, I heard how ridiculous it sounded.

"Honey!" Ashley patted my dad's hand insistently, glancing at her diamond watch. "We need to leave for the airport *right now* and we haven't finished packing, haven't showered . . ."

My dad stood and held out a strong hand to help up his

fiancée. Ashley continued to fill the void among the three of us with busy talk until they escaped inside, leaving me alone on the edge of my seat, straining my ears for the familiar breath-sounds of the ocean.

Dizzy and sick, I wandered into my bathroom and found a bottle of over-the-counter pain pills. I took two. Examined the label. Under absolutely no circumstances was I to take more than two at a time. I shook out another and swallowed that. Read the label again and wondered who had written it and how serious she was. Then slammed the bottle into a drawer. It was too much, calculating the line between reasonable under the circumstances and overdose.

I filled the bathtub. This would use all the hot water and ruin the showers for my dad and Ashley, but they probably were taking one together anyway. Then I pulled off my damp clothes. And got another shock when I caught a glimpse of myself in the mirror.

Mottled purple extended from my left shoulder diagonally down my breast and disappeared at my waist on my right side.

I squinted into the mirror and tried to picture the wreck. It was dark. It was raining. A deer appeared in the road. I swerved and stomped the brakes. My car skidded on the slick road and crashed into Mike's Miata, hard enough to heave me forward and snap my seat belt. My head whacked the rearview mirror. I sat up and saw the boys past the crumpled hood of the Miata, in the front seat: Mike trapped behind the wheel, fumbling for his phone, Doug in pain and struggling to open the passenger door.

No, I didn't remember a bit of this.

I shook my head—mistake, renewal of throbbing—and sank into the bathtub. This would make me feel better, to scrub off the dirt and germs and God knew what from unknown people and places. I wanted clean, dry clothes. I wanted straight, smooth, tangle-free hair.

But first I wanted to soak. Not to relax, exactly. That would have been impossible with the noise of Ashley and my dad in their room over my head, rushing around getting ready for their trip (or just Ashley rushing around and my dad lying on the bed watching CNBC). At a particularly hard *bump* overhead, I jumped, sloshing water against the sides of the tub. That was okay. The way I felt, I would never relax again. I just tried to clear my mind and start over, like rebooting a computer when it got clogged with spyware, so I could make sense of what had happened.

My mind wouldn't reboot. The same window kept popping up, the one snippet of the last twelve hours I did remember: Doug coming to my car and pulling me out of the wreck. I suppose it was because of the concussion, but I didn't recall the snippet with shock or fear or pain or anything but giddiness at being saved by Doug. If my memory of this was accurate, I'd acted like such a dork, no wonder he thought we'd connected and I'd fallen for him for real.

His wet black hair lay against his skin glowing white in the headlights. His voice rumbled in my ear. He smelled like chlorine. After twenty replays, I realized my subconscious was trying to tell me something. The wreck had been awful, but some elements of it I *needed* to be true, only changed a bit. I'd had sex with Brandon last Monday, and despite my best efforts, I hadn't seen him since—or if I had, I didn't remember. What if he'd been in the other car instead of Mike and Doug? What if he were my hero?

"Zoey," said Brandon. Did he have a broken leg like Doug? No, he wasn't hurt—at least, not yet. He reached into the Bug, lifted me out, and carried me across the grass. Behind us, the Bug exploded (the deer was clear of the blast zone). Even as big and solid as Brandon was, the shock wave slammed him to the ground. He twisted in midair so he took the brunt of the landing and I was cushioned on top of him.

"Brandon, I'm so sorry," I murmured.

"Sorry!" he groaned, in pain because of his heroics. "It's not your fault. Hush now." He stroked his fingers across my scalp. My hair didn't tangle. It wasn't raining.

This new and improved scenario was less satisfying. Maybe I'd been with Brandon earlier in the night, and that memory was more appealing than this fantasy, if only I could access it. After making love with Brandon at the beach party and dropping him off at his house in the main part of town, maybe I'd been headed home when I wrecked.

The thought made me flush in the hot bathwater. If we'd done it, would I be able to tell? The first time I'd felt it the next day. How about the second?

I glanced into the corners of the ceiling as if cameras would suddenly materialize in my bathroom, of all places. I pressed my fingers into myself, then outside. I rubbed my fingertips in wider and wider circles. I wasn't sore.

That didn't mean anything. I'd taken painkillers for my head. They might have dulled the soreness. Maybe Brandon and I had done it after all.

What if we'd done it? I was on the pill. I reached into the drawer nearest the bathtub to check and, sure enough, I'd taken my pill yesterday like a good girl. Right after my seventeenth birthday, my mom had suggested I get on the pill. At the time I didn't bother to tell her she had nothing to worry about.

Now she did. God bless the pill. But that wouldn't protect me against a venereal disease. Surely Brandon had used a condom again. I wouldn't have let him do it otherwise. I hadn't hit my head and gone crazy until the wreck after.

The more I invented worst-case scenarios and dismissed them logically, the more deflated I felt. Catching a venereal disease or getting pregnant because of something Brandon had done to me would be the end of me. Yet the idea seemed so normal and teenage and, dared I say, *romantic* compared with everything else going wrong in my life just then. Comforting.

I was scaring myself.

Reboot, reboot, reboot. I sank deeper into the water and massaged myself again. Testing for tenderness gave way to making myself feel better. It helped with my headache. I forgot all about my headache and Brandon as I opened for Doug. He slipped his hands into my jeans and explored me with his fingers, and finally took me there in the wet grass.

I STEPPED FROM THE BATHTUB WITH a smaller headache (marble-sized) and a resolution to stop being so screwed up.

After drying my hair (which still didn't cover the bruise very well), putting on makeup (which did), inserting fresh contact lenses, and pulling on dry clothes, I sat on the living room sofa, waiting for my dad and Ashley to leave. As I painted my fingernails, I brainstormed for ways I could find out exactly what I'd done last night without revealing the extent of my amnesia and getting myself committed.

I would ask around carefully. If that didn't work, I would hope Doug wasn't out to get me after all, and admit to him that I'd lost my memory not just of the wreck but of the whole night. If, and only if, I exhausted all my other possibilities, I would trust him with this.

I smudged the paint on that fingernail and had to remove it and start over.

And otherwise, I would keep my own counsel. In middle school I dreaded the rare times I rode somewhere in the car alone with my dad. He wouldn't say a word the whole time.

Maybe I remembered it wrong (and I sure wouldn't place any bets based on my memory *now*), but it seemed we'd gotten along fine when I was little. He wasn't home much, but on weekends he would play with me. Swim with me in the ocean, before we built this new house with a pool. Lie on his back in the sand, balance me on his feet raised above his head, and let me play airplane.

Something happened when I was in grade school—the opening of Slide with Clyde, I suppose—and suddenly he was in a bad mood all the time. My mom would say that unlike her, unlike me, he was a quiet person. He didn't want or need to talk out his observations about life or his problems. He kept his own counsel. I resented him for that. But considering that my mom had gone insane, it wasn't wise to continue along *her* path. I would keep my own counsel from now on.

And I would get started on my investigation, asking Keke and Lila what happened, if my dad and Ashley would hurry up and leave already. Waving my fingernails in the air to dry them, I glanced up at the cameras every ten seconds. There was no reason for the cameras to irk me. No one would be watching me but my dad. Like he said, it would be as if he were here in the house with me. And I'd never done anything to alarm a parent anyway. Except have sex with Brandon.

But now, with the cameras rolling, I wanted what I couldn't have. I wanted to take advantage of my dad leaving me alone for a week. I wanted to throw a wild party, roll a joint on the cutting board in the kitchen, make love to Brandon on my dad's bed. Anything bad. I wanted to make out with Doug right here on the sofa where he'd sat an hour ago. It still smelled faintly like him, of chlorine and sea.

Finally they came downstairs. My dad's arms were full of Ashley's luggage as he blustered through the room, but I called to him anyway. I had to take care of myself and my own needs, because clearly nobody else was going to. "Dad, if I get an insurance check in the mail while you're gone, can I shop around for another car?"

"You owe me out of that check," he said. "I paid to have your car towed to the junkyard from the road into town."

I filed away this information: he'd just told me where the wreck happened. And I nodded, trying not to make waves. "I'm pretty sure I can get another classic Bug for the same price as the first."

"Absolutely not," he said. "No Bug."

I looked to Ashley. She looked out to sea. She couldn't see it through the living room wall, but she looked in that direction.

"Why not?" I asked.

"You're not buying another heap," he said. "That Bug had no air bag. The aftermarket seat belts broke on impact. That's how you got so banged up in the first place." He gestured to my forehead. "Next time you'll be dead."

I realized I'd been rubbing my head. I put my hand down, took a deep breath, and asked reasonably, "If you want me to use my own money for a car but you won't let me buy an old car I can afford, what do you expect me to drive?"

He shrugged. "You can drive my Mercedes next week while I'm gone. Next summer you can work again and add to your money."

"And in the meantime? How am I supposed to get around? Is Ashley going to homeschool me?" Never let the jury see how angry you are. My mom had taught me that. Never let them see you lose your cool. However, my mom did not argue cases in court while people whacked her in the head with marbles.

Ashley laughed. "I'm sure it will all work out," she said, patting my dad's butt to scoot him on out the door. He had to make a second trip upstairs to carry down all her luggage. They were lucky to fit everything in her Beamer. In the end Ashley seemed fonder of me than she'd ever been before, while my dad glared at me like it was my fault he had to worry about me dropping dead from brain damage, thus ruining his vacation. I wanted to reassure him that when I started school a few weeks ago, I'd listed only my mom as an emergency contact. If I dropped dead at school, they wouldn't have a phone number for my dad anyway.

I decided to let him sweat it. I kept my own counsel. Cheerfully I waved good-bye and best wishes to them as Ashley executed a seventeen-point turn in the courtyard and sped through the gate. Then I sank onto a teak bench on the porch and called Keke and Lila.

* * *

"Where were Mike and Doug headed when you hit each other?" Lila asked from the backseat as Keke sped their rusty Datsun through the warm morning. Hitching a ride with them was the best way I could think of to reconstruct last night. They could take me by Brandon's for a visit and debriefing. Then I'd go with them to the swim meet and grill the team about what happened, though I wouldn't compete. And I didn't think I should drive myself. The headache was still marble-sized, but I felt like I was standing on marbles too. I might lose my balance at any second.

"I don't know where they were going," I said, hoping I wasn't supposed to know. I'd been trying to get Lila and Keke to tell me what happened since they'd picked me up. It was harder than I'd thought. I'd admitted to them only what I'd told Doug: that I didn't remember the wreck itself. More than this and I was afraid they would report it to their mother, she would try to report it to my mother but get my dad instead, and he might actually make good on his threat to have me committed.

The twins didn't automatically offer a recap of events. Very frustrating. And as I prompted them, I had to choose my words carefully so I didn't give away how little I knew. I couldn't say *I had such a great time at the football team's party* or *I had such an awful time at the football team's party* because the opposite might have happened. After a few seconds of a boy band wailing on the CD player, I settled for, "Wow, what a party. I'll remember it for the rest of my life."

"Why?" they asked at the same time.

I threw up my hands like they were *so dense.* "Because of what happened. You know."

"No," Keke said, "we *don't* know. You told us you couldn't find Brandon, and then you disappeared. Then it started raining, so Lila and I came home. What happened?"

"Oh, just the usual," I said.

"What was so great about it that you'll remember it for the rest of your life?" Lila persisted. "Maybe I was drunker than I thought, but it sounds like we weren't at the same party."

"My head hurts," I said out the open window. We'd reached the straight stretch of the road into town, where my dad had said I'd wrecked. Sure enough, black tire tracks careened across the road, and broken glass twinkled in the grass on the shoulder. A deer stood in the trees, chewing, watching traffic. I shook my fist at it.

"You're nuts," Keke said.

We reached downtown. The high school and the football stadium. City hall. The police station. The county courthouse where my mom worked. A historic town square with striped awnings on storefronts, including the police station and my mom's office. The dried skeletons of petunias in pots outside her office door, because no one was there to water them. It was a quaint little downtown like any small town's, built in an era before tourists cared about the beach. The only difference was that ours was built on sand.

Keke turned the Datsun off the square, down the road with new housing developments: the one where Gabriel lived, then the one where Keke and Lila lived. After a couple of miles, the impressive entrance to Brandon's neighborhood appeared, an enormous facade of an antebellum mansion with faux marble columns painted to look like they were smothered in wisteria. The neighborhood itself was a grid of brand-new identical brown brick houses, one story, on such narrow lots that they'd put the front door on the diagonal, set back from the wide two-car garage door dominating the front.

"And I thought all the houses on *our* street looked alike," Lila said. "How do you find him in here?"

"Count three streets over and then six houses down," I said. Not that I came over much. We'd been together only a week, and he'd been busy. I had cruised by a few times on my way home from swim practice in case he was outside. His family didn't seem to be outdoorsy types. His house was always shut tight.

Today we didn't need to count. Clouds parted. Angels trumpeted. In the grassy strip that passed for his lawn, powerful spotlight beams crisscrossed, advertising his house. An airplane flew overhead like the ones that dragged advertisements for tourists at the beach, proclaiming BRANDON LIVES HERE.

He stood in his driveway, soaping slow circles along the Buick, with his shirt off.

"You can say that again." Lila breathed at the sight of the muscles moving in Brandon's back. I wondered what strangled noise I'd made that she was agreeing with.

"Stephanie Wetzel can say it again," Keke declared, nodding toward the house across the street from Brandon's. A curtain in the diagonal front door fluttered shut.

"Do you think she needs us to give her a ride to the high school?" I suggested.

"*She's* the one who's been giving *Brandon* rides," Keke said.

Lila hit her.

"Hit her again for me," I grumbled.

"I don't mean *that* kind of ride," Keke said. "I mean, she's been giving Brandon rides to school since Brandon's Buick broke. You didn't know that?"

I had not known this. I had not known the Buick was broken. It explained why Brandon hadn't popped over to my house for a visit during the week. It didn't explain why he hadn't asked *me* for a ride.

"If the Buick is so broken, how'd he back it out of the garage?" Lila asked.

I whirled in my seat to face her. "What happened to Brandon and me being perfect and dreamy?"

"Only if you keep up the maintenance," Keke said. She parked the Datsun in the street because Brandon's driveway was too small for two cars. "Flirt hard."

I turned to Lila for verification. She shrugged. "We're just saying."

This was not exactly the pep talk I needed. But Brandon had already stopped scrubbing and turned his muscled trunk toward us, wondering who might emerge from the somewhat crusty Datsun 280z. I gave myself one last glance in the side mirror. It seemed my makeup was still caked nicely over the bruise. But I got only a glimpse. I didn't want Brandon to catch me looking at myself, like I cared too much. From my angle stepping out of the car, most of my face was hidden by the words OBJECTS IN MIRROR ARE CLOSER THAN THEY APPEAR.

"Hey, baby!" I called.

"Hey!" he called back, and he did *not* glance ever so briefly at Stephanie Wetzel's house. I did not see that. Keke had put that idea in my head, and how could I tell anyway, with the bright sunlight glinting off his pecs?

I walked toward him. He threw his soapy sponge onto the hood and met me halfway, just like he was supposed to. He wrapped me in his muscular arms, squeezed me, and let me go, running his damp hand down my arm.

I said, "We were just on our way to the swim meet" (and took a detour several miles out of our way) "and I stopped by to tell you I had a wreck last night!"

His eyebrows shot up. "With Doug?"

Someone had told him about Doug and me in the emergency room! Only . . . if that were true, Brandon wouldn't have been rubbing his thumb back and forth across my forearm.

Maybe he'd heard a less incriminating version of the story, and I could still pass the whole incident off as what it was: lust induced by brain damage. I punched him playfully in the shoulder. "You heard already and you didn't call me!"

He stared at me for a moment with his mouth open. "I didn't hear *you* were in a wreck. I heard *Doug* was in a wreck." Now he looked over the top of my head, toward Stephanie Wetzel's house. This was not my imagination.

It crossed my mind that he was lying about something. I knew he lied. He'd lied to every single girl he'd had sex with over the summer. But I was the one he told *about* the lies. I wasn't the one he lied *to*. Of course, that meant I wouldn't know what he acted like to the girl when he was lying to her. He might very well be lying now.

No, I was just paranoid about everything today. Because of our history, Brandon's relationship with me was different. We were good friends, and we could trust each other. I saw there was more to him than beachy-clean good looks and a buff body. I told him about swerving to miss the deer and hitting Mike and Doug.

While I talked, he continued to stare toward Stephanie's house. I thought he wasn't paying attention to me. I verified this by asking, "So, you're not mad about last night?"

He didn't seem very concerned about my wreck. He hadn't lifted my bangs to peer at my bruise. But he must have reasoned I couldn't be too bad off if I was here, talking to him. Right?

Then I realized he was unwittingly about to tell me what happened last night. I asked carefully, "Mad? Should I be?"

"Definitely not." He frowned down at me, blue eyes looking straight into my eyes. "I told you not to come to the party."

"You did," I agreed. That much I remembered.

"I missed you, though."

I heaved a satisfied sigh. He hadn't told me what I'd been up to last night. But he *had* told me what I *hadn't* been up to. If he'd missed me, we hadn't spent a lot of time together. Probably we'd had a big argument about me crashing his man-party.

"You could make it up to me," I said, stepping closer to him again. My flip-flop was inside his big bare foot, my thigh inside his thigh. My neck hurt, standing this close to him and looking up—which reminded me of doing the same thing last night at the football game with Doug.

WRONG ANSWER.

"I want to *see* you," I said quickly. By *see you* I meant *get down and dirty with you in the back of the Buick.* Or whatever car was handy. He stared blankly at me, so I wasn't sure he got it. I clarified, "I want an encore of Monday night. But I'm still feeling a little dizzy from the wreck. I don't think I should drive tonight. Could you borrow a car and come see me after the swim team gets back from the meet? We could go to the beach park again. Shirt optional." I giggled as I slid my fingers across his chest. I noticed the fingernail polish was smeared on my pinkie.

"Mmmmm," he said. At first this seemed like a purr of approval at my touch. But no, it was a rejection of the encore idea. "My parents are going out in their car." *And not a single one of my hundred friends on the football team can lend me his wheels.* Say it!

"How about tomorrow?" I persisted. "I'm sure I'll feel better by then, and I can drive us in my dad's Benz."

He looked toward his house. "Tomorrow's a school night. I have to study. My parents have been on my shit about my grades. I already flunked an algebra test."

It seemed to me that he could go out with me tomorrow night if he studied now rather than sudsing a broken Buick. But Lord knew parents were weird. I didn't want Brandon's parents to think I was pushy because I'd forced the issue. "Then maybe you could come to my swim meet on Wednesday at six?"

"Mmmmm," he said.

"School night?" I asked. It came out bitter and I could have kicked myself.

"School night," he agreed.

"Could you catch up on your studying before then, since you have so much time to plan for it?"

"Mmmmm," he said.

At this point I think I was about to tell him to stuff it. But that would be crazy. Brandon was my friend. He had legitimate issues with seeing me. He was not screwing me over. He would not do that to me.

"Yeah, maybe I could make that," he finally grumbled. "I know it's important to you."

"And maybe I could take you out after? I'll let you drive the Benz." I was under strict orders from my dad not to let anyone drive the Benz. Too bad. He should have installed an onboard ClydeCam. This was important.

"I'll try." Brandon put his heavy arm around me. His skin was warm from the sun. He had put his arm around me a lot during the summer, inducing friendly tingles. Though I didn't want to be his girlfriend back then, he was hotness incarnate, and I loved it when he touched me. Now that I *was* his girlfriend, I should have felt positively giddy with his arm around me, a little taste of the next time we went parking.

Instead, I felt the slightest bit nauseated, like on Monday night. This was because our relationship was so new, and sex was so new to me. I would work on this.

Never mind. He gripped my hand in his big hand and popped my knuckles one by one. When he'd tried to do this during the summer, I'd squealed and jerked my hand away. Now I should have let him do it because feeling so vulnerable, I welcomed any show of affection from him. But with the dizziness and the headache, I simply couldn't stand him popping my knuckles. I pulled away and was surprised at how easily my hand slipped out of his.

6

"Tardy!" Ian hollered as I stepped through the sliding door onto the swim team van. Other boys chuckled and echoed, "Tardy!"

"I have a minute to spare." I checked my watch to verify this, then laughed like I didn't care. Part of my job as team captain was surveying and closing up the women's locker room before we left. Keke had offered to take over for me today, but I didn't want Coach or the team to think I was down for the count, which would be bad for morale. I made sure the faucets in the locker room were turned off and the heavy doors were locked. Naturally I was the last one out.

But after the whole hullabaloo with the team complaining that Doug was tardy, and me telling Coach yesterday, and Doug dissing me at the game last night, and me turning down Doug for a date this morning, the likes of which you did not see around here every day, I did not need a tardy joke erupting every time I made an appearance, like those pop-up prompts suggesting keyboard shortcuts whenever I sent an email. Zoey's here = tardy joke. The tardy joke would remind Doug ten times a day that he was mad at me. Of course, I didn't expect him to be on the van *now*, but he'd show up at school in a few days to a chorus of tardy jokes. I shivered at the very thought of those cold green eyes burning a hole through me.

I shrugged it off and rolled the van door shut behind me. I just wanted to blend in, sink into a seat on the van, and play my electronic sudoku for the forty-minute drive to Panama City. I scanned the van for an empty place. Usually there was just enough room for all of us. I got along with everyone, so being the last one on the bus wouldn't be a problem unless I was stuck next to Stephanie Wetzel—whom I had no real reason to dislike, I reminded myself. She lived across the street from Brandon. It made perfect sense for her to give him rides.

Seventeen of us plus Coach in the driver's seat filled the van. A Zoey-shaped space should have remained on the second or third bench. Today the first three rows were packed—more than packed, with girls sitting on top of boys and giggling about it. The backseat was empty. There must be something wrong with the seat to drive people away. Something dark and dirty. I peeked over the third row to find out what the problem was.

Doug.

He stretched across the entire seat, asleep. His leg in the splint was propped up on his backpack. His crutches lay on the floor beside him.

To allow him to have the whole seat, the team must have figured it had taken a lot for him to drag himself to school for the trip when he couldn't compete. Or they were shocked senseless by this show of team spirit from him.

Or they were afraid for him. Lila shrieked as Mike tickled her. Doug didn't flinch at the noise. His face was smooth, slack, his eyes hidden beneath heavy lids and long black lashes.

Had anyone checked his vital signs?

Doug was not dead. Doug had not overdosed. If he were that bad off, he wouldn't retain the muscle tone to clutch the prescription pill bottle in one hand. This was what I told myself so my teammates couldn't see that my heart strained in my chest and I was back in my mother's bedroom, trying to fix everything. I slipped off my backpack, crouched near Doug in the aisle, and tilted my head to read the label on the bottle.

"Touch my Percocet and you're dead."

I started at the rumble of his voice. His bright eyes pinned me to the floor.

And then I found my legs and escaped back up the aisle, hurrying before Coach started the van. The argument with Doug this morning was too fresh. I didn't want to continue the same argument all the way to Panama City, trapped in the backseat with him.

I stepped around Gabriel sprawled across an armrest and reached Coach in the driver's seat. Coach examined a map of the area even though he'd grown up here and had probably driven to Panama City one billion times. Ian had snagged the seat next to Coach, but he had earbuds in so he couldn't hear me. I bent to whisper in Coach's ear, "Doug shouldn't be here."

"He *should* be here. He should not be *broken*. Next time, hit the deer." Coach gazed up at me and used one finger to brush my bangs away from my forehead. Apparently I hadn't done as good a job with my makeup as I'd thought. Or he could see things Brandon couldn't. "You shouldn't be here either."

"Yes, I should." I needed to find out where I had been last night. Anyway, even on a healthy day my biggest contributions to the team were cheerleading and keeping records, and I could do that with a concussion. Probably.

He shrugged. "We need to get going. Roll Fox out the door into the street if you want to, but you take responsibility for that. I don't want to meet his padre in a dark alley down by the waterfront." He threw the map at Ian, who jumped out of his music-induced trance and spilled his Gatorade. Coach started the engine.

I had no choice. Knowing Coach's driving, if I stood my ground I'd go through the windshield, taking out another rear-view mirror. "While I'm up here, I'd like to say something to the team about the party we went to last night. So don't drive until I'm done, okay?" I bent down and looked Coach in the eye to make sure he'd heard me.

He eyed me right back. "What kind of party? Were there bad things going on at this party?"

Beats me. "I assume."

"I don't want to hear about it."

"Cover your ears." After Coach had gamely covered his ears with his hands and relaxed against the driver's seat for the duration, I called out to the van in general, "May I have your attention, please."

"Speeeeech," said several boys.

"Right," I said. "I just want to thank all of you for going to the party with me last night."

I paused, waiting for the comments under boys' breath that would give me hints about what really happened. For once, the van was silent. Every member of the team (except Doug) gazed at me, rapt, waiting for me to continue.

"It was such a memorable party," I ventured.

They stared at me, unblinking, chewing their cud like deer.

"Though it didn't end well," I finished.

"The van's about to wreck!" Connor yelled. "Quick, Doug, save me!"

"Doug, the van's exploding! Carry meeeeee!" pealed more boys. Doug's hand popped up from behind the last seat back, giving them all the bird.

I had lost their attention. "Anyway, thanks for going to the party with me." So much for finding out what had happened. I pulled one of Coach's hands away from his ear. "The coast is clear." I turned and made my way down the narrow passage between the door and the seats, holding on tightly to each seat back as I went. Coach was not the safest driver. Sure enough, he swung around the high school sign at full speed and *erk*ed to a stop just short of the highway through town, tossing everything on the van to the left, including me. My grip on the seat back slipped, and my bruised ribs found out just how solid the edge of the seat back was. "Fuck!"

"What did you say?" screamed Keke and Lila.

"Zoey!" squealed the junior girls.

"First tardy, now this," mumbled assorted boys.

"I beg your pardon." I rounded the last seat back to face Doug.

"Language," he said with one eyebrow raised. "I've never heard you cuss before."

"You're a bad influence."

"Fucking A."

With growing suspicion that I was stuck here with him for the whole trip, I tried to lighten the mood. "Must be the brain damage."

"Why didn't you tell me this morning? That explains everything." I should have known he'd come up with a nasty one-liner. Or two. "I think the brain damage actually happened Monday night, when you did it with Brandon."

I knew he was in pain, but this was too much. He couldn't insult what I had with Brandon. I tried to stomp my foot in the aisle in frustration, but my flip-flop stuck to the floor seasoned with a decade's worth of spilled Coke. "Bitter much?"

"Oooooh," said Connor and Nate, leaning over the seat back to watch us, like they were a couple of deer watching the road. Slowly they sank down, and Doug and I were alone again. Relatively speaking.

But Doug had closed his eyes. I was dismissed.

I watched him for a few seconds more. Then I gazed at the floor. Dared I sit down there? The corrugated rubber for traction showed darker stains with scraps of paper and grains of sand embedded in them, which meant double-sticky with unknown substance. Coke was optimistic. But it wasn't the sticky that turned me off so much. It was my teammates watching me sit in sticky. Down on the floor, below them, like a nut job. Because Doug Fox wouldn't move over for me.

"Doug," I said. "Scoot. You can't take up a whole seat."

"Yes, I can," he said without opening his eyes. "My leg is swollen and I'm supposed to keep it elevated. Head or feet? Pick one."

I looked doubtfully at his splint and his free foot, both of which seemed reasonably clean. His battered flip-flop must be somewhere on the floor. Again, I wouldn't mind having his feet in my lap so much. It was the idea of other people seeing his feet in my lap. A sane girl with high self-esteem wouldn't allow this to happen.

But I hadn't forgotten the strange way Brandon may or may not have acted when he mentioned Doug in the wreck. Did he suspect Doug and I had gotten lovey-dovey in the ER? Was he jealous? If I held Doug's head in my lap for forty miles, Brandon would find out.

The van braked hard.

Every girl screamed. I caught the seat back with both hands

so I wouldn't fly up the aisle. Doug wasn't as lucky. The length of his body hit the seat back all at once, and he fell onto the floor on top of his crutches.

"Coach!" everyone yelled.

"Damn deer in the road," Coach yelled. Actually we were at a stoplight.

"Point taken," I hollered. "Enough already." I slid across the seat and held out a hand to help Doug, who eased up from the floor. "Are you okay?"

"Thank God for Percocet." He ignored my hand. But he asked, "Are *you* okay?"

"This time."

"Well, we're almost to the four-lane. Sit the hell down before Coach kills you." Doug crawled back onto the seat. He was precisely as tall as he'd been before he fell down, and there was just as little room for me.

So I edged along the seat back with my backpack ahead of me, trying not to step on his crutches. When I drew even with his head, I gently slid my arm around his shoulders and eased him forward. He didn't resist, but he didn't help either. He was heavy. I slid onto the seat, crossed my legs under me, and laid his head in my lap.

I walked a fine line here. I trusted Brandon, but what if Stephanie Wetzel really was after him? I didn't want to give her any ammunition to help break up Brandon and me.

On the other hand, I wanted Doug to like me. As much as

he *could* like me now that I'd apparently seduced and then jilt-
ed him in a twelve-hour period. He knew way too much about
me and my problems, and he was too much of a loose cannon
to be allowed out into the world with a grudge against me. Everyone would expect me to take care of him while he was hurt.
That's how I functioned. And as long as he'd kept our secret,
no one knew what had gone on between us at the wreck or in
the hospital.

I looked down at him in my lap. He squeezed his eyes shut,
hurting and wired. To me this didn't say *Percocet.* "Doug."

"Zoey," he said evenly. His very evenness dripped sarcasm.

"Are you okay? You don't seem okay."

He licked his lips, just a tiny pink stroke, upside down. "I
didn't want to take these pills because they're addictive. It'll be
hard enough for me to get a swim scholarship after all this.
The last thing I need is a painkiller addiction. But the hospital
warned me if you wait until the pain is unbearable, the pills
don't take the edge off."

"Oh." My concussion was bad enough. I could only imagine what Doug's broken leg felt like when the IV wore off, he
hadn't taken Percocet yet, and he realized he was caught.

I placed my fingers on either side of his forehead and
rubbed his temples. Even though he was upside down, I could
tell he reacted properly. He tilted toward my fingers, tensing at
the pressure and relaxing all at once. He went still. I kept mas-
saging him for a long time. His skin was hot.

Finally I reached into my backpack on the floor and

snagged my electronic sudoku. Ahhh, I still had problems, but nothing more pressing than where the nine went on the grid. Minutes passed. The conversations on the bus settled into a lulling hum. The van reached the four-lane.

Just when I'd exhausted my possibilities horizontally on the grid, Doug sighed. Without opening his eyes, he rolled just enough to turn his head to the other side on my leg. I returned to sudoku. The land of numbers was stark, with white columns towering in a white room, but familiar and predictable. I relaxed here, wiggled my toes in the sand.

I hadn't yet exhausted my possibilities vertically when he sighed again. This time when he turned his head, he shook it a bit as if to place as much as possible of his longish black hair behind him to cushion his hard skull on my harder leg bone.

The van was freezing. Coach didn't play around when he turned on the air conditioner. But I pulled off my swim team sweatshirt—carefully, so I didn't wake Doug. I folded it in fourths.

I paused, sweatshirt in one hand, the other hand poised beside Doug's head. We were already taking up the backseat of the van together. He lay in my lap. Putting the sweatshirt under his head would be the next step in making him comfortable. It was the least I could do after what we'd been through together last night. Yet my arms tingled and my face flushed hot. For the first time ever I was glad *not* to be wearing a sweatshirt on the van. I looked up to see if anyone was watching me. It didn't seem possible I could be blushing like this for no reason.

Fourteen backs were turned. Even fifteen and sixteen didn't pay attention to me. Mike and Lila arm wrestled with their elbows on a calculus textbook, which I thought was weird. They'd brought their calculus homework on the bus. I usually finished my calculus homework during class, though sometimes I did extra problems for fun. And Mike was actually speaking to Lila. Mike never spoke.

But no one was watching me.

Gently I scooped up Doug's head with my hand and slipped my sweatshirt underneath.

As I laid his head down, his eyes opened. Intense green stared up at me in the afternoon sunlight streaming through the van's back window.

And then he was gone again, head turned on the sweatshirt pillow.

I picked up sudoku and tapped it to turn it back on. But now I didn't feel comfortable holding something hard so close to Doug's face. U.S. 98 wasn't the most evenly paved highway, and I didn't want to bang his nose with my electronics in addition to whacking his leg with my Bug. I didn't feel comfortable touching him either. There was no place to put my hands. I tucked them under my thighs.

And stared down at Doug, drugged, sleeping hard. Black stubble barely shadowed his upper lip and chin and cheeks. His eyes were closed, his eyelashes long, his lips soft with sleep. He was a beautiful boy. It was hard to imagine him going to juvie in ninth grade, or getting suspended in tenth grade for fighting in the hall outside history class, or calling me a spoiled brat last night.

Even though he wore his own swim team sweatshirt, he was cold. His arms were folded tightly across his chest. His sweatshirt bunched around his ribs and stopped there, exposing a flat expanse of tanned stomach and a *V* of fine black hair that started around his inny belly button and pointed downward.

I wondered if blond hair dusted Brandon's belly, and whether he was an inny or outy. I'd seen him without his shirt plenty of times. In the hot afternoons behind the concessions counter at Slide with Clyde, sometimes he'd bare his chest. My dad let him do this because we sold a lot more ice cream that way. And I'd rubbed my hand across Brandon's bare chest not half an hour ago. But all I'd ever noticed was how big and muscular and tan he was. Little things like fine hair and his belly button hadn't occurred to me. Strange that I could share the ultimate intimate moment with a boy without any intimacy at all.

He hadn't even taken his shirt off when we'd done it last Monday. I had always thought my first time would be more of an event, with more leading up to it. Brandon had had enough sex with enough different girls that sex with me didn't reach event status.

But I knew we would get there. I never would have pictured us as a couple before, but now that we shared this bond, I could see us staying together through high school gradua- tion and even into college if he got his football scholarship to FSU.

Doug had nobody. Other than that girl from Destin, I'd never heard of him asking someone out since—well, me, in ninth grade. I wondered if he'd ever had sex.

Despite myself, my eyes traveled back to his flat stomach dusted with fine black hair. From underneath his cargo shorts peeked the gray heathered waistband of his underwear. I won- dered whether they were boxer briefs or maybe plaid flannel boxers, but I couldn't see farther than that waistband. His un- derwear disappeared into the dark.

Now it wasn't just my face burning and my arms tingling. I was tingling in places that Doug was nowhere near touching, so why did I feel guilty? This had nothing to do with Doug. The non sequitur tingling must be what happened when you had sex for the first time and then got a concussion and thought you'd had sex again when you didn't and then found out you wouldn't be alone with your boyfriend for at least a few more days. That is, *brain damage*.

With a gasp I returned to the swim team van jerking across "repairs" in U.S. 98 that had done more harm than good. Doug snuggled his cheek deeper into the sweatshirt in my lap but didn't wake.

Then I looked up at Stephanie Wetzel staring at me over the back of the second seat. I wondered how long she'd watched me look down Doug's pants, and how quickly *this* would get back to Brandon.

Looking isn't cheating. Brandon had said this to me a million times on our lunch break at Slide with Clyde. He would seem deeply absorbed in relating his troubles to me about the latest girl he really liked. Then his eyes would follow an entirely different girl's ass across the food court, and I would punch him playfully for being a hypocrite. *Looking isn't cheating,* he would say. The only difference was that those girls had looked back at Brandon and given him a knowing smile. Doug had no idea I was looking, and if he knew, he would just laugh and say something in that sugar-sweet sarcastic voice of his. *Zoey Commander thinks I'm hot. Hoo-ray.*

Except he'd asked me out this morning.

In the end I stopped torturing myself and allowed myself to look at him. Stephanie couldn't tell what I was staring at. I could say I was staring into space. And Doug was a lot more interesting than sudoku's white landscape of numbers. The landscape of numbers made me feel more sane and the contours of Doug's body made me feel less sane. But in this controlled insanity maybe I could exorcise what was eating me. I let my eyes and my mind wander.

"Go, Lynn!" I called. If she could find an iota more power inside her, she could win the women's 100 fly. On second thought, I screamed, "Go, Stephanie!" She was part of this heat too, and I didn't want anyone to think I was dissing her because she was giving my boyfriend rides.

But before Stephanie or Lynn touched the wall, I sank to the front row bleacher. I'd felt disoriented since I'd followed Doug limping into this fancy natatorium. I'd thought the problem might be that for the first time since I'd joined the varsity team, I was in the stands with screaming friends and parents from five schools rather than in the locker room, getting ready to swim. Or that instead of focusing on the pool in front of me, my mind was on Doug lying on the bleacher behind me, still half asleep. Now that I was getting really dizzy, I decided to cheer from a sitting position for the rest of the heats.

My muscles tensed. My body ached to stretch out and swim. I watched my teammates so closely that I was down in the water with them. I could feel their muscles work, then burn and tire, and the cool water swirling past their bodies. I could tell how fast their times would be before I saw them. I didn't take notes on my clipboard because the host school would give Coach a computer printout of the times for the whole meet, but I was so keyed into times that I guesstimated them automatically.

Even when I wasn't watching the clock, I knew which runs would be personal records. And not because of some internal clock I'd constructed from attending so many practices, but because I knew my teammates' bodies, the ways they moved when they were on, or tired, or distracted. That included

Doug. Before the boys touched the wall at the end of the 200 free, I knew they were slower than Doug's personal best, which he'd bettered every meet this season before we came to a screeching halt in the wreck.

I bet Doug never watched anyone this way.

At the end of the meet, my headache came back. It was kind of funny actually. Watching Connor and Ian in the final heat, I felt a twinge at their first turn. By their second turn I knew the culprit was the headache and not the fact that I'd stared at the pulsing water too long with my eyebrows in knots. By their third turn the golf ball was back, banging against the inside of my skull. By their fourth turn I was looking at my watch to see whether the recommended four hours had elapsed since the last dose of painkillers I'd swallowed during the meet. I stared at my watch dial for a long time. People with concussions needed digital.

The heat ended. Everyone knew what the finish meant toward the point count. Fans of the home team sprang from the bleachers, cheering that they'd won the meet. We came in third out of five. Normally I would have gone with my teammates into the locker room and bitched with them about the officiating, and that one chick from Apalachicola who was like a Creature from the Black Lagoon, and the fact that we would have won or at least come in second if we'd had Doug.

The headache anchored me to my seat. I couldn't have withstood the escalating pitch of the excited girl-squeals in the locker room. And if Mike sang the boy-band falsetto on the van, I would kill him.

Four tall boys from other schools called to Doug. He brushed past me, maneuvering down the bleachers to the floor to talk to them. They pointed to his splint. He held it out to show them, nodding and then laughing. They'd come to the meet expecting to lose to Doug. They couldn't believe their luck. They wanted to know how long he'd be out—that is, how long their luck would run. I knew this though I couldn't hear them. Their voices mixed with the echoes of the crowd in the natatorium. Every word sounded five times.

Suddenly Doug's finger was under my chin, tilting my face up so he could look into my eyes. I had no idea how long he'd been crouching in front of me, propped on his crutches. "This is why I came," he said. "I figured you were running on adrenaline this morning but you'd crash tonight. And I knew you'd come to the meet, because you're such a dork."

"I love it when you talk dirty." This was not the thing to say. Doug was telling me he cared about me. He'd come to the meet to watch over me. I should say the right thing and then we would have a little conversation. He would feel comforted because he'd connected with another human in the very small way that was the only way Doug ever connected with anybody. He'd limp back to the van and fall asleep to sweet dreams. I couldn't think of the right thing to say.

"Go take some Tylenol," he told me.

"I can't," I whispered. "It won't be four hours for another hour."

"Go—take—some—Tylenol," he said in the stern voice of my mom when I talked back.

I found the bottle in my backpack and swallowed three pills at the water fountain. Relaxed against the painted cement block wall (ah, nice and cool) and stared into space for a while. Followed my teammates to the van. Leaned heavily on each seat as I passed. Thank God the backseat was empty. I would still need to argue over it with Doug, but at least I could argue lying down. He was welcome to share the seat with me. Lying down in more cramped quarters shouldn't bother him. With Percocet on his side, he could fall asleep in a mosh pit.

7

"Zoey! Doug!"

"What," I grumbled into the seat. I could tell from the way my face resisted movement that the fabric texture had imprinted itself on my skin.

"Captain Anderson's!" Keke sang. Captain Anderson's in Panama City was my favorite tourist trap seafood restaurant. And there was no way I was getting off this van. My headache had faded, but I was asleep. Gone. Checked out of the ocean-side resort.

"Fuck off," Doug said. His voice came from right beside me. I was lying on my stomach, so he must be lying on his side against the seat back.

The front doors slammed, and the side door rolled shut.

A stuffy silence settled. Even though night had fallen, the van was too warm with the air conditioner off. Welcome to Florida.

Doug slid along my body, backing out one end of the seat without disturbing me. Now that plenty of seats were available, he wanted his own. Fine. I spread out over the whole seat like an ice cube melting, liquifying faster as my fingers touched the upholstery still hot from his body. Dreams of him were better than the real thing.

A creak and a thump. He cranked open one window, then another.

His weight flattened the seat padding as he slid next to me again. It made sense for him to return. He'd have to lie with me when the team got on the van anyway. And if he felt as bad as I did, he wanted to move as few times as possible.

Back to dreams of him. He probably couldn't help his knee touching my thigh.

"Zoey," he said, reaching into the Bug. He lifted me out and carried me across the grass. Behind us, the Bug exploded (the deer had wandered to the shoulder and was peering at us through the trees). Even as tall and solid as Doug was, the shock wave slammed him to the ground. He twisted in midair so he took the brunt of the landing and I was cushioned on top of him.

"Doug, I'm so sorry," I murmured.

"It's not your fault," he whispered. "Hush now." His knee pressed my thigh. His knee nudged my thighs open as his tongue opened my mouth. He kissed me hard in the soft rain. I shivered.

I took one more breath through my nose as the van came to life around me. Without opening my eyes I knew exactly what had happened. I'd gotten cold when Coach turned the air conditioner on, and I'd snuggled close to Doug. I recognized his scent of sea and chlorine. Now we'd parked at our high school. The lights were on and the team gathered their bags and shuffled through the door. Every one of them probably peered into the backseat to see what Doug and I were up to.

But maybe Doug wouldn't know I'd snuggled up to him. Maybe he was still asleep and I had nothing to worry about. I opened my eyes.

He was staring down at me.

I jumped in surprise.

"Sorry," he said. "I wanted to make sure you had normal pupil reflexes."

I started to ease up into a sitting position, but something held me down. Doug's long fingers circled my arm. His thumb pressed my wrist.

"Checking your pulse." He let me go. "Now it's sped up."

Was he telling me he knew I'd dreamed about him? I asked casually, "What would my pulse tell you anyway?"

"Do I look like a doctor?" He bent down. I bent too, to grab his crutches for him, but he'd already snagged them from the floor.

He crutched up the aisle. At the sliding door he paused to say something to Keke. She nodded. Then he placed the tips of his crutches carefully on the pavement outside the van and heaved himself down. I couldn't see him fall but I heard him yell, "Fuck!"

"Zoey, girlfriend," Keke called back to me. "You're spending the night with Lila and me so we can keep an eye on you."

Gabriel said something about girl-on-girl-on-girl action. Lila vaulted over two seat backs to slap him. Everyone remaining on the bus gathered around them to watch. Everyone, that is, except Mike. Right in front of me, he bent to stuff his belongings into his bag, then turned for the door.

As he turned, he looked straight at me. Then he looked away just as quickly so I'd think his eyes were simply wandering as he exited the bus.

But I'd seen it. And he'd blushed. As if he'd witnessed everything I'd done to Doug in the grass beside the wreck, and he was embarrassed for me that I'd do such a thing while I had a relationship with Brandon.

Or as if he were angry Doug had asked him to lie to everyone, including Brandon, and pretend he hadn't seen what I'd done.

Or . . . like he wanted to get out of the van before I could ask him any questions about the wreck. Like he knew something I didn't.

"Come on, girl." Lila pulled me.

"I can't stay with you," I murmured. "My dad expects me home."

"Doug said your dad is gone and your mom is out of town and we need to keep an eye on you," Keke informed me.

Your mom is out of town. I laughed at this euphemism. At least Doug wasn't spilling the beans about her. As long as nobody knew about it, I could keep pretending it hadn't happened.

"My dad expects me home," I insisted. "He has ways of checking on me."

"Call him," Lila said. "Or we'll get our mother to call him if he doesn't believe you."

I waved this idea away with both hands. Their mother would find out my dad was gone and my mom was way gone. Their mother would report me to Child Protective Services.

"Then just email him and tell him what you're doing and why," Lila said. "Here's my phone. Type him an email message and we'll take a picture of you looking . . ."

"Used," Keke said.

I took Lila's phone, typed my dad's email address and the message, *I am fucked*, and handed it back to her.

"Zoey!" she shrieked.

Keke snatched the phone from Lila and looked at the screen. "You're going to get yourself grounded. No parking with Brandon for you, ever." She pressed a key over and over with her thumb, backspacing.

"Speaking of," I moaned. "Do you think anyone got the wrong idea about Doug and me back here?"

They stared at me blankly. Lila prompted, "Like . . . ?"

"Like Stephanie Wetzel would tell Brandon."

Keke prompted, "That . . . ?"

"That Doug and I were making out or something."

"You *were?*" Lila shrieked.

"No!" I wailed, slapping my hands over my ears.

Lila laughed hysterically. "You and Doug? That's so random!"

Keke patted my knee in sympathy. "No, nobody suspected you were making out with Doug Fox. You hit your head harder than we thought."

I'd always lived on the ocean. I mean, *right* on the ocean, with the noise of the surf drowning out the TV when I opened the windows. But I never, ever took the ocean for granted, because most people in our town lived inland. Including Keke and Lila.

I woke on their den sofa at my normal time in the morning, which was pretty early. A lot earlier than other teenagers who told me they slept until the afternoon on weekends. I didn't understand this. I had homework to do and books to read and data to enter. Keke and Lila's younger siblings weren't even up watching cartoons yet.

Now the headache was bad enough for painkillers, but not so bad that I was careful about moving my head too quickly. I was getting back to normal. So I approximated my normal routine. Routine was important. Since my mom tried to kill herself, routine reassured me that my life was still perfectly normal. First thing in the morning at my dad's house, I always stepped out on my balcony to watch the ocean and breathe the air. Here, after picking off the Lego pieces stuck to my face, I stepped out the den door into their backyard.

I'd been here a lot. I should have known which direction their house faced. But it was in a labyrinth of a neighborhood like Brandon's with even less structure, winding curves rather than right angles in the roads. I always got confused coming here. And this morning, low gray clouds blanketed the sky, almost as if it were winter. Where was the glowing patch indicating east and the sun? I had no idea which way was south and the ocean.

Whirling from back door to swing set to garden gnome, I choked out a cry and slapped my hands over my mouth. There *was* no direction. I held my breath to keep from panicking. My heart thumped in my chest. Tears stung my eyes.

Finally I turned back toward the house. One of Keke and Lila's little brothers stood in the open doorway in his Superman diaper, pink elephant under his arm, watching me. Oh, I knew what he was feeling, watching a Big Person go crazy.

I sniffled and made a quick pass under my eyes with my fingertips to dry up. "Good morning!" I called. "I just realized I lost something. But no worries. I'll find it."

Superman eyed me warily.

"Do you want to help me make breakfast?" I asked, imitating Keke's enthusiasm.

That got his mind off my erratic behavior. Soon Princess Diaper joined us in the kitchen. I ended up making breakfast for what seemed like fifteen or sixteen children. I liked kids. I ran the birthday parties at Slide with Clyde, and of course as a lifeguard I watched kids all day long. But at Slide with Clyde I blew a chirp on a whistle when I needed their attention. I gave them a command with a nod of my head, and they followed orders because I was scary with my face stern and my eyes hidden behind my sunglasses.

In contrast, these kids didn't understand the meaning of, "Don't do that." I cleaned up a lot of flour from the kitchen floor and inadvertently thought really hard about the new half sibling I would have soon. Ashley's baby was due on Valentine's Day.

Then I read to the kiddies until I was hoarse. But I could only stand so much of this. I wanted to go home. I had no toiletries except what I'd taken in my backpack to the swim meet, and I was too tall to wear Keke and Lila's clothes.

More than this, I wanted to find out what had happened to me. And that required a visit to the place where I'd wrecked.

"Is your mom going to sue Mike?" Keke asked. My friends lumped all lawyers into one category and made a lot of lawsuit jokes, forever asking whether my mom was going to sue people. My mom was a public defender. She'd never filed a lawsuit in her life (disappointing my dad, who said only a spoiled brat would go to school all those years and choose to make as little money as possible). I was glad Keke asked this, though. It meant she thought my mom was still working. News hadn't gotten out yet.

"No, the wreck wasn't Mike's fault," I said. "Or mine. My mom just wants me to take some measurements while the evidence is still here. She might be able to get me more insurance money." I hated lying to my friends, especially since they'd taken care of me last night and they were helping me now. I was getting desperate.

Seeing the tire marks crossing the road in the distance, I parked Keke and Lila's Datsun on the shoulder. They pulled out buckets and sheets of poster board that we'd bought at the drugstore and printed with HIGH SCHOOL SWIM TEAM FUND-RAISER. I didn't expect to make any money. The signs would slow cars down and keep them from creaming me while I did my research. We left Keke near the Datsun. Lila flounced a hundred yards down the road to stop traffic on that end.

I walked more slowly after her, careful not to jostle my still-fragile brain. It was strange to walk somewhere I'd driven past a million times. The smells were different, melted asphalt and warm hay. The sounds were different too: the whisper of my footsteps through the long grass, chirping birds, buzzing insects, the sweep of wind in the trees. And *crunch*. I looked down. My flip-flops ground pieces of my Bug's headlight into the sandy soil. Or pieces of Mike's Miata's headlight—that was the question. I'd reached the tire marks in the road.

I glanced up and down the road before venturing into it. Lila was in place with her sign. Keke had already stopped a sucker in a pickup. Satisfied I wouldn't get hit, I followed the tire marks to the spot where they intersected with a second set of marks and the cars had kissed. The marks weren't very long. Mike and I had been surprised. We couldn't see well in the dark and the hard rain, and the deer came from nowhere.

This is what must have happened. This is what I reconstructed in my mind. But my memory was just as blank as it had been yesterday when I woke up. It started and stopped with Doug.

A cool wind blew at my back just then, tossing my ponytail forward over my shoulder. The day was still overcast. Even though the air was warm as usual, this cool breeze kept creeping up on me. It tangled up the gray clouds in turbulence and filled the otherwise innocuous day in the countryside with foreboding. When the robes started billowing in movies about wizards, that always meant something ominous.

I was scaring myself again.

Taking Keke's dad's mini tape measure from my pocket, I set the end at the outer edge of one tire mark and walked along the metal tape, keeping it from drawing up on me, until I reached the outer edge of the other tire mark and set the measure down. Sixty and a half inches in width. This was the car that had come from the direction of Brandon's house. When I got home I'd look up on the internet whether sixty and a half inches was the width of a Bug or a Miata. Then at least I'd know which way I'd been driving. Simple.

To triangulate my data, I put the end of the tape measure at the outer edge of the tire mark for the second car and calculated that width the same way. This was the car that had come from the direction of the beach.

Sixty and a half inches. Both cars were the same width.

"Fuck." Panic welled up inside me and my heart knocked against my chest wall, trying to escape. I told myself to calm down, calm down. I couldn't wig out here in sight of Lila and Keke. I would find some other way to figure out what had happened to me, and then my life would be back in order. I told myself this, but my heart sped up instead of slowing down. I was on the verge of panic with the sky still overcast and the view south and north on the highway looking exactly the same, until luckily I was distracted by Keke yelling into the distant pickup. My heart slowed down.

At that distance I couldn't tell what she was saying to the people inside, but she shook her poster at them, then her bucket. She threw her poster and bucket into the payload and climbed in after them. I began to see that she and Lila shared something with all their siblings. It was hereditary and they couldn't help it. They were not good at following instructions, such as *do not throw flour* or *stand here in the road until I call you.* The truck must have contained hot boys.

Sure enough, as it drew closer, I saw it was Officer Fox, with Doug in the passenger seat. My heart sped up again.

I released the tape measure so it wound back up into its metal coil, slapping my legs as it went. Then I stuffed it into my back pocket like I wasn't already caught.

"Busted!" Keke squealed at me as the truck pulled onto the shoulder in front of the Datsun. Doug opened the passenger door and stepped out, crutches first.

"Soliciting charitable donations is not illegal," I called past him into the cab to Officer Fox.

"It's not safe to do it on the highway," Officer Fox said. "But you're right, being stupid isn't illegal. Otherwise half this town would be behind bars, and Doug would have gotten the death penalty by now. Hey—" Officer Safety opened the driver's side door and fell out of the cab onto the highway with the engine still running to avoid Doug reaching across the seat to grab him.

Doug gave up, slammed the passenger door, and righted himself on his crutches, hopping a little. "What'cha doing?" he asked me in his sweet, sarcastic voice, pretending he hadn't seen the tape measure.

"Getting some fresh air," I said. The wind at my back flipped my ponytail over my head. I brushed it away. "I've been hanging out at Keke and Lila's house. They have, like, fifteen or sixteen siblings."

"We have *three*," Keke called from the payload as the pickup drove past to retrieve Lila.

"Seems like more," I called back. I stared after the retreating pickup, and Keke knocking on the window to bother Officer Fox, so I wouldn't have to meet Doug's gaze. I should thank him for insisting Keke take me home with her last night. I didn't thank him because all I did lately was thank him and apologize to him and hope he wasn't ruining my mother's life behind my back. I wished we could go back to the way we were at the beginning of the school year, when we avoided each other. Before he called me a spoiled brat at the game. Before he knew I liked to snuggle in the grass. Before I knew what he smelled like.

Because now the wind swirled around us both and wound me up in his scent of chlorine and ocean.

He reached for my mouth. I didn't know what he intended, so I willed myself to stay still and not make a big deal out of his hand moving in slow motion toward me, beside my cheek, almost out of my line of sight. With his pinky he brushed a strand of my hair from the corner of my mouth where the wind had blown it into my lip gloss. His fingertip trailed fire across that tender corner.

And then he put his hand down and smirked at what he'd done to me. At least, that's how it seemed. He stood in the hot air and the cool wind, taller than ever on his crutches, and looked me up and down with his distant green eyes. "So, a little hair of the dog?"

"Where?" I glanced around. Now that Keke and Lila weren't guarding the road, a car could fly by and cream whatever wandered into its path.

Doug whistled and passed his hand in front of my eyes to get my attention. "Hair of the dog. Bloody Mary after you've spent the night drinking. As in, revisiting something helps you get over it."

My eyes followed the path of his hands down as he grabbed the handle of his crutch before it fell over. Did he mean we'd spent the night drinking? I didn't drink. Doug didn't drink while he was in training. Mike did drink. However, he hadn't been drinking before the wreck, or Doug would have been driving Mike's Miata.

Doug's fingers caressed the worn wooden handle of the secondhand crutch. My gaze trailed up his big hand, his wide wrist, his strong forearm meant for pulling his body weight through the water rather than maneuvering himself on land. Slowly I realized he was speaking metaphorically.

And I lashed out. "I do *not* need to get over you," I said more forcefully than I'd intended, because I was lying. Oh God, I was lying again, and now I was confused, but this had to stop. "I am happy dating Brandon. I didn't know you would drive by while I was here. How could I know that?"

He stared at me without blinking, and tilted his head ever so slightly to one side. "I meant you're getting over the *wreck*."

"Right!" I turned toward the skid marks in the road to hide my red face. He would use this to embarrass me in public. Embarrassing me in private was bad enough. *Zoey likes me after she swore she didn't. Zoey has been fantasizing about my knee on her thigh.*

Miraculously, instead of pressing the subject, he gave me a way out. "That's where my brother and I have been, looking at the Bug and the Miata in the junkyard." He waved past me, inland. Then he glanced pointedly at my pocket. "I didn't take a tape measure, though."

I watched past his shoulder, way down the road. In the distance, Lila set down her bucket and poster board, put her hands on her hips, and argued with Officer Fox inside the truck. I willed her to stop arguing and come back to save me from this conversation and this beautiful, snarky, way-too-perceptive boy. The cool breeze caught the poster board and blew it down the shoulder. Lila abandoned her act with Officer Fox and galloped after the poster. No help there.

"I . . ." I said, thinking hard.

Doug raised one black eyebrow at me.

"I'mmmmm still a little confused about what happened. What time did we wreck?"

The suspicious look he gave me let me know I shouldn't have asked this. "About two thirty," he said.

I'd made him suspicious with this question and the answer didn't even give me any information. When I'd lived with my mom, every curfew had been negotiated in detail, taking into account the activity, location, and company associated with said revelry (and sometimes I typed out a contract in legalese like this just to poke fun at her).

But my dad didn't care what time I came in. When we'd wrecked at two thirty in the morning, I could have been headed south for home. Or I could have been headed north to Brandon's house, or elsewhere.

Where?

Officer Fox had gathered Lila and cruised back in our direction. I could slip one more question in and then escape quickly if Doug's eyebrow rose again. I brushed past him and walked along one of the skid marks. I asked over my shoulder,

"So, I was driving along like this? And then, all of a sudden—"
I threw out my arms. "Deer drama! Right?" I turned around to
grin at him.

Uh-oh. His eyebrow was up. "You don't remember which
direction you were driving?"

So I'd aroused his suspicion again. At least I knew now that
I'd been driving in the *other* direction, north toward Brandon's.

Or did I? Maybe Doug wasn't telling me I was wrong. He
was only saying it was a weird question for me to ask. I was
getting dangerously close to admitting I didn't remember the
whole night.

The pickup reached us and pulled to a stop, bringing the
cool breeze with it. I shut my eyes against the sand in my face.

Lila sobbed from the payload, "Now we'll *never* collect
enough money to fund the swim team trip to District!"

"There's no one here for you to bullshit," Doug told her.

"Oh, right." She and Keke climbed out and ran for the Datsun, hampered by the breeze against their poster boards and
their buckets.

I beat them to it. Before Keke could slip into the driver's
seat, I pushed the seat forward and dove into the back, which
smelled strongly of used bubble gum. I owed Doug some kind
of good-bye, but maybe the surprise escape would take his
mind off my blond questions.

No such luck. He crutched forward and knocked on Keke's
window until she cranked it down. (This was a very old Dat-

129

sun.) "Zoey," he said, angling his head to look past Keke and the headrest, straight at me. "You don't remember which direction you were driving?"

I leaned between Keke's seat and Lila's, out of his line of sight, and hissed, "Go, Keke, before Officer Fox arrests us."

"I thought you said this was legal!" Lila whined. "Your mom is a lawyer!"

"It might be just a *little* illegal," I admitted. Keke was already spinning the tires in the soft sand of the shoulder to make our getaway.

Doug had wisely maneuvered out of our path. As Keke sped away and she and Lila both bitched at me for getting them in trouble and wondered aloud whether the wreck had given me brain damage, I stared out the back window, between the old-fashioned defrost stripes, at Doug watching us go.

If he asked me again at school tomorrow, I would deny everything while maintaining a friendly distance so he didn't get pissed at me and give away anything about what we'd done together after the wreck. Or about my mom.

In the meantime, I would go to my father's house and take a long swim in the ocean. Stroking against the tide would restore my strength and help me think. As I planned my next step in finding out what had happened to me, I would swim away from shore, and my dad's house on the beach would grow smaller and more distant. Just like Doug leaning on his crutches in the middle of the country highway, smaller and smaller until his green eyes disappeared.

8

"Zoey!" the three chicks on my relay team screeched at the same time Coach bellowed, "Commander!" Then I hit the water.

I knew I'd jumped the block almost before I jumped it. Starts were one of the key parts of relay practice. Swimming fast and growing stronger were important, but I also had to make sure I didn't dive into the water before the person ahead of me touched the block I was standing on. If I did, I let down all three teammates in the relay with me.

I surfaced quickly so the team would have less time to talk trash about me. I caught Stephanie in the middle of, "Not *again!*" Then I swam to the edge of the pool and held on to the side, waiting for Coach's rant.

He didn't rant or even kneel down to give me a talking-to. He barked, "Dry off, Commander," like that was the end of our discussion.

"Coach!" I shrieked. "I'm fine. I won't do it again."

"You've done it three times in a row," Stephanie pointed out. Swim caps and goggles didn't enhance anyone's natural beauty, but I thought Stephanie looked particularly googly-eyed and sea-monsterish as I hoisted myself out of the pool and slapped to the bleachers to drip-dry in the afternoon sun.

Swim practice started the last period of school and extended an hour and a half after school was over. I'd done fine at first. And my head wasn't bothering me. As a precautionary measure I'd taken painkillers all day—only two every four hours, exactly the recommended dosage. Maybe Coach would let me back in the water after a few minutes.

Because I could focus now. I'd finally accepted that Doug wasn't coming to swim practice. He'd skipped English this morning. I'd spent a long hour in fear that he wouldn't come to school at all, I would stay in the dark about our accident for another day, and something had gone wrong with his leg. Gangrene.

Then he showed up in biology after going to the doctor to get the splint off and a cast put on. You couldn't miss him when he entered the classroom. He was enveloped by boys hooting, the weak ones capitalizing on a strong boy's downfall. The thought crossed my mind that he would punch them for this, and I wondered if it crossed theirs. I wasn't sure why he had attacked that guy outside history class and had gotten suspended for it two years ago.

I didn't cross the room and talk to him myself. After sleeping with him on the bus Saturday, I didn't want to give anyone reason to tell Brandon something was going on between Doug and me. Besides, now that Doug was back at school, I knew I could talk to him during swim practice without so many people around.

And now he'd gone missing. When I'd taken roll at the beginning of swim practice, Gabriel had told me Doug was in Ms. Northam's class making up the English test he'd missed this morning. That accounted for his absence last period. It didn't explain why he still wasn't here after school.

I shivered in the cool autumn breeze that had settled in despite today's hot sun. We would need to put up the massive dome over the pool this week if the wind kept up. Then I sat on the bleachers, pulled my phone out of my backpack—as always, checked first for a message from my mother—and pressed Doug's number. Cringed in anticipation of his voice mail announcement, which is what I usually got when I called him about a change of swim team plans. Sighed with relief when his phone rang. Tensed again after the third unanswered ring, hoping he was okay, revisiting thoughts of gangrene. The rest of the swim team splashed back and forth across the pool in front of me. Doug should be in the pool with them.

The wreck hadn't been my fault. He'd said that himself. So why did I feel guilty?

"Zoey!" he yelled through the phone, and I jumped. "Are you okay?"

"Well, yeah," I said. "Did you think I wasn't?" He sounded like he was as worried about me as I was about him. But that was impossible. Doug didn't care that much about *anybody*.

Static sounded on the phone as he let out a long breath. "I didn't expect you to call me."

"I wanted to make sure *you're* okay," I said. "You're not at swim practice."

"Oh, *swim practice*." The bittersweet sarcasm was back. "You know me. Normally nothing could keep me from supporting my teammates. But my dad got a charter for the afternoon, and I need the money. I guess I haven't totally given up on the idea of going to college someday. Hold on." There was more static, and his muffled shout at someone with his hand over the phone. Then he was back. "I need to go. We're trying to land a marlin."

"Do you plan to avoid swim practice for the rest of the season because you don't want us to see how upset you are?"

In the background, a man shouted, "Doug! A little help!"

When Doug didn't answer me, I rushed on before he hung up on me. "You're overreacting. Yeah, six weeks in a cast is a setback, but you were so far ahead already. College scouts know that you had an injury and that you'll recover. You need to come to practice and show Coach how committed you are instead of catching marlins and feeling sorry for yourself. Break your leg, take one day off, fine. Now get back to work." I got more excited and louder than I'd intended. Coach looked over at me from the edge of the pool and gave me a thumbs-up.

"Doug!" shouted the man on the boat.

Without putting his hand over the phone this time, Doug hollered back at the man, "What the fuck? I'm on crutches."

Then he lowered his voice for me. "I guess I was waiting for somebody to tell me that. Coach hasn't told me that."

"How could he tell you? You didn't come to practice!"

Silence fell, except for the calls of seagulls through the phone, circling Doug's boat. Or maybe they were the seagulls swooping above the school. I couldn't tell.

"I'll come tomorrow," Doug finally said. "Thanks for calling, Zoey. I'll see you in English."

"Wait. That's not what I called about," I said quickly, cupping my hand over the phone. Stephanie and the others were pulling themselves out of the pool to line up behind the block again. There was no reason to keep it a secret that I wanted to see Doug. I *needed* him for information, to figure out what had happened to me Friday night. But I didn't *want* him. Brandon had nothing to worry about. Still, I tucked the phone away behind my hand so the swim team couldn't read my lips. "What time are you getting to shore? Could I meet you? Maybe take you to dinner? Just as friends. Just to talk."

His voice turned dangerously sweet. "What do you want to talk about? Us?"

"No," I said. Definitely not us. "The wreck. I still don't remember everything."

"Do you want to talk about your mom?"

I sucked in a breath and held it, my mind reeling, grasping for something to say. He hadn't brought up my mom all week. He'd lulled me into thinking he wouldn't.

"That's why I came to swim practice late every day last

week," he said. "I knew you didn't want to talk about it in public, and I was afraid to call you and make your dad mad and get my brother fired. I was trying to get you to call me."

"Doug!" The man on the boat was cursing at him now.

"I planned to sit by you on the van to Panama City on Saturday," he said in a rush. "But on Friday you turned me in to Coach for being tardy. Logically I knew you hadn't betrayed me. How could you betray me when we'd never been friends? But that's what it felt like. I figured you'd go to the football game to see Brandon play. I paced around the parking lot forever, planning exactly what to say to you. And then I came in, and I said the wrong thing, and you mentioned Brandon, and I was an ass."

"You called me a—"

"Spoiled brat," we said at the same time.

"And I apologized for calling you a spoiled brat," he said. "I wish you remembered *that*."

I clung to the underside of the bench with one hand, trying to breathe normally, refusing to go back to my mother's bedroom and try to fix everything. It had been a week since I'd found her. I couldn't melt down every time somebody mentioned her.

"All right," Doug said kindly. "Yes, Zoey, I would like to meet you after I get to shore, and go with you to dinner, and talk about the wreck, and nothing else."

* * *

I PARKED THE BENZ AND WALKED around the docks crowded with polished yachts and dilapidated fishing boats until I found the empty space and the big wooden sign for the *Hemingway*. Taped to the sign, a sheet of green paper advertised the rates for fishing trips. The trip this afternoon appeared in a special box with the caption YOUR HOST BY SPECIAL REQUEST, PEGLEG DOUG.

I glanced at my watch. It was exactly time for the cruise to be over, yet they weren't here. Maybe a storm had popped up and they'd capsized. What if Doug couldn't swim with one serviceable leg? What if his cast took on water and weighed him down?

I told myself to get a grip. Friendly white clouds puffed across the hot autumn sky. The *Hemingway* was running a little late, and why hurry? No one was waiting for it. Except me.

I paced under the *Hemingway* sign. Then I walked up the dock to the shallower water, reasoning that moving away would cause the *Hemingway* to sail closer. On the bottom of the shallows, hermit crabs, all legs and claws under borrowed shells, picked across the rocks and oysters. I counted five of them in the small section I could see before the sand fell away from the shore and the water grew deep and dark. Five crabs moving in different directions, each headed where another had just been. If I knew what their goal was and what destination would best help them achieve that goal, I could line them up and send them there in an orderly fashion. Doug would scoff at me for this.

I longed for him to scoff at me. It was awful. I was only

attracted to him because I couldn't have him. I was with Brandon. If I broke up with Brandon to be with Doug, even if Doug did want me, I wouldn't want Doug anymore and I'd pine away for Brandon. This was how it worked, being a cheater. I hoped Ashley was enjoying her time in Hawaii, because her days with my dad were numbered.

I knew this, yet the sign that said *Hemingway* pulled me back down the crumbling pier. I examined the water hoses, the plastic buckets, and wondered whether Doug had touched them. Had he taped the Pegleg Doug sheet to the *Hemingway* sign? I pictured him balancing on one leg, dropping his crutches, and bracing himself against the sign with one hand, a stapler in the other. In school today I could tell he'd already grown accustomed to his crutches and had developed a routine for letting them go, throwing himself into a nether realm without balance, and gracefully taking his next handhold just before falling. I knew the movements of his dance as if I were dancing it myself.

And there was Doug, facing away from me, braced against a rail around the bow of the *Hemingway*. The boat glided fast through the green-blue inlet, already so close that I stepped back in surprise. Then, because Doug was arguing with his dad, I kept backing up. I sat on a clean space on a nearby bench, between blobs of dried seagull poop, to wait.

I didn't recognize Mr. Fox. I didn't think he'd ever been to a swim meet. But I knew who he was right away because Doug argued with him. And because even though Mr. Fox was blond with a ponytail and a beard, he was built like Officer Fox, a tad shorter and thicker than Doug. As Doug ducked below the rail, working, Mr. Fox scanned the shoreline. His eyes moved over me without stopping.

The boat bumped gently against the padded dock and backed up a little, engine churning and water boiling. Over this noise I heard Mr. Fox cursing the boat pilot. Then he watched Doug struggling for a moment and said, "Put your weight into it. What are you, a fag?" He turned on his heel, disappeared into the cabin, and came out with a beer can in one hand and a lit cigarette in the other. Holding the beer perfectly level so not a drop spilled, he jumped from boat to shore and headed for a small charter office behind me without a word to any of the passengers or crew, and without a glance at me.

Every few seconds Doug's head popped up from beneath the rail. Still struggling.

On the phone he'd said at first that he didn't want me to pick him up here. He'd suggested he crutch up to Jamaica Joe's on the corner and meet me there. Then he'd suggested he crutch up to his house, which he'd said was not inland, as I'd assumed, but on a bluff nearby. Neither of these suggestions had made sense to me. Why should Doug hobble when I could drive? I'd insisted on meeting him as close to the boat as possible. Now I understood the problem. Everybody was embarrassed of crazy parents.

The crew and the fishermen and the fish they'd caught spilled from the boat onto the wharf. Doug came after them, pushing a barrel in front of him and holding on to the boat rail with the other hand to keep from toppling over. He bent to retrieve his crutches and hobbled into the boat's cabin. He came out in a different T-shirt and shorts. He crutched to the side of the boat, paused a moment to consider the bobbing bow and the two-foot gap to the wharf, and finally hopped across the gap as if he'd been on crutches all his life. When one of the crew tossed a hose to the concrete, Doug picked it up and squirted off his good foot, flip-flop and all.

Then he crutched toward me. "Hello," he called without smiling. Just as he stopped in front of me, the cool breeze whipped around him, carrying his scent to me. No chlorine today. He smelled of soap and ocean.

I stood up. "Hi," I tried to say casually, as if I were still innocent and hadn't heard what his dad said to him. The dark look he shot me let me know I was a bad actress.

I cleared my throat. "You didn't get the marlin?"

"We did. We like to take a picture of it and then let it go. When men bring home a seven-foot-long dead fish, their wives don't want them to come out with us again. What happens on the *Hemingway* stays on the *Hemingway*." His words were light, his tone somber.

I laughed. "I take it you've seen a lot happen on the *Hemingway*."

One black eyebrow went up ever so briefly, then back down. His mouth twisted into a tight bow. This sober mood of his worried me. Doug was frequently angry but rarely down.

His anger was explosive, like his happiness. His depression was something only a parent could cause.

"So." He gestured with his head toward the parking lot. "More hair of the dog."

"Hair of the deer." I walked slowly beside him so he wouldn't have to exert himself as much. I saw it was just hard for him to crutch, propelling forward six foot two inches of height and a hundred and eighty-six pounds (I knew his stats from swim team) with his upper body only. Each time he put his weight on the crutches and swung his good foot forward, his biceps bulged against the material of his FSU T-shirt—a different one from Saturday, faded gold rather than faded red.

I unlocked the Benz with the remote and stood on the passenger side to open his door, or hold his crutches, whatever he needed. But I could have predicted he wouldn't let me help him. In a few deft moves he swung into the car and tossed his crutches into the backseat, shaking his black hair out of his eyes. I started to close the door for him, but he reached for the handle first.

I rounded the car and slipped into the driver's seat. Cranking the engine, I pressed buttons to lower all four windows and let the heat out. I paused a moment more to make sure I was comfortable driving. This was my third time behind the wheel today and I kept expecting to feel shell-shocked, with heart palpitations and sweating hands. Nothing. No post-traumatic stress disorder, no memory of the accident. There was nothing but a drive to find out what had happened to me, an itch to be evil, and a soft spot for Doug.

"Sweet ride," he said.

"Thanks. My dad's," I said as I steered the car up the hill past Jamaica Joe's. "I only get it until he comes back from Hawaii next Saturday."

"What are you driving after that?"

I explained the conundrum of having a loaded father who bought expensive cars for himself and his mistress but not his daughter and disallowed his daughter from buying a cheap car either.

"He's as crazy as *my* dad," Doug marveled. "If he's so concerned about your safety, why *won't* he just buy you a car?"

"He says he doesn't want me to be a spoiled brat."

A few seconds passed, cars whispering beside us in the other lane of the main beach road, before I realized what I'd given away. I'd asked Doug to dinner so I could find out what happened Friday night, *not* so I could make him feel bad about what he'd said to me at the football game. And I certainly didn't want to get in another argument with him.

"If it makes you feel better, you can call me a fag." He pressed a button until the seat motored back as far as possible. Then he pressed a different button until the seat back reclined, he was low-riding, and he could stretch his broken leg out straight. The seat motor moved excruciatingly slowly, heightening the silence that had fallen between us.

"Do you want to talk about it?" I asked.

142

"No."

"*Fag* as an insult is so nineties," I said. "Nobody cares about that anymore. Ian's parents don't have a problem with him being gay."

"My dad means it as an insult. It would be impolite not to take it that way."

I nodded. Once when my dad had called me a spoiled brat, I'd informed him Bratz dolls were quite popular. But all that got me was another rebuff for having a smart mouth. If my dad was hateful, he was hateful, and there was no point in helping him toward lingo for a new generation. I knew what he meant.

I pulled into the parking lot for the block of gift shops and restaurants that included California Eatin'. "This okay?" I asked, walking slowly beside him as he crutched toward the door.

"Yes, but since we're here . . ." He glanced down the sidewalk. "Would you mind if we ate sushi next door? I mean, they have more than sushi if you don't do raw. It's just that my leg's swollen, and at the tatami table I could stretch it out."

"The tatami table is for parties of six or more." I knew this because my mom and I had tried to snag it on a daring girl-outing. Even when daring each other, we did not do raw.

He passed me and balanced on his crutches to hold open the door of the sushi restaurant for me. "Let me take care of this. Old ladies are suckers for guys on crutches. I've milked this with my teachers at school all day. I can be very charming."

"Which is the act?" I asked as I brushed the front of his T-shirt going in. "Charming or dour?"

He threw back his head and laughed—such a beautiful, musical laugh that the dour version of Doug from a minute ago was hard to imagine, though I figured it would make another appearance shortly. It always did. "I like to keep you guessing," he teased me, hobbling forward to the hostess podium.

I wondered whether keeping me guessing was just another part of charming mode, or he was actually flirting with me.

I wanted him to flirt with me.

Which was too bad, because I had a boyfriend.

Doug leaned on his crutches, and he and the Japanese hostess talked animatedly with their hands. Doug threw back his head and laughed again. Girls at school would not recognize this Doug. I certainly didn't.

Finally the hostess led us into the crowded dining room, past the enormous tanks full of fish not native to this area of the ocean, and up two stairs and through a paper screen to the low table. We kicked off our flip-flops in the doorway. I rounded to the far side with Doug to help him ditch his crutches and ease down to table level, but the hostess did this instead, fussing over him in Japanese that he seemed to half understand. I was in the way, so I retreated to the other side of the table and sat down on a cushion. The lady winked at me and left.

Doug stretched to snag a paper menu and a tiny pencil from the edge of the table with two fingers. "Do you come here a lot? Would you like me to order you a good roll with nothing raw in it? They're just bringing me whatever's fresh." When I didn't answer, he glanced up from the menu at me. "Okay, okay, I'm not that charming. The hostess and my mom were friends."

I let him peruse the menu again, or pretend to. I waited for him to end this facade on his own.

Finally, without looking up from the menu, he said what I'd been puzzling through: "My mom was Japanese."

I felt stupid and unworldly not knowing this, but it had never come up before. There weren't any Asians in my high school. Or so I'd thought.

"My dad met her when he was stationed at Pearl Harbor," Doug said. "Cody was actually born in Honolulu."

I examined him as he examined the menu. Of course he was Asian and white. This explained his beautiful sea-green eyes with a deep tan and black hair. But I could still see how his dual heritage had never occurred to me. His face scintillated as I watched, like the optical illusion of a vase and two faces, flickering between known and unknown.

I said, "I didn't know you were half Japanese."

"I can tell."

A waiter popped through the paper screen. Doug made a few marks on the paper menu and handed it to him. As the waiter bowed and disappeared again, Doug said, "I ordered you rice and shrimp and avocado, basically. We could have gone for California Eatin' for that."

"Do you try to keep your . . . ethnicity a secret from people?" I should not have been so fascinated by Doug turning up

Asian, but I couldn't quite get my head around the fact that I hadn't known something so basic about him.

Leave it to Doug to turn his response into a defensive insult. "I don't try to hide anything. People know all my business anyway, or think they do. You're just not paying attention."

Screwing up my courage, I struck right back at him. "Nobody seems to know why you went to juvie."

9

A burst of laughter from behind the paper screen made both of us jump. It was easy to forget we were in a public place, enclosed only in the illusion of privacy. Now I wondered if I'd spoken loudly enough for other diners to hear me through the thin screen.

I adjusted my position on the cushion. Doug didn't move. His body, laid back against the cushions and the wall with his broken leg straight out to one side, said *relaxed*. His fingers, frozen in midfidget on his good knee, said *people aren't supposed to ask me that*. Either that or *I have just been shot through the paper screen*.

He wasn't bleeding. But I began to see his point about catching a marlin and then letting it go, because honestly, what were you going to do with a marlin? He was a six-foot-two fish out of water behind a miniature dining table. Even slouched down, his shoulders were broad, his head was even with mine, and his legs took up the entire space in front of him. No wonder the wreck had broken him. If he was too big for the tatami table, he was way too big for Mike's Miata.

"They don't?" he croaked, then cleared his throat.

"Even Keke and Lila don't know, and they know everything."

He laughed bitterly. "I didn't belong there, if that's what you're asking. But I learned a thing or two. If you ever want to sell crack, I can show you every possible place to hide it."

I cringed. "No, I'm asking why you went."

"I thought *you* knew," he said flatly.

"How would I know?"

"Your mom defended me."

The waiter came back and placed rectangular plates and small dishes in front of us. After he left, I did what Doug did, poured soy sauce into the small dish.

Doug deftly nabbed a block of raw tuna with chopsticks and held it in my direction. "Try?"

I shook my head and concentrated on balancing a piece of my roll between my chopsticks. I was not good at this. And I hated to ruin the beautiful design of the plate, perfectly matching circles of rice encasing dots of pink and green. Finally I dipped one in soy sauce, chewed it slowly and swallowed, to give myself time to think. "I didn't know my mom defended you."

"Of course she did. She's the public defender. My dad sure as hell wouldn't pay for my lawyer. He was the one who wanted me to go to juvie."

"For . . . ?" I was glad we were eating. We looked at our food instead of each other. That seemed to be key for Doug and me to have a conversation. The conversation was so charged that I couldn't taste what I ate, but that was a small price to pay for what I was dying to know.

"I went to juvie because I ran away," he said.

I thought I'd misunderstood him. "From home?" I clarified, frowning into my soy sauce.

"Yes, I ran away from home, like you do when you're six and you get mad because your dad turned off *Scooby-Doo*."

This story didn't make sense to me. I began to realize that Doug kept his own counsel, and that he probably viewed this terse conversation as "opening up." I would need to drag every detail out of him. "Why'd you get sent to juvie just for that?"

"My dad asked the judge to send me. You know, to straighten me out once and for all." In his bitter tone I recognized the bark of his father calling him a fag. I had lifted up a stepping-stone to find snakes teeming underneath.

"Straighten you out. What was so crooked about you?" I pictured him shoplifting, smoking pot. Someone who didn't spend a lot of time around him might suspect him of these things now, as a senior. He had that edgy personality, that cavalier expression to his eyebrows. But he would never do anything to jeopardize his chance to swim. And back in ninth grade . . . as I remembered him, he was even less likely to make juvie-worthy moves. Laughing and clueless, he hadn't yet developed the honeyed sarcasm. I remembered being floored the first time someone told me Doug Fox was in juvie, not out of school with the flu.

"Oh! Pffft." He waved his chopsticks in the air, shifting again to the voice of his father. "What *wasn't* crooked about me? I read too much. I wanted to swim instead of playing tough-man team sports like football. And my dad couldn't convince me to join the navy."

"The navy! You?"

"Exactly." His hands moved in the air in front of him. "He would conscript me on my eighteenth birthday if that were still legal. But I know I couldn't stand people telling me what to do. And actually having to do it. On a submarine, where I was caught." Still gripping his chopsticks in his fourth finger and pinky, his pointer fingers and thumbs closed around an imaginary throat. Then his hands fell to the table in defeat, submerging and sinking.

I laughed, because a little part of me still clung to the hope he was kidding.

He wasn't. He pinned me with an angry look. "My brother acts half dead since he came back from the navy, like he's been lobotomized."

Then his angry expression faded. He realized what he'd said. Lobotomies and other treatments for mental illness were one of the topics we did not want to talk about.

The key was to avoid looking at each other. I gazed at my plate again, dipped another slice of roll in soy sauce, and hoped he would follow suit.

"Why'd you run away?" I asked offhandedly, slipping the bite into my mouth.

"My dad hit me." His finger tapped double-time on his knee, twice as fast as the beat of Japanese rock music whispering on the speakers overhead. "Sorry to lay all this on you. No wonder no one's ever asked."

No one's ever dared, I thought. I put my chopsticks down on my plate. Throughout high school I'd been a problem solver and a good listener. But I wasn't sure I could handle this marlin I'd reeled in. "Does he still hit you?" I murmured.

"No. I'm bigger than I used to be." His voice was tight. His hand on his knee had stopped. "Anyway, it was this weird time. When my mom died, Cody was still around, and the three of us were okay. It was only after Cody got shipped to the Persian Gulf that my dad and I found out there's nothing between us. Nothing." He struck the ends of both chopsticks on his plate to even them, then turned them over and struck them again, considering his last bite of sushi. He put it in his mouth and chewed slowly. "Eight months to graduation."

I picked up my water glass. "To graduation."

We clinked glasses and sipped, watching each other.

"Well," I said, "I had no idea why you went to juvie or that my mother was your lawyer. She's very big on attorney-client privilege. I'm sure she has dirt on half the town, and I've never heard a peep about it."

"She wouldn't have told you she was defending your homecoming date?"

We eyed each other. The look on his face was one I recognized. It was the glare he gave me right before he rolled his eyes at me, the expression Keke was so good at imitating.

"You didn't tell your mother we were going to homecoming?" He sighed.

I shifted on my cushion. "I don't remember exactly. It was three years ago."

It was his turn to stare me down, one black brow cocked, until I confessed.

"If I didn't tell her," I said quickly, "it wasn't because of you. I felt gangly. I didn't involve my parents in my social life when I didn't have to. I felt embarrassed about that sort of thing." Still had, until last Monday night. "And when you came back to school and acted like I didn't exist, I didn't possess the social skills to waltz up to you and demand to know what happened."

"I was mad at you because you'd gone to homecoming with Carey Lewis!"

Come to think of it, so I had. I hadn't even remembered that boy's name. His family had moved inland to Alabama shortly afterward. They were scared of hurricanes.

"You were gone," I said. "You didn't notify me. As far as I knew, we were over. Like nothing had ever happened between us."

He put his chopsticks down on the table and leaned back against the wall, frowning at me. He looked so hurt that I thought back over what I'd said—and realized it sounded an awful lot like what I'd said to him Saturday morning.

"If I'd notified you," he said slowly, "called you up and said,

'Hey, Zoey, I won't be able to take you to homecoming after all because I'll be in jail,' would you have gone out with me later?"

I thought, *No*. I said, "You never gave me that chance."

"You're right. I didn't. I was an excellent judge of character. Because three years later, you're still holding it against me, and keeping me from getting hired as a lifeguard at your dad's park." He raised both eyebrows at me, daring me to deny it.

In the week since my mother had done what she did, I had never felt more like crying. I swallowed and leaned forward over the table. "Doug," I whispered, "I know you have a lot of reasons to be mad at me. But please don't tell anybody about my mother."

He blinked. "I won't."

"If not for me, for her, because she was your lawyer. Maybe not a very successful lawyer, since you went to juvie—"

"She got me a light sentence," he broke in. "It could have been a lot worse."

"Please."

"I said I won't," he repeated, watching me somberly.

I licked my lips and took a breath to tell him thank you.

"So!" he burst before I could get the words out. "We've talked about your mother, which we said we weren't going to do. We've talked about us, which we definitely weren't going to do. You haven't asked me a single question about the wreck. And you know what that means. You've taken me on a date. Brandon is not going to like it, because as we all know, Brandon is your boyfriend."

Why were we suddenly back to this? I sat back on my heels and huffed out a sigh of frustration. "I don't understand you."

He took a sip of water. "I don't understand *you*," he said without looking at me.

"Have we been sitting here forever? How do I get a check?" I turned around to look through the opening in the partition, at the other diners on real dates with less drama.

"There's no charge. The hostess loves me."

"Oh, I want to pay." I opened my purse to pull out a credit card. "I told you I was taking you out, and I'm paying." Boy was I.

Doug reached around the corner of the table for his crutches and braced himself on them, struggling to stand. By now I recognized the pain in his eyes.

I threw a five down for the waiter, at least, and hurried around the table to help Doug. "Here." I held out my hands to him.

"I don't need your help." He braced his shoulder against the wall and slid up it, but now he dropped one crutch. He grabbed for it and caught my wrist instead.

We both stopped moving and stared at each other. His big hand was warm and solid and tight around my wrist. His face turned red. Saying *boo* to Mike would make his face turn red, but Doug did not blush for just anything.

In this instant, Doug was my boyfriend.

"Okay." I twisted my wrist out of his grasp and bent to

pick up his fallen crutch. I had *just gotten* one boyfriend—Brandon—and I didn't need another. I wasn't like that.

I followed Doug as he crutched slowly down the steps from the platform and through the dining room. I stood nearby as he exchanged a few last words of broken Japanese with the hostess in the doorway. I walked next to him down the sidewalk to the Benz, edging closer to him to let other laughing couples pass. All of which gave me ample time to stew about him making fun of me.

I had to stay with Brandon. I *had* to. Brandon was the only good thing in my life right now, and the only thing that made perfect sense. If I broke up with him just because Doug Fox had taken a shine to me for some reason and threw jealous fits, I was a cheater, a ho who'd slept with a boy she didn't love, and nuts.

Trouble was, I *was* nuts. I was beginning to see that now. Because every time Doug complained about me dating Brandon instead of him, I wanted to agree. And that hurt.

In the car, we sat in silence until I turned from the highway onto the main road through town. Doug muttered, "Things were going so well."

I ignored him and kept driving. During the summer I would have navigated through the backstreets built on bridges between inlets, reminding myself just how tenuous our town's hold was on the shifting ocean and earth. I would have swerved left and right through a maze of low beach houses overgrown with hotly scented flowering vines, just to avoid the strip. The main road through town ground to a halt at this time of night when the tourists were in town, eating at Tahiti Cuisine, browsing the books at Beach Reads, taking advantage of the half-off sunset admission to Slide with Clyde. The tourists were gone now, store hours shortened, Slide with Clyde closed, sidewalks empty, roads clear. The faster to drive Doug away.

"I don't know how this happened," Doug said.

"What you mean is, 'I'm sorry, Zoey.'"

"I'm sorry, Zoey," he said immediately.

I turned in at the road to the wharf, then realized I might be driving to the wrong place. "Do you want me to take you to your house, or—"

"The wharf's fine. I have some paperwork to finish for the business. My dad can't do math."

"But you can't do math either." Calculus was the one class I didn't share with Doug. He was in a lower-level class and still didn't make the grade for National Honor Society, which was probably why he was so desperate for an athletic scholarship.

"I come by it honest," he said as I pulled the Benz to a stop at the docks.

I waited.

He waited.

The motor was running. Did he want me to get out and open the door for him? I stared straight ahead at a streetlight until my eyes watered.

And then he was hugging me. Half hugging me, really, because I didn't hug him back. His cheek rested against my shoulder and his arm reached across my chest to my far side. "Okay then. I had a great time," he said, syrupy and sarcastic. He squeezed me hard and let me go, sliding out of the seat and slamming the door.

Soon I realized I should drive home or he would come back and ask me why I was still sitting there. But for a few moments I enjoyed the residual tingles rippling along my skin like the fireflies leftover from summer, zooming and firing in the dusk. I watched him crutching into the streetlight. He disappeared under the brightness.

A boy who was such a threat to my mental health and happiness should not be so tall.

In English the next morning, he hobbled in on the bell, avoiding my eyes. This surprised me. After last night I'd thought I had the upper hand and he would come early to class to suck up to me. I needed him to suck up to me. I hadn't gotten any new information from him about the wreck. I had to try again. I would visit the Bug in the junkyard and take him with me. If that didn't prompt him to talk, nothing would.

I stole a glance up the rows of assigned seats, checking for spies watching me. Keke and Lila were way across the room. Stephanie was a junior so she wasn't in this class. And Brandon in AP English would be a disaster, a deer in the road. Still,

I scribbled the note on a full sheet of paper and passed it to Doug unfolded so it would look to the people around us like I had nothing to hide. Swim team business.

I need you again today after practice.

I considered adding a *please* or a smiley face but decided against either. This would be admitting I'd had second thoughts about overreacting when he'd turned on me. Especially after he'd spilled his story about his family like a marlin gutted on the wharf.

He passed the paper back with a note scrawled under mine.

No

My face burned as if he'd called me a spoiled brat in public. But people around us weren't tittering behind their hands. There was only Ms. Northam droning about E. M. Forster.

In front of me, Doug moved. The black curls inched up his neck, and I caught a sliver more of his tanned cheek. My adrenaline spiked. He was turning around to whisper that he *wanted* to go with me, but he couldn't go right after practice because he had an octopus to wrangle. Maybe we could go later?

He didn't turn. He tilted his head until his neck popped, then hunched his shoulders. He put his elbow on his desk and his chin in his hand, listening to Ms. Northam's lecture.

Not so fast. I scribbled across the sheet and passed it back to him. This time he didn't grab it when it grazed his shoulder, so I gave it a little toss and hoped it ended up on his desk rather than the floor.

That is not the correct answer.

He raised his hand. Without waiting for Ms. Northam to acknowledge him, he interrupted her. "Ms. Northam, Zoey is disturbing me."

The room exploded in laughter. I calculated just how this incident would be distorted by the time it got back to Brandon.

"Zoey," Ms. Northam called, "whatever the problem is, maybe you'd be more comfortable in another seat. I'd make Doug move but he'd take an hour."

"Ooooh," said some of the boys. I didn't think this was a particularly good line on Ms. Northam's part, but boys would say *ooooh* to anything.

As I stood, I snatched the paper back from Doug, lest it fall into the wrong hands, and tried to calm down before anyone noticed my panting. People probably thought Doug and I were having yet another disagreement about the swim team. No one would suspect the girlfriend of the star of the football team was falling for the boy who went to juvie. And the boy who went to juvie wasn't returning the favor.

*   *   *

As I walked from the women's locker room onto the pool deck for practice, Doug stood and limped toward me on his crutches. "Let me do that for you."

I looked down at my clipboard. "Why?" Every night I checked over the carefully penciled race times, traced them in pen, entered them into my computer at home, and finally emailed them to Coach with instructions on how to download them, because he forgot every time.

"I'm a team player," Doug deadpanned. "You have a meet tomorrow that you need to train for, and I'm just sitting here. Don't you trust me?"

No, I thought, handing the clipboard over.

He stuffed it down his pants.

Okay, take two. With the crutches still shoved firmly into his armpits, he held out the waistband of his cargo shorts with one hand. I got a good look at his underwear, not just a heathered gray waistband but heathered gray boxer briefs that disappeared as the clipboard slid over them.

When he half turned and crutched back toward the bleachers, I saw how carrying the clipboard in his pants this way made sense. His backpack wasn't around. He needed both hands for his crutches. And to move, he swung his good leg forward without shifting his pelvis, so the clipboard stayed in place.

I was surrounded by boys in bathing suits. There were nine of them out here, and I wore a bathing suit myself. And I got this hot and bothered when Doug Fox flashed me his undies? This was a testament to how sad my sex life was with Brandon.

I hadn't seen Doug give my mostly naked body a glance—but then, I'd had my eyes down his pants. On the off chance the clipboard stunt was more flirting with me, I followed him to the bleachers and sat down beside him.

"No," he said, pretending to be absorbed in the numbers on the clipboard sheets.

"I want to go to the junkyard to give the Bug last rites, but I don't know where the junkyard is."

"Look it up in the phone book." He lifted a sheet to check the second page of times. "Doesn't the Mercedes have GPS?"

I glanced toward the pool. Everyone was here now, including Stephanie, who *appeared* to be deep in conversation with another junior girl, but you never knew. I couldn't take a chance on touching Doug's knee. I'd touched him to get him on my side at the game Friday night, but that was before I felt guilty about my fantasies.

I studied the side of his face, the shadow of a beard just beginning to show through his tanned skin, the ends of his black locks curling around his ears.

"Please," I said.

He turned and looked down at me. His green eyes took me in. They seemed friendly. I wanted to fall into them, even though I knew the next thing he said wouldn't sound like we were friends.

"You hardly spoke to me when you dropped me off last night," he reminded me.

"I slept on it," I said. This was not quite true, but it was in the ballpark. I had *lost* sleep over it. "Talk about a change of heart. You were all apologetic last night, and now *you'll* hardly speak to *me*. And stony silence is not your modus operandi. What happened?"

Coach emerged from the building then, blowing one chirp on his whistle. Reluctantly I stood and headed for the pool.

"I slept on it," Doug called after me.

Practice was long. I had to come up with a way to get Doug to go with me to the junkyard. At the same time, I was determined to swim better today than my disaster yesterday. As long as I took the recommended dose of Tylenol, my head didn't even hurt now, so that was no excuse.

In the middle of a 400 individual medley, as Stephanie pulled ahead of me, I needed extra power from somewhere. So I reached inside myself and grabbed what I'd been tamping down for a week and a day. I grabbed that anger at my mom and swam right over the sensation of drowning. I held on tight and let it propel me forward through the fly. I was madder at my dad than I was at my mom, and that got me through the backstroke.

Brandon pushed me through the breaststroke. Whoever heard of a serious senior boyfriend who put obeying his parents and studying algebra over sex with his new girlfriend? This was a mature and responsible decision on his part, but let's get real.

And last but not least there was Doug, who had ruined my

life. If it hadn't been for Doug confusing me about my loyalties and priorities, I wouldn't have been mad at Brandon in the first place. Doug made me dissatisfied with Brandon. Doug should pay. The force of that anger shot me through the free so quickly, I felt out of control, on a roller coaster gone wild. It was a great feeling. When I touched the wall for the final time, I was almost disappointed the heat was over.

"Way to blow it out, Commander!" Coach hollered, pumping the air with his fist. A few seconds later, when the other girls touched the wall, surfaced, and figured out what I'd done, they shouted, "Great time!" Even Doug on the bleachers gave me a thumbs-up before writing on the clipboard.

"You're so awesome," Lila said between heaving breaths in the lane beside me. "What's your secret?"

"If you told Lila, it wouldn't be a secret," Keke advised me from the other side. Keke and Lila had been fighting all day. I had no idea why. In my normal state I would have delved into their problem and solved it by now.

"If Keke shut up, she wouldn't be such a beyotch," Lila said.

Keke dove across my lane into Lila's to slap her. Coach blew his whistle and the boys moved toward the pool. Ian observed the twins throttling each other for a few moments, then called to no one in particular, "Cleanup in lane two."

Bracing myself against the wind—it wasn't as cold as it had been the past few days, but anything felt colder when I was wet—I stalked right over to Doug and said, "I want you to go with me to the junkyard. I've asked you nicely, and you have no reason not to."

He let me stand there dripping, waiting, while he penciled in a few more times. Long enough that I looked toward the girls on the other end of the bleachers giving Doug a wide berth. I felt self-conscious about talking to him alone.

Finally he said quietly, "I don't think we should spend any more time together unless I have a chance with you."

I shivered, a movement big enough that he saw it. His eyes met mine. Then he looked down at the clipboard again, paging through the times.

"I'm dating Brandon," I told his bowed head.

"Really?" he asked without looking up.

"Yes!"

"I'll print you a wallet card to whip out every time you need to say that, so you can save your voice."

"Could you laminate it?"

Finally he lifted his head and raised one eyebrow at me. "Don't push your luck."

Coach chirped on his whistle. Apparently the boys had disgusted him with their weak leg work (or with their poor showing last Saturday without Doug), so the whole team had to pile into the pool with kickboards. I stomped away from Doug, grabbed a float, and plunged into the water. I had plenty of anger to propel me. And I had a fact-finding plan to reevaluate.

Finally practice ended. Coach told us we would get killed at the meet tomorrow night because we had a bad attitude (translation: because Doug was out). Coach blew his whistle and disappeared inside the building.

Dragging my kickboard with me, I ducked under three floating dividers and reached Mike's lane before he escaped from the pool. I'd decided that if I couldn't take Doug to the junkyard, I would ask Mike what had happened that night.

When I surfaced, Mike saw me out of the corner of his eye and half turned, then realized it was just me. He assumed I was headed somewhere else. And then, when I said, "Hey, Mike," he actually jumped.

"Sorry," I said, laughing so he'd think it was perfectly normal for boys to jump when girls came near them. I *had* sneaked up on him from underwater. "We haven't gotten the chance to talk since the wreck. After we change clothes, would you visit the Bug in the junkyard with me? I wonder if it fused to the Miata in the wreck and the tow truck hauled them both away in once piece."

As I watched, Mike developed a severe sunburn. "I can't," he said.

I'd approached him as nonaggressively as I could, predicting he'd turn red like this. And I wasn't about to let him go. I put my back to the edge of the pool so he'd have to climb over me to get out, which he would *not* do. "Come on," I coaxed. "Doug and I went to dinner to talk about the wreck yesterday, and that was nothing." Lie.

"Mike has a date," Lila called, walking over from the bleachers while toweling her hair. "With me."

"Okay," I sang, attempting to hide my shock at Mike going on a date, Lila going on a date, and Mike and Lila going on a date. "Have fun—"

"Go ahead and ask Zoey for what you need, Mike," Keke yelled from the locker room door. "She has a whole discount club–sized box of condoms." The door thudded shut behind her.

I'm not sure whether the rest of the team milling around the pool got Keke's dirty joke, but I got it. And Mike got it. His sunburn transformed to well-done for a lobster. And Lila got it. Going on a first date—not just a first date with a particular boy but a first date *ever*—was awkward enough. But to have your twin sister joke that you needed a condom because you would have *sex* on the first date? How humiliating.

Wait a minute. I *had* had sex on the first date with Brandon. But at least I didn't have a sister joking to the boy about it! Lila, avoiding our eyes, frowned at the fluffy clouds scuttling across the blue sky. "Excuse me," she muttered, scampering for the locker room in her bare feet, towel clutched around her. A second later we heard screams through the school's hurricane-resistant brick walls.

"I can't give you a condom," I told Mike. "I left my condoms in the Bug." I pulled myself onto the deck, pried off my swim cap and goggles, and dripped my way over to Doug.

I caught him. He'd been watching me, and when I walked toward him he didn't look down quite fast enough. I sat right next to him on the bleachers and scooted against him, soaking the hip of his shorts and leaving a bright red patch on the side of his faded red T-shirt.

He was busy writing something on the top sheet. I decided to be obnoxious and lean my wet head on his shoulder to see what he was doodling. A heart with *B.M. + Z.C.* inside.

"You shouldn't start fights," he said. "It's bad for team morale."

"Give me that," I muttered, snatching the clipboard from him. When I had trouble taking another breath, I realized how tired and how stressed I was. With effort I breathed as deeply as I could through my nose and let out a long sigh with my eyes closed. "I *really* want you to come with me to the junkyard," I said.

"And I *really* think we shouldn't spend any more time together."

I didn't know what to do. I needed him to come with me so I could find out about the wreck. And I'll admit, even if I'd figured out everything there was to know about the wreck, I would have invented an excuse to spend more time alone with Doug.

I opened my eyes and told him the truth. "I'm dating Brandon—"

He slid his wallet from his back pocket, slipped out an imaginary card, and tried to hand it to me.

I thumped at his fingers with mine. "But sometime in the future, if things didn't work out between me and Brandon . . . I don't want to say you'd have a chance with me, because that sounds like I'm some pink and orange stuffed animal at the county fair that you'd pay a dollar fifty to throw darts at."

He rolled his eyes. Then he reached for me. The rest of the team had flowed into the locker rooms by now. The pool deck was empty. No one saw him run his middle finger across my forehead, tracing what was left of the bruise. All my hair stood on end as he tucked one wet strand behind my ear and whispered, "That's good enough."

10

I walked yet another slow circle around the Bug, then another circle around the Miata. Examining the diagram of the wreck I'd drawn on the clipboard, I leaned back against the Miata. I leaped up again when it groaned and shifted under me. "So, I saw the deer and jerked the wheel to the left." I held the clipboard in front of me and turned it left like a steering wheel.

Doug shrugged as well as he could while leaning on his crutches in the weedy junkyard. He slapped at a mosquito.

"Mike, headed the other way, simultaneously visualized said ruminant and relocated the steering device leftward."

"I *am* listening," Doug insisted.

I put my hand gently on the crushed front panel of the Miata. "Seems like both of us would have turned right automatically. As a driver, you'd try to crash on your side rather than the passenger side, since you're the one responsible."

"Let's not go there," Doug said, shaking his head. "It was dark, it was raining, the roads were slick. There was a fucking deer, for God's sake. You don't remember the wreck, so you have to trust me. I do remember it and I couldn't even tell you who turned the wheel where. It happened so fast. Deer, *bam*, and it was over."

Deflated, I let the clipboard sag. And not just because Doug couldn't give me details about the wreck. I wanted details about *him*, too, and he thwarted me at every turn. One of the few things I knew for sure about him was that he and Mike hated each other. Whenever they found themselves sitting next to each other in the swim team van, they made someone else move so they could get away from each other. And now it sounded like he was *defending* Mike.

"What's this?" he asked, hobbling over to the car next to the Bug, this one protected by a canvas. He peeled back one corner of the cover to reveal the sparkle of red metallic paint. "Holy fuck, it's a 1987 Porsche 944."

I ventured closer. "I thought you didn't know anything about cars."

"But I *am* male, and I recognize a 1987 Porsche 944 when I see one."

From the reverence in his voice, I could tell this car was something special. It didn't look like much, though. "That's some paint job."

"Yeah, that's probably part of the reason a Porsche is sitting in a junkyard. That color is definitely not found in nature." Then he grinned at me. "Wanna go parking?"

"Ha ha ha," I said nervously.

He snapped his fingers. "You told Mike you left your condoms in the Bug. Did you want those?"

"Ah, right," I said, moving to the front of the Bug (the engine was in the trunk). I turned my key in the lock, but the hood didn't pop open—not surprising since the front right fender was demolished. I pushed it, pried it. "Thanks for remembering my condoms," I said as I struggled. "Do you have plans?"

In answer, he let his crutches fall, prodded me aside, and threw his whole weight into forcing the hood open.

"Don't hurt it!" I pleaded.

He looked at me.

"Okay, you're right," I admitted. The Bug was toast.

With a groan from both Doug and the car, the hood popped open. I blinked back tears at the sight of my pristine trunk, which I'd covered in fresh carpet from the remnant store a few weeks before. The inside space was concave. Poor Bug.

The vat of condoms had slid to the back wall. I reached in for it and half fell into the trunk. Doug put his hand on my lower back to steady me.

The vat of condoms was suddenly just out of reach and strangely hard to grip. Doug's warm hand burned through the skin of my lower back.

When I couldn't draw it out any longer without being painfully obvious, I grabbed the big box and backed out of the hood. Very slowly. Doug's hand smoothed up my back, under my shirt, all the way to my bra.

I turned to him.

He gazed down at me with absolutely no expression on his face while tracing his fingers down my back, out of my shirt. "What?" he asked innocently, daring me to mention Brandon again.

"I guess I should get all the stuff out of my car before it's crushed into a metal cube and lost forever." Dropping the box of condoms at his feet, I ducked away from him and ran to the driver's door, which opened easily. On the floorboard and under the driver's seat, there was nothing. I had trouble wedging my head into the space between the bashed-in passenger side dashboard and the seat, but once I did, I saw nothing. The glove compartment, permanently popped open with the force of the crash, was empty. None of this surprised me. I kept a very clean car, unlike Keke and Lila's Datsun, which was knee-deep in candy wrappers. I folded the seat forward and slid into the back.

Doug pushed the driver's seat into place and sat down, grunting a little as he hoisted his cast into the car. "Looking for something?"

"I was half hoping I'd find my diamond earrings in here," I admitted, my voice muffled against the carpeted floor. I righted myself and brushed my hair out of my face. "I was wearing them the night of the wreck, and I haven't seen them since."

He reached in front of him and popped open the ashtray in the dash. Diamonds glittered inside.

"Eureka!" Leaning through the space between the front seats, I scooped the diamonds out. My fingers hit an unexpected bump, and I leaned forward to look. The ashtray had caved in with the dash. One of the earring posts was bent. The same force that bent a platinum earring post had also done a number on Doug's leg over in Mike's car. It was a wonder he still had a leg at all. But Doug didn't need to be reminded of that, so I swallowed my nausea and smiled. "How'd you know my earrings would be in the ashtray?"

"In old cars with ashtrays, everyone puts everything in there." He looked at the earrings rather than me and held out his hand for them. I placed them gently in his palm, my fingertips caressing his skin so briefly before coming away.

He cranked down the window and tossed the earrings outside.

"Doug! Move!" I shook his seat back so he'd let me out. "I may need to replace the settings, but I'm sure the stones are okay."

"You mean they're *real*?" His voice cracked as he opened the door and half fell out.

"Of course they're real." I stepped over him and scanned the sandy ground. Luckily they hadn't disappeared beneath the Porsche. I scooped them up from the sand and turned.

He sat in the driver's seat again with the door open, foot and cast on the ground outside the car, looking pale and sick.

"You look like you just saw a ghost. Percocet treating you okay? Or— Here, I found them." I held out the earrings for him to see, in case he envisioned paying me back for losing them. I would never make anyone do something like that.

He pressed his middle finger hard along his eyebrow like *he* was the one with the headache. "I just had an idea. You think you could get a couple thousand bucks for those? Because you could sell them and use the money toward a newer car your dad would approve of."

"That's a great idea," I admitted. "I can't do it, though. My parents gave me these earrings." I dropped them into my pocket.

"They wouldn't let you sell them? Even to get something you need more? I couldn't make that kind of logical argument to my dad, but I'll bet you could make it to yours."

"I mean, they're the last thing my mom and my dad gave me together, before they separated last summer." I was pulling on both earlobes, which made me seasick. I put my hands down.

He frowned at me. "Why haven't you been turning the world upside down looking for your real diamond earrings?"

I shrugged. "I figured they'd turn up. Like my virginity."

He laughed. I laughed with him, but mostly I wanted to watch him laugh. He blushed like a real boy and wiped tears from the corners of his eyes like a real person. I couldn't step closer because Brandon was my boyfriend. But I wanted to laugh with Doug, hug Doug. A little part of me wanted to *be* Doug.

Over his laughter I said, "Tell me about losing yours. Was it with that girl from Destin?"

The sun shone into his eyes so the green seemed transparent, like looking into the shallow water and watching the sand shift underneath. He stared over my shoulder at the Porsche, but I knew he saw the girl from Destin. He took her hand and they splashed into the ocean together. He put his arms around her and held her body loosely in the warm water as the tide came in. Late in the afternoon they dried off and walked into town, wandering the tourist trap gift shops and marveling at the wondrous sculptures of pirates that could be crafted out of coconut shells nowadays. He bought her a hamburger and they shared a milk shake at the Grilled Mermaid. Trying to act carefree and beachy, she'd been foolish enough to walk the hot sidewalks barefoot. She cut her toe on a shell in the pavement. He carried her piggyback to his Jeep in the dusk. They drove to the city beach park and made love. It was the first time for both of them, they were in love with each other, and it meant something.

He blinked and looked straight at me.

I swallowed and tried to say smoothly, "What happened to her?"

"Mike told her I'd been to juvie."

I nodded. "That's what I heard, but I never heard why he did that."

He shrugged. "I guess he liked her or some shit like that. Can't talk to a girl himself so he has to steal somebody else's."

I nodded again, as if I was a good listener. Not as if I was a highly interested listener pumping him for information. "Up until then you and Mike had been close friends, right?"

"Right," Doug said carefully. He knew I was up to something.

"And since then, you've hardly spoken to each other?"

"Until after the wreck, yeah."

Depending on what had happened Friday night, asking my next question might expose that I had amnesia. I was running out of options for finding out the truth. I chose to trust him. "Then why were you riding in Mike's car?"

He stared at me. Not a mean stare burning a hole in my head or a vacant stare over my shoulder, but a big-eyed stare in surprise. With his eyes so deep green and his black lashes so long, he'd never looked more hot. And I'd never felt further from him, because he'd just figured me out.

Or not. "When we wrecked?" he asked, like he'd been momentarily confused rather than bowled over.

I stamped my foot. A cloud of fine sand rose around my flip-flop. "*Yes*, when we wrecked."

He rubbed his hands on his thighs and looked around the junkyard, suddenly uncomfortable. "You know how Gabriel always says he's not going to get drunk, so he drives to a party, and then he gets drunk?"

I nodded.

"I left my Jeep at school and rode to the party with Gabriel so I could drive his Honda to his house afterward. Then I could walk over to the school for my Jeep."

That made perfect sense. Doug never drank while he was training. He served as designated driver for people all the time. "But?" I prodded him.

"But somebody else took Gabriel home early, and Mike

was the only person left to drive me back to school to get my Jeep."

"So you and Mike were driving north," I mused. "Which means when we hit each other, I was driving south, toward the beach. Toward home. Brandon says I wasn't with him. Where could I have been?"

"It's a mystery."

I glared at Doug. The constant snark was one thing. I'd put up with it because I felt like I'd done him wrong times a hundred, even if I couldn't quite put my finger on why. But for him to make fun of me about *this* . . . It was too much to take.

Scooping up my megabox of condoms and wrapping both arms around it, I stalked across the junkyard toward the Benz.

Behind me I heard the door of the Bug slam. I could tell from the screech of metal and the *thud* that the door had fallen off its hinges, but I didn't turn around.

"Zoey," he called.

I stopped between a tower of TVs and a pile of wheelchairs. The tricky thing about trusting Doug was that I had to stay on his good side so he didn't tell everyone in my school about my mother despite his promise not to. I didn't walk back to him, but I did turn with the condom box in front of me like a shield. I waited for him to maneuver down the narrow path winding through the trash.

The afternoon wasn't hot as Florida went, but when he crutched to a stop in front of me, two drops of sweat loosed themselves from his hairline and raced down his cheek. "I didn't realize how much memory you lost, Zoey. Why didn't you tell me?"

"Because losing your memory sounds crazy! Like my mom."

He tilted his head way over to one side, as if looking at me from a different angle would help. "This is nothing like your mom."

"It feels the same." I transferred the box to one hip and chewed on my thumbnail—normally something I did *not* do because it ruined my manicure and projected weakness, said my mom.

I was finally talking about this with someone.

Even if it *was* Doug Fox.

"My dad told me it was the same. He threatened to lock me up with her if I ruined his trip to Hawaii."

Doug closed his eyes, looking pained. He shook his head. Then he leaned on a crutch and spun the other on its rubber tip in the dust, one of the many tricks he'd invented over the past few days. Gazing at the spinning crutch rather than me, he told me, "You said you didn't remember the wreck. But you did remember me pulling you out of the car. And you remembered me calling you a brat at the game."

I laughed. "I remember all the good stuff."

He stopped spinning the crutch and looked up at me.

"That's why I was so confused when you came over Saturday morning and acted like we were together," I explained. "I don't remember what happened in the emergency room."

He stared at me.

"So . . . ?" I prompted him.

He didn't say a word.

"So, what *did* happen?" I insisted.

"Don't worry about it," he said gruffly, elbowing me just a little as he crutched past me, toward the Benz.

I watched him go, my face and chest burning with anger in the hot sun, not *believing* he had just blown me off.

He rounded the Benz and executed the five-step process of entering a car with crutches.

That's when I ran toward him. I ran at full force like I was swimming the fly, powered by fury. I jerked open the driver's side door and threw the box hard over the headrest into the backseat. The box hit the rear window, and a few condom packets slipped out as the box tumbled to the seat, then the floor. "Don't worry about it!" I yelled. "What the fuck, Doug?"

His arms were crossed, head against the window, eyes closed. "Right—" he started.

I slid into the driver's seat and slammed the door as hard as I could. "I've already told you—"

"Okay—" he said without opening his eyes.

"—this is really important to me—"

"Yes—"

"—and it's not fair for you to withhold information!"

"What happened was, I told you I loved you." Without moving his body or his head, he opened his eyes and gave me a look that said *so there.*

I cranked the car and backed it carefully out of the junk-yard parking lot. Or, I backed it carefully out from between the junk cars where I'd parked it. I couldn't tell whether the other cars parked near the office were working or not, but the Benz certainly looked out of place between them.

Doug shifted his shoulders away from me and gazed out the window.

It took me until we'd passed the high school and maneuvered through the courthouse square to say, "I'm having a hard time believing you."

"Thanks," he said flatly.

I drove down the country highway, toward the beach and the wharf, puzzling this out. I believed him. He had no reason to lie. I simply couldn't picture it. We lay in the wet grass together and he said, "Zoey, I'm sorry for calling you a spoiled brat and I love you." We held hands between stretchers in the emergency room. He kissed my fingers, whispering, "I should never have called you a spoiled brat, and by the way, I love you."

As I turned onto the beach road I asked, "Did I say it back?"

"You said it first."

He braced himself against the seat and the door as the car bumped over the curb. I jerked the wheel to steer back onto the road, eyes darting left and right, hoping Officer Fox wasn't watching from his police car.

"Doug," I finally exhaled. "I don't know what to do. I hope

you'll give me a while to get my brain around this. I mean, I'm dating Brandon—"

He whacked his head against the window.

"Ouch, please don't do that." I put my hand out to touch his head. I even wiggled my fingers, but I couldn't quite reach. I put my hand down. "I don't want to lose you. I realize I don't have you, but I don't want to lose that chance. Like you said, I want a chance with you."

"You do?"

"Yes," I said, "but not right this second. Because I'm dating Brandon—"

"Jesus!"

"—and I don't want to be a cheater."

"You're not married, Zoey!" Doug shouted. "Yet. Just wait. It's this kind of fucked up thinking that will make you wind up married to Brandon Moore."

I tried to laugh, but it came out more of a choked gasp. "I'm seventeen!"

"My point exactly."

I felt him looking at me, but I didn't dare turn my head for fear of running off the road again.

I parked at the wharf and asked as pleasantly as I could under the circumstances, "Is this okay? I could drop you off at your house instead. Do you have paperwork to do?"

"Yes." He opened his door and pulled himself out, leaning on the car.

"Well, wait. It's still early. We could grab a burger and talk some more. Do you have a *lot* of paperwork?"

"Stacks, and then I need to swab the deck and scrape barnacles off the bow." He closed the front door and opened the back to slide his crutches out.

"I'm serious," I called over my shoulder. "We need to talk this out or it'll fester."

"What do we have left to talk about?" he demanded. "Why don't you say 'I'm dating Brandon' ten times fast to get it over with? When that changes, *then* you have my number." He slammed the door.

I SHOULD HAVE DRIVEN HOME, HEATED up a frozen dinner, finished my homework, read ahead for English, and watched TV until I fell asleep.

The idea of this night at home with myself twisted my stomach. Over the past few days I'd had more and more trouble concentrating on homework or English or even TV. I was never alone. Doug and Brandon stood at the periphery of every room, scowling at me with their arms folded. And of course I really was being watched by my dad on candid camera.

Instead, I drove thirty minutes along the oceanfront road, to the mall in Destin. I bought dinner and ate it in the open-air food court while I worked on calculus. If I couldn't be alone with myself, the next best thing was surrounding myself with a happy crowd who had serious concerns like what gifts to give and what clothes to wear. I stayed there, drinking refills of Diet Coke, doing extra calculus problems from the back of the book, until groups of shoppers passed me for the third time and whispered about me because I'd sat at the same table doing calculus so long.

I went shopping. I didn't need anything. I never wanted anything. My mom always had to convince me to buy new clothes to present an organized and confident appearance to the world. She would arrange her schedule so she wasn't catching up with work on Saturday afternoon, bribe me with a promise of a Starbucks frappuccino, and bring me here.

So it's more accurate to say that this time, rather than shopping, I walked through the stores, inhaling their familiar scents. My favorite anchor store smelled just a tad like mildew. The boutique next door reeked of dizzying perfume, a chemical brainwashing me into buying something more fashion forward than my usual comfort zone. Macramé leggings. I didn't fall for it this time, but I might have fallen for it with my mom working on me too. The sales chick smiled with dollar signs in her eyes, said she recognized me from other shopping trips, and asked where my mother was.

She wasn't being catty, I told myself over and over as I swam through the vast parking lot under the mile-high streetlights to the Benz, trying to reach that life raft before I drowned, struggling to stay on the surface. The sales chick didn't know about my mom. Nobody knew but me, and my dad, and Officer Fox, and Doug.

* * *

Baby, r u still coming to swim meet tonight 6 pm?

I shouldn't have sent the text before English. Then I wouldn't have ached for class to end so I could turn my phone back on and see whether Brandon had answered. We turned our phones off during class or they were confiscated. A fishbowl on the counter in the school office swam with phones on vibrate.

And I wouldn't have glared quite so hard at the back of Doug's head. Somehow he knew I hadn't heard from Brandon since Saturday. He knew I'd texted Brandon this morning out of desperation. Brandon *did* give a shit about me, I could have sworn.

When the bell rang I grabbed for my backpack and clicked on my phone. No message.

Doug didn't turn around. He hadn't met my eyes the whole class. But he glanced over his shoulder, looking while trying to look like he wasn't looking. If I'd been half an actress I would have busied myself thumbing my phone, composing a fake response to Brandon's fake answer. I didn't think of this until history class.

Finally, during break, after Doug had already limped out of the room so it didn't even matter, I got Brandon's response:

Glad u remindded me. Ill ask Stepane.

184

For a ride, I finished for Brandon. Surely he only meant he'd ask her for a ride.

I PLUNGED OFF THE BLOCK INTO the water and glided until the precise moment when stroking would propel me faster. Then I broke the glide and kicked for all I was worth, with my anger at my mom and my dad and Brandon and Doug behind me.

I had fresh reason to be mad at Brandon. Stephanie Wetzel had brought him to the meet, all right. And she had visited him in the stands several times. Once I glanced up from the pool deck to wave at him and caught him sipping from her Coke, then passing it back to her.

Right then I vowed that I would win the 400 IM—which I had never done before. Usually I came in sixth or so. I would recapture Brandon's attention. I would make him feel the pride I felt for him when I watched him score a touchdown. Actually I hadn't seen it happen last Friday because Doug had distracted me, but I would be sure to see it this Friday.

And I had a fresh reason to be mad at Doug, like I didn't have enough reasons already. After his show of caring about the team yesterday, he'd spent most of tonight's meet texting on his phone. I wondered whether he was LOLing and ROFLing with another girl from Destin who didn't know he'd been to juvie. He'd decided I wasn't worth the wait.

That got me to the first turn in record time. Between strokes I couldn't raise my head far enough to see the clock on the wall, but it *felt* like the cool water slipped past my skin faster than ever, and the chicks from Crestview and Niceville in the lanes on either side of me were nowhere in sight. Anger was a beautiful thing.

I pushed off the wall hard. Every time I took a breath, I heard Doug yelling my name. Amazing that I could pick out one voice from the hundred or so in the bleachers and around the deck, especially when my ears were full of water. If he thought hollering for me would refresh my anger and make me swim even harder, it was working. Then it occurred to me Brandon might not like Doug cheering himself hoarse for me. I decided Brandon was not as jealous as I'd thought. Brandon had shared a Coke with Stephanie Wetzel. Brandon did not in fact give a shit about me. My kick was powerful, my whole body in sync. Angrier and angrier, I would win this race. At the next turn I flipped toward the wall.

Something grabbed me like the cold tendrils of the under-tow snagging me in the ocean. It grabbed me and wouldn't let go. I screamed underwater, inhaled pool, and thrashed to get away until I didn't know which direction was up. The thing dragged at me, pressing me against the side of the pool. But now I could tell from the warmth of the setting sun that my head was above water. Gulping air, I pushed up my goggles and came face-to-face with my mother.

11

"Zoey," she gasped. She was lying on her stomach on the pool deck. With both arms around my back, she still pressed me toward her, into the hard cement of the pool. "Oh God, Zoey, are you okay?"

Other than the fact that she was lying down in a public place, she probably looked normal to the other people there. She looked like the other moms in their track suits, only with a better figure. But I knew the difference. Normally she would have done herself up gorgeously. No track suit, no way. Trendy jeans with an age-appropriate top. Her makeup would have been immaculate. She was wearing *none*. Her long blond hair was caught in a careless ponytail. Then I noticed something strange in her bangs, something I'd never seen before on her. Gray roots.

"Breathe," she said. Her grip tightened around me. The sinews in her arms flexed. "Let me hear you breathe."

"Mom, I'm fine." Between gasps I said this quietly, like maybe if I kept it down, nobody would notice my insane mother lying on the pool deck and clinging to me. The girl from Crestview and the girl from Niceville each had an elbow up on the wall now, treading water and watching us. "Mom, let me get out."

She released me around the back but kept one hand firmly around my wrist and pulled me. I crawled one-handed onto the pool deck and stood to exactly her height. Coach was right behind her, questioning me with his eyes. Behind him was a ref—he must have stopped the race, but I hadn't heard the whistle. All the swimmers held on to the wall and looked up at us. All three swim teams huddled together in three bundles of bathing suits in three different colors, folding their arms against a sudden wind. All the people in the stands looked over at us. Brandon whispered to Stephanie. Doug was on the phone.

I told Coach, "I'll take care of it." I told the ref, "I forfeit, whatever, sorry." Then I put my arm around my mom's waist, wetting her but I doubt she noticed, and steered her out the gate to the front of the school. I'm sure we looked like an odd promenade because she still hadn't let go of my wrist. Behind us the whispers of the crowd swelled. My eyes stung with tears.

The second the gate closed and the crowd couldn't see us, I jerked my wrist out of her hand and whirled to face her. "What the fuck are you doing?"

She blinked and actually took a step back. "I had a dream you were drowning."

I put my hands on my hips. "They let you out of a locked mental ward because you had a bad dream?"

She cleared her throat. "I guess I escaped."

"You *escaped from the mental hospital?*" My voice echoed across the high school parking lot, over the cars and a few buses gathered around the pool entrance.

She shrugged. "It wasn't brain surgery."

"It's a forty-five-minute drive. How did you get over here from Fort fucking Walton?"

This time she didn't even blink at the F-word, which was a bad sign. "I took a taxi."

I ran my hands back through my hair, or meant to, and stopped when I felt nothing but rubber swim cap and goggles. "What am I going to do with you?" I asked, exactly what she'd asked me once in seventh grade when she caught me trying to run out the door to meet Keke and Lila at Beach Reads wearing argyle kneesocks with my gym shorts. What did I do now? I looked out over the parking lot and watched a police car cruise toward us.

Officer Fox to my rescue again.

He parked at the curb right next to us and got out. "Hey there, Counselor," he called.

"Hi, Cody," she said without smiling.

He strolled over and joined us like we were three old friends who'd run into each other at the homecoming parade. "I hear they're worried about you at the hospital. I can drive you back, or"—he glanced over at me ever so briefly, then focused on my mom again—"Zoey can take you."

My mom nodded. No argument. A bad, bad sign.

He jerked his thumb toward the pool. "Zoey, why don't you go change into some dry clothes and meet us back here. Tell Doug what we're doing."

"Okay." I let Officer Fox take charge, just as he had when I found my mother the first time.

Doug leaned on his crutches inside the pool gate. He'd called his brother to turn my mom in. That's why he'd been on the phone during my heat. Or his brother had texted him first to tell him there was an alert out for my mom. I was the last to know.

Past Doug, in the pool, another heat had started. They must have repeated the one I'd ruined and begun a new one, because BENNETT was on the board. I wasn't sure whether this was Keke or Lila. I couldn't remember the order of the heats or who was swimming in what race. I was losing it.

The crowd didn't mind. They cheered for the racers in the water. Only a few spectators nudged their friends and pointed at me. Brandon sat in the stands with Stephanie like nothing unusual had occurred. Maybe nothing had.

"What happened?" Doug asked, maneuvering in front of me like he thought I might escape too.

I waved vaguely toward the outside world. "She's with your brother."

"Is she okay?"

"If she's not, maybe I can have her car," I joked.

I'd walked five steps beyond him when the nausea hit me, and *I can have her car* throbbed in my throat. My mom would spend the rest of her life in an insane asylum, and I could have her car!

My clothes were in the women's locker room, but I headed for the one-stall bathroom just off the pool for swim event spectators. If someone had been inside and I'd been locked out, I don't know what I would have done. I *could not* vomit in front of a hundred and fifty people on top of everything else. Luckily the bathroom was open and empty and cool. I calmly closed the door behind me, turned the dead bolt, and dashed for the toilet.

Retched and retched and dry heaved, doubled over with the sharpest pain in my stomach and the unbearable nausea. Started sobbing to go with it, because dry heaving wasn't horrible enough. Cried and retched with my face inches from a public toilet. At the same time, I saw myself. From across the room I watched a girl with family problems losing it in a public bathroom. That girl was not me.

A sound like machine-gun fire strafed the bathroom wall. Jerking my head up, I realized it was just someone knocking on the metal door. "I'm okay," I called over the racket, standing up straight. I'd really hoped I could vomit so I'd feel better after, but I knew now that nothing would make me feel better, ever.

God, they would not stop pounding on the door. "I'm okay," I said again. Something hard and cold moved against my cheek. I was on the floor. I must have fainted. I lay on the public bathroom floor in my wet bathing suit. Glorious.

Slowly I sat up. I braced myself with my hands on the

floor—nasty—but better my hands than my face. I took two deep breaths before scooting my back against the wall and easing my way up, standing again, eyes on the door. Something told me the persistent knocker would come through the door soon whether I liked it or not, and I needed to be standing up when that happened.

Sure enough, the dead bolt turned by itself as I watched. And I probably had floor cheese on my cheek. I ran for the sink and splashed cold water on my face, bracing myself against the wall with the other hand so I didn't fall down.

The door popped open a crack. The school's elderly janitor lady peeked in. "Zoey?"

"Hey, Ms. Roberts," I sang, reaching for a paper towel to blot my face. "Thanks for checking on me."

Her face disappeared from the crack. Doug burst in, shouldering the door aside. "What are you doing?" he demanded.

"Looking for privacy!" I screamed hard enough that I felt dizzy again. "Can't I have a little fucking privacy?"

"No," he shouted back, "you *can't* disappear and lock the door, not when your mom—"

I squeezed the paper towel into a tight ball and hurled it at him. It bounced off his chest. We watched it roll across the floor. I knew I was not crazy, I was completely normal, because I suppressed an overwhelming urge to pick up the ball and put it in the trash can. I did not litter.

"You passed out, didn't you?" he said.

"No."

"Come here," he said, switching both crutches to one arm and holding out the other arm for a hug.

"No," I barked. "Don't touch me. Get out of my way."

He was surprised enough that he scooted aside. I walked out the door.

And faced almost the entire swim team, everyone who wasn't in the pool, shivering in an arc around me.

Without meeting their eyes I edged past them against the wall of the building and headed for the locker room.

"Go with her," Doug said quietly.

I didn't turn around to see who he was talking to. It didn't matter anyway. Inside the locker room, I wound my combination lock with fingers shaking from sudden cold. When I turned with my clothes, Lila was standing there with a towel tight around her and her arms folded to keep it in place, scowling at me, staring me down without a word. Lila or Keke or Stephanie, it was all the same. Everyone knew about my mother now.

We both jerked our heads at what we couldn't see: Doug shouting somewhere in the hall between the women's and men's locker rooms. "Brandon, get the fuck over yourself." And then, "Great timing, motherfucker."

Doctors could keep brain-dead patients alive on heart-lung machines. If they could also get those brain-dead folks up walking, talking, and driving to the produce stand for a pine-apple smoothie, that would be me. I was aware of what was going on around me, but my brain had shut down, and zombie

Zoey did not have any reaction to Doug Fox calling her alleged boyfriend a motherfucker. I pulled off my goggles and swim cap and hung them from the top hooks in my locker. Quickly combed out my damp, tangled hair. Dressed and walked past Lila still glowering at me, out to the pool.

This time Brandon met me at the door. Really, I didn't want a hug from him either, but he took up the whole doorway, and pushing past him might cause a fuss. I walked right into the front of him. He folded me in his huge arms.

Over his shoulder, Doug leaned on his crutches, watching me. Or watching Brandon, making sure he didn't get away from me. I'd hugged Brandon and helped him through countless affairs all summer. I'd always listened, never complained. Once he woke me up in the middle of the night, calling me to whine about woman trouble, drunk. I'd spoken soothingly to him, not because I had a crush on him then—I didn't—but because I'd cared about him.

And now I suspected Doug had to yell at Brandon to get him to hug me.

This was how it would be with people from now on, now that they knew about my mother.

I counted to ten because that seemed like a long enough hug, then pulled back and smiled up at Brandon. "Thanks so much for coming. Maybe I'll see you later."

He put one big hand back through his golden hair. "Call me anytime," he told me. As if this were not an automatic privilege of being his girlfriend. As if he were doing me a favor.

I walked past him to march between the pool and the bleachers, running this gauntlet one last time. Keke's heat was over, and now she stood shivering with the rest of the team. She and Lila might not be identical twins, but their outraged glower was amazingly similar. I kept my eyes on the gate ahead of me.

Outside the gate, I saw for the first time that the sun had set. My mom and Officer Fox sat on a low wall around a palm tree in front of the school, illuminated by the parking lot floodlights. I couldn't hear what they said at this distance, but they seemed to be chatting casually. Officer Fox's feet were far apart on the ground, his hands on his knees. Just as I would expect Officer Fox to sit on a planter. My mom should have crossed her legs elegantly in front of her, or even refused to sit on a cement wall. But her knees were tucked to her chest with her arms around them, in the fetal position. If she started rocking back and forth before I reached her, I was headed right back to the bathroom to throw up.

The gate clanged behind me like the bars of a jail sliding shut. "Zoey," Doug called.

I stopped and turned to face him.

"You ride in the police car with your mom," he said. "My brother will bring you home."

I shook my head. "That's not the plan. I'm driving her. Your brother said I could drive her."

"You are *not* driving to Fort Walton when you just passed out in the bathroom," Doug informed me.

"I wouldn't drive if I wasn't okay to drive. What do you think I am, crazy?" I walked to the planter, watching my mom carefully for rocking. "Let's go."

I didn't look back to see whether she followed me. Officer Fox was there to Taser her if she resisted. But I heard her footfalls crunching the sand that covered everything here, even the concrete parking lot. Her footfalls stopped at the back of the Benz. "Where's your car?" she asked.

"I totaled it."

No reaction. None. Next she asked in a monotone, "Where's your father?" Of course she wouldn't remember that he was in Hawaii, marrying his pregnant mistress. My mother was crazy.

"Away on business." I hit the button to unlock the doors of the Benz, and we slipped inside. As I pulled from the parking lot onto the road, I glanced in the rearview mirror and saw Officer Fox's patrol car with Doug in the passenger seat, following me closely.

I headed north and took the highway that hugged the bay, the fastest way to Fort Walton from here. There was absolutely nothing to see—just the patch of highway visible under the headlights, fading into an impenetrable tangle of plants with sharp tips and briars on either side of the road. If I'd turned the wrong way, east toward Panama City, I wouldn't have been able to tell. It all looked the same.

"You realize what you are?" I burst.

No reaction. She sat as she had the whole drive, staring out the window into the scrubby wilderness, hands rubbing her thighs slowly like her palms were sweating and she needed to dry them before shaking another lawyer's hand in court.

"You're an escapee from the loony bin," I said. "You're the butt of every joke ever told. You might as well be the chicken that crossed the road."

"It's a chemical imbalance," she whispered to the window.

"Right. And you poured your chemical imbalance into an Erlenmeyer flask, shook it up"—I bobbed my hand violently to show her—"and *spewed it all over my school!*" My arms circled as wide as the explosion. One part of me felt so, so guilty for saying this to her. I couldn't stop myself. Anger was a million times better than panic.

She didn't move. She didn't speak. But when I glanced over at her again, the tracks of tears down her cheeks glimmered in the glow from the dashboard of the Benz.

I HALF EXPECTED MY MOM TO bolt toward the forest surrounding the low mental hospital building and disappear into the palmettos. Officer Fox would dash after her. My mom would prove surprisingly elusive and they would pick her up a few days later walking along the highway, legs torn to shreds by the unforgiving Florida woods, arms thrust through holes she'd poked in a garbage bag like it was the latest fashion in outerwear, eyes vacant. This time there would be a photo in the newspaper.

But she walked quietly into the hospital with me, without

once pulling a razor blade out of her shoe or collapsing into a seizure. When I told the receptionist who we were, four security guards descended on us and swept my mom away down the hall, all business and alacrity to prove they had their shit together even if a brilliant loony did slip through their grasp every now and again.

The receptionist asked me to wait. Eventually a shrink took me into a courtyard garden. Amid the music of bubbling fountains and the heady scent of oleander bushes that were probably pruned by lobotomized men with fingernail clippers, the shrink told me many things that were ironic, perfect as punch lines, even better than the chicken that crossed the road. I walked to the hospital exit reviewing the punch lines over and over in my head so I could repeat them to Doug exactly the right way.

When he saw me coming across the parking lot, he got out of the police car—door open, crutches out first, then his good foot, heaving himself upward. He crutched around the open door and slammed it shut with his hip. Then he rounded to the front of the car and hopped onto the hood, sliding his butt around to find a comfortable spot in a way I knew was meant to piss his brother off. He patted the hood beside him. I looked to Officer Fox for approval to sit on his police car, but he stared up at the roof as if praying for strength.

I slid onto the hot hood beside Doug. Though the night had settled, the air warmed me now that I wasn't hanging out in a wet bathing suit. And the hospital corridors had been refrigerated like they needed to preserve their human specimens for study. I relaxed into the hot hood defrosting my ass.

Doug watched me.

I recited the punch lines I'd memorized. "The doctor said at first they thought my mom was depressed, since she attempted suicide. So they put her on an antidepressant, but it pushed her into a manic episode, which causes people to do things like escape from the psych ward and jerk their daughters out of pools when they are winning a heat. And do you know *why* the drug pushed her into a manic episode?"

No, why? Doug was supposed to say drily, setting me up for the next punch line. Instead, he only watched me with his big sea-green eyes and shook his head.

I delivered my line anyway. "Because my mom isn't just depressed. She has bipolar disorder. It took them a week and a half and a jailbreak to figure this out, when I could have told them in the first place. I mean, I didn't know what was wrong with her, but I could have told them she'd been depressed for a few weeks and then so high for a few weeks that she'd gone to the doctor to get a prescription for sleeping pills, which of course came in handy when she got depressed again and needed to commit suicide. They could have figured it out before now."

This time Doug knew his line. "Why didn't you tell them before?"

"They didn't ask me. They wouldn't let me see her. They told my dad that when people attempt suicide, their families are part of the problem, so they don't let the crazies see their families while they're being treated."

Doug didn't laugh or even gape at me in disbelief. He just kept staring at me. He got the highest grade in the class on every English test, yet he didn't understand the exquisite irony of this situation. I *knew* he didn't understand when he said, "They didn't mean *you* helped make her crazy. They meant your dad screwing his employee. But they don't know stuff like that when a patient first shows up. They have to keep everybody away from the patients just in case."

"You're not getting it," I said. "If the doctors had given me some credit instead of viewing me as a bothersome child when I came to the emergency room with her, I could have prevented this whole problem!"

Now Doug watched me with his chin down like a librarian or a badass nanny examining me through bifocals. He was passing judgment on me. Worse, with his chin down he was looking up at me through his long black lashes. He was passing judgment on me in a very sexy way without even meaning to. And I had a boyfriend back home who hugged me only when prompted.

Sliding down from the hood, I grumbled, "I shouldn't have told you anything."

"Hey." He grabbed my hand before I could step out of his reach. "I'm not acting like you wanted me to act. What did you want me to do?" He leaned forward and his grip was strong. Unless I read him wrong, he was serious.

I shook my hand loose and folded my arms on my chest. "I wanted you to laugh with me and be outraged with me and do something other than sit here and stare at me and feel sorry for me."

Still he stared at me, not understanding.

"It's hereditary," I continued in a rush. "The doctor told me what the warning signs are. Depression . . . that's obvious. Then people cycle to mania. They're workaholics. They want to take care of everything."

"But you're like that naturally."

"They're impulsive," I added.

Doug cocked his head. "Like what? Having sex on the first date?"

I squealed, "Brandon and I are in lo—"

Doug reached out and put two fingers over my lips. "You had sex with Brandon the same night your mom swallowed a bottle of sleeping pills. To me that doesn't sound like you have bipolar disorder. It sounds like you're just run-of-the-mill screwed up. Not crazy."

"She *is* crazy," Officer Fox rumbled from inside the police car.

12

I squinted at Officer Fox, but I couldn't see him clearly through the windshield reflecting the lights from the hospital. This was probably the fourth thing I'd ever heard him say. I wanted to double-check that I'd heard him correctly before I disrespected a police officer by cussing him out.

Apparently he *had* said what I thought he'd said. Doug smiled. "My brother thinks that you're crazy and you need to get checked out yourself."

I closed my eyes, took a deep breath through my nose, opened my eyes. "Why?"

Doug spoke in his usual sarcastic tone. If I'd listened to him without watching him, I wouldn't have known anything was wrong. But as he spoke, he held his head still, like he balanced on a tightrope. "When you found your mom that day, you were very calm. You didn't cry."

I hadn't thought about it. But now that I allowed myself to consider it . . . A seventeen-year-old discovered her mom after a suicide attempt, and she didn't even cry? That *did* sound crazy.

I concentrated on Doug's green eyes. "I knew she was there

because her car was in the lot, but when I went in, the lights were off and the air was cold." I felt goose bumps prick up at the memory of stepping from the broiling afternoon into that cold, dark space.

Doug slid down from the hood and moved toward me, balancing on one crutch.

"I found her on her bed and I knew she was dead. I knew exactly what she'd done. She'd been taking a lot of naps in the middle of the day, but there was something about the way her hand lay on the duvet." I moved my fingers to that position, duplicating what death had looked like to me, fingers relaxed, palm open and vulnerable.

Doug's hand covered my palm.

"And then I touched her and knew she was alive," I told our hands, "so I was relieved. You can't imagine how relieved I was, and happy. I'm probably laughing on the 911 recording. I felt like the luckiest person alive. I still felt that way when your brother came and I rode with him behind the ambulance to the hospital. It wasn't until later, sitting in the waiting room at the hospital, that I started to get scared my mom might be stuck this way. Oh God."

Even before my face crumpled, Doug shifted forward to give me a hiding place. I sobbed into his FSU T-shirt. Once I started I couldn't stop, and I made a choked noise my mom could probably hear if she were sweeping the paths in the hospital courtyard, pausing over one stepping-stone in particular, sweeping the same stone over and over, spotless.

"Shhhhh," said Doug. He stroked his fingers at the back of my head until his fingertips penetrated the thickness of my hair and he touched my nape. He looped the other arm half around me at an odd angle so he could keep hold of his crutch too. And he kissed the top of my head.

That made me cry even harder. I was caught in the current dragging me along the ocean floor. I struggled to the surface to gasp, "Why did you do this to me?"

"Shhhhh. I just wanted to make sure you're okay."

I cried for a long time. Every few minutes I'd pull away from him, sniffle, and try to dry up. Then I'd look up at his face, the tears in his eyes, and I'd lose it again. At least no one stared at me. The parking lot was empty except for us and Officer Fox, and anyway someone bawling their eyes out was probably an hourly occurrence outside the mental hospital. All this time Doug worked his fingers in circles at the back of my neck.

I took one final sniff and exhaled, exhausted but safe for now. We slid back onto Officer Fox's hood and held hands.

I stared straight ahead at the low brick building that gave away nothing. "What do I do now?"

"You wait," Doug said.

"I did that already," I sighed. "I'm not allowed to visit her, but I've known since she got here that she could call me whenever she felt ready. She hasn't called. She's only come to my swim meet and freakishly pulled me out of the water and shrieked like the mother of Grendel."

"Hm." Doug laughed the smallest laugh. "Now that they know what's wrong with her, maybe things will be different." He squeezed my hand.

I wondered which window of the hospital was hers. Whether she had a front window and could see me right now. Whether she had a window at all. "What were the people at the swim meet saying about her?"

"What you'd expect." With both hands on my shoulders, he turned me toward him and shook me a little. "Zoey, a lot of people didn't know. No one on the swim team knew. They were"—he chuckled humorlessly—"surprised. But your mom is a public defender. She worked at the courthouse with fifty people. She's been missing for more than a week. People were going to find out. Your dad could threaten to have Cody fired all day, but he never could have contained this. Now you know people know. That's the only change. You and your dad never had control over the information. You only had control over the illusion that you had control. And if the illusion is all you want, you might as well be crazy."

I rubbed my forehead, which had begun to throb. I'd forgotten to take painkillers.

"It's not the end of the world, Zoey. Yeah, it will be hard for her to go back to work with everyone in town knowing what happened, but what else is she going to do? And she'll get through it. In three years it will be almost like it never happened."

"It will?" I asked, because I suspected that he wasn't talking about my mother anymore. He was talking about coming back from juvie.

Then I glanced at my watch. "Oh, look. My dad just got married." I'd kept Officer Fox from his duties long enough. I asked Doug, "Are you riding back to town with your brother? I can give you a ride instead."

His thumbs moved on my shoulders. "Sure. But you don't have to take me straight home. We could hang out."

I took a long breath, thinking over how to phrase this carefully. After everything he'd done for me tonight, I didn't want to piss him off.

Before I could speak, he let me go. "You're going to Brandon's, aren't you."

I knew it didn't make sense to Doug. It didn't really make sense to me either, except Brandon was my good friend from before all this happened. "I need to know whether we're still together or he's too horrified."

"Can't you just call him or text him or something?" Doug grumbled.

"No, I can't tell anything from that. I can't *see*."

He laughed shortly. "You can't *see* anyway."

I whacked him lightly on the chest. "What is that supposed to mean?"

"You just want to go parking with him," Doug accused me.

"Well, what if I do?"

Well, what if I did?

Doug held his arms out toward the Benz: *Be my guest.*

"Coming with?" I asked. I wished he would come with me, just ride back to town with me so we could talk and make this better.

He shook his head.

I slid off the hood and prodded his good knee with my hip. "Don't be mad."

He shrugged and looked away from me, at the moon rising over the mental hospital. It was almost full, missing just a sliver.

I rounded the police car and peeked through the open driver's side window to thank Officer Fox for all his help. He was snoring.

Wishing that something else would happen, that Doug would change my mind, even insult me to draw this out a little longer, I walked slowly through the silence to the Benz and slipped inside. My mom hadn't been wearing perfume but I smelled her anyway, something I recognized beyond her usual soap and shampoo, which she wouldn't have at the mental hospital. The scent of my mother. I turned the key in the ignition.

Nothing.

I was going crazy. I probably couldn't tie my own shoes anymore either. I took the key out, put it back in, turned it.

Nothing. No dash lights, no radio, definitely no engine.

Looking over at me, Doug knocked on the hood of the police car to wake up his brother.

*   *   *

FIFTEEN MINUTES LATER OFFICER FOX STRAIGHTENED from peering into the engine and let the hood of the Benz fall back into place. "Only thing I can tell you is, my friend owns the garage around the corner. He works late. I'll call him and ask him to tow it for you. Maybe it's something simple." When I nodded, he went back to the police car and spoke into his radio.

Doug had held the flashlight for his brother. Now he turned the beam on me. "I need to lie down. My leg's swelling again."

I winced for him.

"Lie down with me." He leaned so close, I felt the heat of the flashlight beam on my cheek. "You're tired."

I *was* tired suddenly, bone-tired and sore, as if I'd swum a hundred races. Or was this Doug's power of suggestion?

I couldn't lie down with him, though. Lying in the back of a police car with him would not be my consolation prize after I couldn't go parking with my boyfriend. That would make me a ho.

Keeping one hand on a crutch for balance, he put the hand holding the flashlight on my shoulder. I couldn't see him as well anymore in the dim light of the parking lot, but my other senses took over. His hand was hot through my shirt and his low voice vibrated in my gut as he coaxed, "Come on, Zoey. You look like death. Lie down with me. I won't try anything."

I left the keys in the Benz and walked with Doug to the police car. Doug spoke a few words to his brother, who stuffed a couple of pillows through the window between the front seat and the back. Doug must have been using the police car as a sleeping car quite a bit. He had the whole drill down. He put one pillow on the seat for our heads and one at the other end to elevate his leg, and folded his tall frame into the space.

I lay in front of him, just as we'd lain together on the swim team van. Except the police car seat was smaller than the van seat, so we couldn't lie together without touching each other. We touched. He didn't put his hands on me or anything obvious like that, but I couldn't help that the crooks of my knees hugged his knees. His thighs pressed the backs of my thighs. My butt was tucked against his pelvis. His chest radiated heat against my back, and his warm breath whispered in my hair. My headache slowly dissipated. Officer Fox cranked up the thrash metal on the radio and cruised out of the lot.

"Doug," I said softly.

"Zoey," he whispered.

"When you ran away, where did you go?"

He sighed into my hair. Chills raced down my neck. Finally he said, "Seattle."

"That's a long way." I tried to picture Doug at fourteen, as innocent as I'd been at fourteen, alone in Seattle. Smaller than he was now, just a kid. His Florida-weight jacket was no match for the wet breeze off the Pacific, and his wallet was empty.

"I went as far away as I could." He nuzzled the back of my neck—inadvertently, I was sure—as he made a bigger hole for his head in the pillow.

We didn't say anything else. The car hummed, build-

ings flashed by. We must have been taking the longer southern route through Fort Walton and Destin, along the beach.
Streetlights flashed in and out of the car. And Doug's breathing at my back fell into a deep rhythm.

He touched me all over, down the length of me, yet his
hands touched me nowhere. He didn't mean to touch me. I
shouldn't touch him either, because I had a boyfriend, and I
didn't want to lead Doug on. But my hand lay along my side,
resting on my hip. I wouldn't need to slide it far to touch Doug
in a place I *really* shouldn't touch Doug.

The closer to home we got, the stronger the urge grew. Every car we passed swished a sexy Doppler effect: *do it, do it, do
it.* If I did it and he was awake, I would die of mortification. If
I did it and he was asleep, it would seem almost criminal, like
I was taking advantage of him when he was most vulnerable.

I could not do it. But just thinking about it, I was hotter
than when Brandon and I had actually done it.

Familiar landmarks flashed by—Slide with Clyde, the
Grilled Mermaid. We were close to home. Doug would wake
soon. I would miss my chance. Slowly, slowly, a millimeter at
a time, I slid my hand down into the space between my butt
and . . . him. Let him think *I* was asleep and my hand had
slipped there. Let him be surprised.

No. I did not dare.

And then, as I watched Jamaica Joe's flash past out the far
window, his mouth took the back of my neck, kissed it like
it was my mouth or my ear or my breast. I wasn't sure where

these ideas came from. A boy had never put his mouth on my breast before. The thought frightened me and I loved it. His tongue massaged circles across my neck and made me lose my mind. His hand found my hand and pulled me back against him until I rubbed him as I had imagined, then harder.

The engine and the thrash metal on the radio switched off.

We both sprang up, blinking under the dome light, as if we shouldn't have been lying down together in the first place. Guilt is a funny thing. If we hadn't been guilty, I wouldn't have noticed how pink and swollen his lips were from kissing me, or how glazed his green eyes looked from the way I'd touched him.

"Don't get out," I said. "I'll see you tomorrow." I climbed out of the seat and stopped at Officer Fox's window. "Thank you so, so much for everything."

Officer Fox touched two fingers to his forehead in a salute, like a complete dork. "Just doing my job, ma'am."

"Uh-huh." I hoped he couldn't tell I was still tingling and swirling from everything Doug and I had and hadn't done to each other. I hurried into my dad's house, past the cameras and into my room, to finish what we'd started.

"ZOEY."

"Mmmmm."

"Zooooooooeeeeeeeeeey, wake up."

I jerked upright in my bed at the sound of Doug's voice.

He'd hovered just above me all night in my dreams, but I knew they were just dreams. Reality wasn't that good. Then I figured out I was pressing my cell phone to my ear. "Yep, I'm awake."

"Are you coming to school?"

I flopped back on the bed and gazed at the clock on my bedside table. "I'm not late."

"I just wanted to let you know you have a ride. I thought it might not occur to you to look for it, but my brother's friend fixed the Benz. It's parked outside your house."

I rolled over and gazed toward the front of the house, but my room didn't have a window in that direction, and I couldn't see through walls. "You're kidding. What was wrong with it?"

"You know how people speak Japanese and you know it's Japanese but you have no idea what they're saying and you definitely couldn't repeat it?"

"You mean you don't know anything about cars?"

He laughed. I pictured him throwing his head back and laughing.

"Wow," I said. "I'm so grateful to your brother. I think. Do you know how much it cost? I have a credit card." I hoped the garage bill wasn't too much—but if it was, at least I hadn't rolled a joint on the cutting board while my dad was gone. Of course, that was the sort of argument I'd make to my mom, not my dad.

"No charge," Doug said. "My brother and his friend may have drag-raced the Benz and the cop car."

"What?" I jerked upright again. "That's illegal! A damn

sight more illegal than collecting donations in a bucket on the highway."

"My brother is a very bad policeman. So . . . you're coming to school, right?"

I was dying to see Doug. The low notes of his voice on the phone gave me chill bumps all over again. But as I ran my free hand through my hair, crispy from chlorine I hadn't washed out, I pictured Brandon giving me that awkward hug under duress last night. And behind him, the swim team watching me like an exhibit at the zoo. "Nnnnnnno."

"Come so you can be around people," Doug coaxed. "I don't think you should be alone today."

"I think I definitely should."

"Come so I won't worry about you."

He'd made the one argument that could persuade me. I owed him big-time. I owed him that much.

WE HUNG TOGETHER ALL DAY—EXCEPT CALCULUS, of course. It was delicious. Like we'd hooked up. Or, okay, like I'd felt him up in the backseat of a cop car.

Really more like he was my dear friend looking out for me. We weren't doing anything that unusual. Since the school year started we'd followed each other along the same path from English to history, from biology to lunch. The only difference today was that we walked together. I wondered whether everyone avoided my eyes or just wasn't looking at me. I wondered whether they whispered about me and my mom. Doug knew how I felt without me telling him. He gave me someone to walk with and talk to so I wouldn't feel alone.

Since school started we'd eaten at the same lunch table too—just at different ends. Today we sat next to each other at the usual table with most of the swim team, his friends and my former friends who acted like I might bite them now. I'd dropped the ball breaking up the fight between Keke and Lila on Tuesday, but I'd brought them back together without even trying. Nothing cemented a relationship like mutual hatred of a third party. Lila sat between Mike and Keke, talking in turns to each of them. Every time she talked to Keke, she ate a spoonful of Keke's frozen yogurt, and the two of them looked at me with hooded eyes, then looked away. They prided themselves on knowing everything about everyone. They were furious at being kept in the dark about their best friend's mother. It was futile to explain I'd hoped no one would ever find out.

"Let's see the clipboard, Captain," Doug said, giving me something to do.

I set down my fork and pulled the clipboard out of my backpack for him. He flipped through the pages of numbers in his handwriting, really looking. "Your times the past few days have been amazing." He cocked his head at me. "Demons chasing you?"

"Maybe." Across the lunchroom, Stephanie Wetzel acted out a little skit with exaggerated motions for her friends. My mom pulling me out of the pool. A fisherman hauling a marlin on board. Hard to say.

"The trick is to get you swimming like that every time," Doug said, "even when you don't have something hanging over your head."

I turned to him. "I don't think that will be a problem for a while." I passed my hand in a circle above my head. "This is very crowded airspace right now. If it keeps up, I might even place at State." Keke and Lila watched me. I put my hand down.

"My dad's picking me up after swim practice today," Doug said. "On Thursdays we have a sunset cruise and then a crew meeting."

"Crew meeting?" I echoed. That sounded too New Age a concept for the ruffians I'd seen working on the *Hemingway*.

"But I hear the swim team is planning a beach party after the football game tomorrow night," he said, "and they're trying to convince the football team to crash it. Keke and Lila aren't subtle. Want to go?"

I couldn't help cutting my eyes at Keke and Lila. They whispered together as Keke gazed at me. I told Doug, "I'm not invited."

"Of *course* you're invited—you're the captain of the swim team—but let's skip that issue. You're invited because I'm inviting you."

"As a date?" I asked quietly enough that no one around us could hear over the laughter and the clinks of silverware.

"Of *course* not as a date, because then you'd have to break up with your wonderful boyfriend who hasn't messaged you all day." How did Doug know this? He'd been watching me more closely than he let on.

"As friends, then?" I clarified.

He lowered his chin and gave me that sexy look through his long black lashes. "As whatever we are."

During swim practice he even convinced Gabriel to drag a lawn chair poolside so he could sit closer to me, protecting me. But as he'd said, at the end of practice he gave me a wave and limped out the gate to meet his dad. He couldn't protect me in the women's locker room anyway.

I knew it was coming. In my peripheral vision I saw Keke eyeing me as we showered, dried off, and dressed.

I could have sped up and beat the crowd out the door, robbing her of her chance alone with me. Instead, I slowed down. I'd had enough of the cold stares from her and Lila. Lila had hurried out of the locker room to meet Mike, but disarming Keke might disarm both twins at once. When the last of the junior girls finally giggled their way outside, I slammed my locker door and whirled to face Keke, catching her—what else?—midstare. "What is it?" I demanded. "Tell me."

Surprised that she wasn't the one to confront me first, she blinked and took a deep breath before dropping her bomb. "You didn't measure the skid marks at the wreck so your mom could get more insurance money for you. You measured them because you were trying to figure out what happened. You obviously don't remember anything about that night. If you did, you would have been freaking out completely. And you flat-out lied to Lila and me about it."

Yes, but only because my dad had threatened me. I opened my mouth to say this to her. I couldn't form the words. My brain fixated on what she'd said. Why should I have been freaking out about that night? *What had I done?*

"Go home and find the accident report," Keke said. "Even after all the lies you've told me in the past two weeks, you need to know what really happened."

13

"Just tell me!" I shouted at her. If a copy of the accident report was at my house, I knew where it would be. And I wasn't allowed in there. "You know this big secret so just *tell me* instead of making me chase around for it!"

"Oh, I don't give away people's secrets." If Doug's words dripped sarcasm, Keke's gushed it like the biggest waterfall at Slide with Clyde. "That's why you didn't tell me your mom—" Even in the middle of confronting me, Keke couldn't bring herself to say it. *My mom was insane.* "And that's why you didn't tell me you had amnesia. Because you don't trust me with something that important. Now everybody knows my own best friend doesn't trust me. You made a freaking *fool* out of me—"

"Just tell me what happened!" I screamed. My voice set the locks buzzing against the lockers. "How did you find out? Who else knows?" As soon as the words left my mouth, I realized I didn't need to yell at her. I knew *exactly* who else knew and how she'd found out. I jerked up my backpack and stomped toward the door to the pool.

As I reached the door, Keke put her hand on my arm and pulled, eyes full of fear. "You can*not* tell them you heard this from me. Doug will kill Mike. Mike will never speak to Lila again. And Lila . . . and me . . ."

"Then tell me what it is."

Keke pressed her lips together.

I jerked open the door before Keke could stop me again. I headed straight across the pool deck, empty except for Lila and Mike sitting close together on the lawn chair. When Lila saw me, she jumped up, holding out my clipboard, almost as if she were ready to make up with me. "I can't believe you forgot this!" She saw the look on my face and stopped.

I closed the steps between us and took the clipboard from her. "Tell me what happened Friday night."

She gaped at me, then wailed over my shoulder at Keke, "You told her!"

"I didn't tell her what *happened*," Keke clarified. "I told her she needs to find *out*. She can't go around not knowing, Lila, and I don't care if it *does* break you up with your boyfriend."

"You just don't want me to *have* a boyfriend," Lila squealed. "You can't get a boyfriend so you don't want me to have one either!"

"Whatever," I mumbled, skirting Lila and approaching Mike, who had edged toward the pool. He watched the twins silently as if he had nothing to do with any of this. I walked right up to him and stopped inches from his face so he couldn't pretend he didn't hear me, one of his usual tactics for saying nothing. "Michael." I smiled, skin stretched so taut across my face that it might break. "Baby. Tell me what happened."

He turned red as a stop sign and shook his head.

"Doug is *not* going to kill you." As Mike's eyes widened, my voice rose. "He is *not* going to beat you up or whatever he threatened to do to you." I wasn't sure Mike was really safe, but I was desperate. "Doug is full of shit, in case you haven't noticed. Now, for the last time, what the fuck happened?"

As a diversion, Mike jerked the clipboard from my arms and slung it into the pool.

Behind me, both twins gasped.

The plastic board floated for a few seconds. The wind stirred ripples that lapped at the pages, soaking them. Then the clipboard nose-dived.

I didn't stay to watch it hit bottom. My arms were still extended like I could grab the clipboard and save it. I put my arms down. Turning for the gate to the parking lot, I called over my shoulder, "Thanks for being true friends."

Never get into a shouting match with twins. They emptied their clips into my back, still shouting at me as I crossed the parking lot to the Benz. *Right back at you, pot calling the kettle black, talk about a true friend.*

Bitch!

That last bullet jogged the keys from my hand as I reached for the door of the Benz. I bent to pick them up and noticed I hadn't repainted my fingernails since Saturday, which wasn't like me at *all*. A huge chip had formed in my thumbnail.

It wasn't like me to talk on the cell phone while driving, either. That wasn't safe. As I pulled out of the parking lot onto the street, I pressed the button to call Doug. I got his sarcastic voice-mail prompt.

Speeding down the straightaway where I'd wrecked, my thumb hovered above the button to call my dad's cell. But what good would that do me? If he had the accident report, it was in his office, which was off-limits to me. He would tell me no, I couldn't go in there to retrieve it. I could ask permission, be denied, and do it anyway. Or I could go ahead and do it. Or I could call to ask him what might be in the report that my ex-friends wanted me to know. But then I'd be admitting I was missing part of my memory and I was crazy like my mom, as he'd suspected all along.

When I reached my house I sat in the Benz in the court-yard for a few last seconds, soaking up the late afternoon sun on my skin. I had to go in, I had to find out, but these were my last breaths being innocent. I was afraid what I found out would change my life forever.

And then I walked into the house. Past the cameras in the living room, the cameras down the hall. My dad's office was so forbidden, *two* cameras were trained on the door.

Here I paused again. The room had become officially forbidden when I was in middle school and my dad found me looking through his office drawers for invisible tape for a school project. He grounded me from seeing Keke and Lila. I screamed and pitched a fit, because the only thing worse than being grounded when you're a kid is being grounded when you know you didn't deserve it, when you were only looking for tape for *school*, and my dad wanted me to go to *school*, didn't he? I remembered every detail of that drama queen day—the school project on the history of daylight savings time, the sheet of scrapbooking paper with little clocks I'd bought as a cute border for the report (thus the tape), the pink polo shirt I was wearing, the pink wristwatch I stared at as I rocked in the chair on the front porch, willing the hands to move and my mom to come home from her Saturday at work. Eventually she pulled up and I ran across the stone courtyard and threw myself into her arms. She told me she couldn't undo the punishment my dad had doled out because parents worked as partners, but she would talk to him. Eventually she got my sentence reduced from a week grounded to two days grounded. And she laughed at my idea that my dad didn't want me in his office because he had something to hide. No, he just needed an oasis. Starting a business like Slide with Clyde was stressful. Living with two women was stressful. He simply wanted one place in the house all to himself. I could understand that, couldn't I?

Looking from one camera to the other and wiping the tears from my eyes, I stepped through their invisible force field protecting the open door. Checked the top of my dad's desk, the in-box, the out-box, the drawers, the filing cabinets, the shelves, the counter. The accident report wasn't there.

Feeling more and more panicky about what could be in

that report, I dashed out to the Benz. I had one more source to try for this report—the police station—but now it was after five o'clock, and with my luck, they'd be closed. I was shaking by the time I parked in the courthouse square, next to my mom's office.

But I heaved a huge sigh as I slammed the door of the Benz and saw I'd gotten my first break all week. Two parking spaces down, Officer Fox was just stepping from his truck in his police uniform. He must be arriving for work.

I hurried toward him. "Hey!" I said, trying to sound surprised and pleased to see him.

"Hi," he said warily.

"I was just coming to get an extra copy of the accident report, you know, for insurance and stuff."

He nodded shortly and kept walking past me, toward the door to the station. "You need to come back during regular office hours with your dad and a check for two dollars made out to the DMV." He disappeared into the building.

I stood there stunned for a few seconds. Then I galloped after him and swung through the glass door before he could escape deep into the office where I couldn't catch him. He was unlatching and lifting a section of the front counter to let himself through.

"Why?" I called to his back. "I'm a licensed driver in the state of Florida. I'm the driver, it's my wreck, it's my accident report, and my two dollars spends like my dad's."

"Hey there, Zoey," a deep voice boomed behind me. The

police chief closed the glass door behind him, carrying a paper sack from the Grilled Mermaid.

"Hey, Chief," I said with a grin, hoping he'd caught only the tail end of me yelling at his deputy. My mom had introduced me to the chief around town when I was growing up. During parades and festivals along the beach strip, he always rode above the crowd on a horse. He and my mom worked together—or against each other, since my mom defended the people he arrested. But I'd never been in the police station before, and I hadn't thought of him when I stalked in here demanding my life back.

"Fox," he snapped. "Get Miss Commander whatever she needs."

Officer Fox disappeared into the back.

The chief turned to me and smiled sympathetically. "Heard about your car wreck."

That was more than I could say. "Yes, sir, it was scary."

"Heard your mom made a big jailbreak yesterday."

This was why I'd hoped no one would ever find out about my mom. I grinned again and pretended I could laugh at it like he could. I needed his help. I needed that report.

"I've been over to the hospital a couple of times in the past few weeks," he said. "They're still not allowing her to have visitors?"

I opened my mouth to speak. For fear of sobbing, all I could do was shake my head no. He'd been to see my mom? I'd thought I was alone.

"You let me know if there's anything I can do for you or for her." He patted me twice on the shoulder and maneuvered through the counter like Officer Fox had. "Fox!" he hollered.

The chief and Officer Fox passed each other in the corridor, and Officer Fox slid the precious document onto the counter. "Two dollars," he grumbled.

I fished in my purse, tossed two bills on the counter, and slapped my hand down on the paper before he could take it away.

Just as quickly, he covered my hand with his. "Don't go to Doug's house."

He might as well have said, *Don't open the box, Pandora.* "Right." I snatched the report and ran.

"I mean it, Zoey," he called after me.

"Why can't I go over there?" I asked as I backed out the door.

"Because it's Thursday."

Whatever. Outside in the orange light of the setting sun, I scanned Officer Fox's diagram of the wreck, his quaint depiction of a stick-deer, and his clumsy legalese until I found what I was looking for.

Doug wasn't the passenger in Mike's car. He was the passenger in mine.

I plugged Doug's address into the GPS from the swim team mailing list stored on my phone. At first I thought it steered me correctly. I drove in the general direction of the docks, then turned left toward the bluff.

But I began to wonder, as the Benz crept through a thicket that threatened to close in over the road. Palmettos scraped the paint and moths fluttered across the windshield. Satellites could be wrong.

I *really* wondered when the thicket opened to the starry sky and the full moon over the rolling ocean, with the docks almost directly underneath me. I drove across a causeway built up between islands so someone could live out here. Someone rich. Someone not Doug. But I couldn't turn around until I reached the other side. I inched the Benz forward, off the narrow causeway and underneath the canopy of an enormous live oak.

In front of me was Doug's house. I knew this because I saw his Jeep pulled to one side of the clearing and abandoned, the open interior strewn with leaves. The house itself was a 1970s split-level with blue paint peeling from the trim work.

And in front of the house, ten men sat in a circle around a campfire. I was close enough to see them shuck oysters and tilt up bottles of beer. In fact, I caught Doug, who did not drink while he was in training, in midswig. What had I driven into? Instinct warned me to back out the way I'd come, but I could never make it in reverse without backing off the narrow causeway and into the sea.

Doug limped toward me on his crutches. I'd thought maybe his dad let him have one beer on special occasions—but no,

I could tell from the way Doug examined the ground before every step that he was buzzed. I parked the car and hurried to meet him before he fell down.

"Zoeyyyy," he called. "Just the person I wanted to see me at my lowest. Come have a raw oyster." When he reached me he set his chin on my shoulder and whispered, "My dad thinks we're together. Not because I lied to him, but because Friday night I thought we *were* together, and I was all happy about it until I went over to your house Saturday morning and talked to you and found out we weren't. But that's way too complicated to explain to a salty dog. So just smile and nod, if you don't mind." He hobbled away from me and made an enormous vertical circle with one crutch, gesturing for me to follow him.

Not buzzed. Plastered.

I caught up with him and whispered, "Is this your crew meeting?"

"Ha. Is that what I called it? Every Thursday all the deck-hands from my dad's boat hike up here for oysters and beer. Also my dad's roughneck friends come, and their cousins who heard the words *free beer*, and anything else that might have wandered up from the wharf." The familiar snarky sense of humor let me know Doug was in there somewhere, but his delivery was low and rapid fire as if his playback control was set too fast, lubed by alcohol. "All of them get free beer, and raw oysters, and the chance to take potshots at Fox the Younger."

"What kind of potshots?" I asked, beginning to worry.

"Insults for not drinking beer," he said huskily. "Because you know that means you're gay. Teetotalling and homosexuality are the twin and intertwined forces of evil."

"But you're drinking."

He stopped not far behind the circle of guffawing men and looked down at me. "Because, as my dad keeps telling me, I don't have no chance on that fag swim team now that my leg's broke. And if you faced a night of ten salty dogs riffing on your cast, you'd drink too. Abstinence is for pussies."

"Salty dogs don't use words like *abstinence*," I corrected him. "They would say *laying off the sauce*."

He gave me a dark look and very slowly popped his neck. Then he looked up and addressed the circle with his honeyed sarcasm. "Hey, everyone, look who's here! It's Zoey!"

"Zoooooooeeeeeeeeyyyyyy," the men cheered. They had heard about me. Only Doug's dad stayed silent, eyeing me and exhaling cigarette smoke.

"Hello," I called back, suddenly aware I was wearing very short gym shorts and a long-sleeve V-neck T-shirt that showed my cleavage. This was what I wore after swim practice. Bullying Mike, chasing down Officer Fox, bonding with the chief of police, I hadn't given my clothes a thought. Now I did. I shifted to one side so Doug was in front of me.

"Do you like raw oysters?" he asked me over his shoulder.

"I've never tried one."

Seven of the ten men hailed me at once, offering to shuck

me one if I sat beside them. I suppressed the urge to take another step backward.

"You are too, too kind," Doug told the men. "Zoey and I have some business to take care of—"

Two wolf whistles.

"Frank, Barry, thanks for making Zoey feel comfortable and welcome," Doug said. "Zoey and I will have a tête-à-tête."

Two more men grumbled, "Teat-a-what?" as they found two folding chairs and dragged them behind the circle for us. They also left a bucket of oysters.

I sank with relief onto one of the chairs. "This property must be worth millions of dollars," I whispered as I reached up to steady Doug.

"Easily," he agreed, gripping me hard for balance. He sat down.

"Couldn't your dad get a loan on it to send you to college?"

"Oh, God! My dad doesn't *own* this." He dropped his crutches to one side, picked up a glove and a dagger the men had dropped, and pried an oyster open with a flick. "He freeloads. He got in good with an admiral while he was in the navy. He's squatting in this house until the admiral retires and builds on the property." Doug tossed the top shell aside. Now that my eyes had adjusted to the dark, I saw the driveway was paved with these shells.

"My dad operates the admiral's fishing boat," Doug went on, "and the admiral gets the profit from the charters. See, that's why my dad wants *me* to go into the navy, to find an admiral of my own to freeload off. That's how Foxes spell success." Expertly he slid the knife between shell and oyster with one smooth motion. He handed the bounty to me.

Several of the men in the circle turned around to watch me. I stared down at the glistening oyster, psyching myself up. I'd seen people do this a million times. My dad sucked down raw oysters by the bushel.

Doug's elbow was on his good knee, chin in his hand, watching me. "You don't have to."

I glared at him, then dumped the oyster down my throat and swallowed swallowed swallowed, trying to keep my tongue out of the way so I wouldn't taste it. It was my bottle of beer, fortifying me for what was coming. I was capable of all things when I was angry.

Several of the men clapped for me.

"Impressive," Doug said. "And you didn't even have the condiments that make oysters go down more easily. Crackers. Tabasco. Lemon. Civilization. Do me a favor."

I swallowed once more to make sure the oyster didn't come back up. "What," I croaked.

"Promise me you will never, ever come over here on Thursday night again. What are you doing here anyway?"

I nodded toward the bucket. "May I have another?"

He raised one eyebrow at me. "Uh-oh. What happened? Is it that bad?"

"I've just been to the police station," I told him. "I found out you were in my car."

Suddenly the men cheered, and Doug hadn't even handed me another oyster yet. A police car ground across the shells paving the causeway and parked behind the Benz. Officer Fox got out and ambled across the clearing. He waved and called to the men as they called to him, but he made a beeline for me and for Doug, who fixed Officer Fox with that laser-stare of his, even through the alcohol.

"Where's your phone?" Officer Fox snapped at Doug.

Doug eased forward, slipped his cell phone out of his back pocket, and handed it to Officer Fox.

Officer Fox peered at it. "It's off, dumbass. I've been trying to call you to warn you she was coming. Why'd you turn your phone off?" He pressed a button and handed the phone back to Doug.

"I didn't want Zoey to call me while I was drunk," Doug said self-righteously, "because *that* would be *embarrassing*." He pocketed the phone.

Officer Fox put his hands on his hips. "You're fucking wasted. You didn't take a Percocet before you drank beer, did you?"

"Come on, Cody, I never do anything foolish." He watched his brother angrily until Officer Fox sauntered over and joined the circle around the fire.

Then Doug plucked another oyster from the bucket and popped it open. "Yes, I went in the Benz."

I opened my mouth to tell him I meant the Bug and the

wreck, not the Benz. I closed my mouth, realizing I needed to know about him going in the Benz too. As always, there was even more going on with Doug than I'd imagined.

"Actually, my brother did it for me," Doug went on. "He used his official police door unlocker hook thing to bust in. Then he took out a fuse to keep the engine from starting. He swore to me it was safe and wouldn't do any permanent damage. He even laughed at me for thinking it might." Doug handed me the oyster.

I slurped it down whole and wiped the juice from my chin with my hand. I thought I'd fortified and collected myself before I spoke, but my words still came out as a splutter. "You—Doug—You broke into my *car*? You *sabotaged* my *car*?"

"Well, I wouldn't use either of those terms when a policeman did it for me. My brother's friend never towed it to his garage to fix it, because there was never anything wrong with it. My brother just put the fuse back. I think they really did drag race it on the way back to your house, but I told you that already." He sucked down an oyster himself.

"But, Doug, why did you mess with my car?" My outraged squeal echoed against the walls of the house, and men turned to stare at me again.

"To stop you from going parking with Brandon." Eyes narrow and vicious, Doug said quietly, "I knew you would."

"All this is news to me," I said. "What I meant was, I got the accident report from the police station. You were in the Bug when I wrecked."

He blinked.

He shucked me an oyster.

I sucked it down.

"Now," I said, "is there a place we can talk about this without being observed? This whole crew meeting is getting a little—"

"Pedophilic?" he suggested.

"Intense, yes."

With a nod he threw the glove and knife into the bucket, retrieved his crutches, and heaved himself upward very slowly. I walked with him toward the house, so close to him I thought I'd tripped him a few times. I kept him between me and the circle of men.

"Going to take care of business, Doug?" one of them called.

"Barry, shut the fuck up," said Officer Fox.

14

Doug's bedroom was the entire basement level of the house. At a glance I took in the walls of homemade bookshelves, boards stacked on cement blocks and filled with paperbacks, with more books piled on the floor. The walls that weren't lined with books were wallpapered with foreign movie posters. Japanese men and women locked in embrace, Japanese men taking on a ring of warriors and kicking ass.

Doug limped toward his bed against the far wall. "You want to find out where we were headed in the Bug at two thirty in the morning," he said. "You were just taking me home, in a roundabout way." He eased down on the bed and patted beside him as a seat for me.

"Oh, well then. That explains everything!" I said in his sarcastic tone. I sat on the bed and poked him in the chest, looking straight into his eyes. "Doug, you were *in my car at two thirty* AM after you called me a *spoiled brat* at the game. You told me you loved me, after I told you first. You *tell me what happened!*"

His green eyes were wide and surprised and serious. He

glanced toward the door, visualizing salty dogs listening in. He reached for the stereo beside his bed. Fell off his bed with a *thunk* and an *oof*.

"My Lord." I slipped off the bed to sit beside him. "Are you okay?"

He detangled himself from his crutches and sat up. "I've got it." He slid a CD off the teetering stack on the nearest shelf and popped it into the player. Hard rock blasted through the room from speakers in every corner. I felt the bass line in my gut.

He extended his cast in front of him and pulled his good knee up to his chest, then leaned his head toward mine so I could hear him over the music. "You know how Gabriel always says he's not going to get drunk, so he drives to a party, and then he gets drunk? I knew he would do that." He flattened one hand like a notepad and used the opposite finger like a pen to draw a diagram—not so much for me as for himself. "I left my Jeep at school" (tip of pointer finger) "and drove with Connor to the beach party" (heel of his hand). "When the party was over I could drive Gabriel's Honda to his house, drop him off" (thumb tip), "and then walk to school to get my Jeep" (tip of pointer finger). "At the party, you and I hooked up, so Ian and Connor got Gabriel and his Honda home. But you still had to drive me back to my Jeep at school when we were done."

"When we were done hooking up," I said, nodding as if this made perfect sense, as if my skin weren't tingling and the room weren't spinning. "Tell me how we hooked up."

He shrugged. "You wanted to leave the party and go parking with Brandon. I talked you out of it."

That was the end of my patience. I leaned forward, grabbed his good thigh with both my hands, and squeezed. "Douglas. Do me a favor and *do not shrug again* like this is all obvious or doesn't matter so much, because when you shrug it makes me *very angry.*"

I'm not sure whether it was his depthless eyes staring at me, or my hands around his thigh, or our heads so close together that I could make out every black hair in the stubble on his upper lip. But the air vibrated with the energy between us. We were still, yet everything moved. The FSU on his T-shirt quivered as he breathed. The tip of his tongue snaked out to lick his lips.

"I wanted to go parking with Brandon," I prompted him. "You talked me into going parking with you instead?"

He shook his head *no* ever so slightly, his eyes never leaving mine. "That just happened. As we were talking."

"But why did you talk me out of parking with Brandon?" I asked. "Brandon is my boyfriend."

The spell broke. Doug collapsed against the bed. "Brandon is your boyfriend, right. You keep saying 'Brandon is my boyfriend,'" he moved his fingers in quote marks, "and it makes as much sense as 'I am balancing the planet Pluto on my big toe' or 'Kumquats make the best nuclear physicists.'"

I knew he was growing more upset because his gestures grew bigger. The finger quotes had exclamation points attached.

Furious as I was at this boy, I smoothed my hands across his thigh, inching farther up. "Okay, okay. Just tell me what happened."

"What happened is, Brandon is cheating on you with Stephanie Wetzel." He clasped both my hands in his big hands, brought them up between us, and shook them. "I don't have to tell you this. You *know* in your heart that Brandon's been cheating on you for your entire tumultuous week-and-a-half love affair, but you pretend you don't see it. You had sex with him *once* but now you'll stay with him forever just so in your mind it will mean something. He'll get you pregnant—"

"I'm on the pill," I interrupted with my logic.

"I know," Doug said meaningfully. "But he'll get you pregnant anyway because shit happens to you, Zoey, and he'll keep right on cheating on you, and you'll keep right on telling everyone including yourself that he's the love of your life. You'll stay here in town and raise the baby while he's off at FSU partying. When he gets kicked out for his low GPA he'll come crawling back to you and marry you. Why not, if your wife doesn't mind you screwing Stephanie Wetzel?"

When he took a breath to go on, I interjected rationally, "You've made this up. You realize that, right?"

My pulse quickened and my blood went strangely cold as he looked straight at me again, green eyes focused on me and deadly serious. "I can see the future."

As quickly as he'd zeroed in on me, he was gone again, gesturing widely. "You'll have more kids with him. He'll get the job in town that doesn't require a college degree and pays the most with the least effort expended. Insurance salesman. Something large and blank, just like Brandon. And you'll get a job too. Eventually maybe you'll even leave him. But your chance to do something bright and beautiful, like you—that will be long gone."

He stared at one of his speakers in the corner of his ceiling, as if a camera hung there like in my dad's house. And I stared at the underside of his chin dusted with black stubble, gathering my self-control around me like my comfy swim team sweatshirt so I didn't burst into tears in Doug Fox's bedroom with ten salty dogs outside. "It doesn't sound so bad when all you really want in life anymore is to get your mother home safe and avoid going insane yourself." I hadn't even realized this until I spoke the words out loud.

Doug didn't skip a beat, like he'd known this about me all along. His tirade continued. "And that's exactly why you need to break up with Brandon. You want to handle your problems yourself. You think you *are* handling them, but you're not. You're leaning on Brandon. He is a poor choice to lean on. You need a stable guy who won't screw you over. Or you need to go to the psychologist, like my brother said—"

"My dad won't let me."

"—or, Jesus, Zoey, talk to somebody at school or the YMCA, something. Every other girl in the universe has a best girlfriend they can talk to about this, but one normal girlfriend has more sense than Keke and Lila put together."

"So it's imperative to you that I find a stable person to lean on in this time of strife," I mused. "Yet the person you steer me toward through various sneaky and downright illegal means is *you*, who went to juvie!"

He pointed at me. "That was three years ago. And those records are *sealed*. No one is ever supposed to find out about that, except of course everyone who's ever known me."

I put my hand on his good knee to bring him back to me, to ground him. To make that connection with him I thought I'd missed when I put my hand on his forearm at the football game last Friday night. "How far did we go?"

He picked up my other hand. Held it loosely. Pressed it to his lips, watching me.

That didn't bode well.

"How far?" My voice broke. "Doug, what did we do? Did we go to third?"

He moved my hand away from his mouth long enough to ask, "What's third?" and then put it to his mouth again.

I jerked my hand back. "Going down my pants. This *matters* to me, Doug. Does it *matter* to you?"

"Yes," he whispered.

Suddenly I understood *everything*. "Oh my God, we went all the way. It's like you slipped me a roofie!"

His eyes filled with tears, exactly as if I'd slapped him. "It is *not* like that," he yelled back, "and don't you dare accuse me ever again of pressuring you into doing something you didn't want to do. You wanted it. You *said* you wanted it. You *asked* for it.

Don't you *dare* accuse me of that." He panted a few times. "I don't belong in jail, Zoey. I've been there and I know I don't. This never would have occurred to you if you remembered Friday night. It never would have occurred to me either. Do you understand?" His hands shook on his knee.

I sat back and took in all of him, broken leg extended out, the rest of him curled into a ball, upset. He was telling the truth, *now*. "Then why didn't you tell me before?" I insisted.

"I didn't know you didn't know! You pretended to remember everything except the wreck."

"But you figured it out on Tuesday, when you found my earrings in the Bug," I said. "One of them must have caught on something Friday night, and you watched me take them out and put them in the ashtray for safekeeping."

"It caught on the zipper of my jeans."

I gaped at him, picturing what we'd done.

He sniffled and looked away. "I'm sorry. That was very crude of me."

"You found out forty-eight hours ago, Doug," I said quietly. "When were you going to tell me?"

He turned back to me, looking haggard and awful. "When I could think straight. When I got off Percocet."

I shook my head. "Poor excuse. Try again."

He swallowed. "Considering how you pushed me away when you thought we'd only felt each other up in the emergency room, I wasn't optimistic about how you'd act if I told you we did it in your Bug at the beach."

I couldn't raise one eyebrow like he did, but I approximated that facial expression as well as I could. The meaning was *Bullshit*.

He winced like I'd punched him in the stomach. "Oh, God, Zoey. I was scared of what you might do, okay? You said losing your memory was like what happened to your mom. I wasn't sure what you meant by that." He stared down at his cast.

I watched him for a few moments, this half-Asian intellectual raised by a pirate. I looked around the room at the posters championing sex and violence in another world. My gaze came to rest on the books on his bedside table, both by E. M. Forster. Right now we were reading *A Passage to India* for English, but Doug was reading two that Ms. Northam hadn't assigned: *Howards End* and *A Room with a View*.

"I want a way out of this," I sighed, "but there's no way out. You lied to me."

He glared at me over his raised knee. "And you've told me some choice ones too. Such as, 'I remember what happened Friday night.' And, 'No, I have not passed out on the floor of the bathroom at the pool.'"

"You went way beyond that, Doug. When you found out I didn't remember, you told Mike and your brother. You asked them not to tell me anything!"

"You'd already made me ask them not to tell anyone that you and I had been together, so Brandon wouldn't find out," Doug said. "You don't mind lies. You just want to be the one to control them."

He had me there.

"And you told me the biggest lie of all. You told me you loved me."

It was my turn to wince like he'd slapped me. "I don't remember saying that."

"You would if it had been true. You would feel something."

"I *do* feel something," I protested.

"You just don't care."

"I *do* care," I insisted. "Doug, you don't understand how badly I *want* to care about you. But for the past few days, you've controlled every move I've made."

"Of course I haven't," he said. "I know how you are. That's the worst thing anyone could do to you."

I watched him, waiting for him to understand the depth of what he'd done to me. Doug was one of the smartest people I knew. Even through the alcohol, he would get it. It took about ten seconds, and then his lips parted. Now he would say something remorseful, but I wouldn't be able to accept his apology. Ever.

He said, "I love you."

I stood. "Guys only say that when they want to get laid."

"Zoey!" he shouted after me, but I was already out the door.

I galloped up the stairs, out of the house, and crossed the shadowy yard to my car. Officer Fox's police car was gone. I worried briefly. But the men cackled around the fire with nary a wolf whistle in my direction as I skipped to my dad's Benz and settled into the cold leather.

I executed a very careful three-point turn that would not draw the derision of the salty dogs, and cruised up the driveway crackling with shells. Just before the live oaks closed in around the house behind me, I glanced in the rearview mirror, half expecting to see Doug crutching after me through the dark. But he didn't appear.

Doug had finally taken no for an answer.

15

Leaving his house, I felt seventeen times as lost as I'd felt Tuesday night when I dropped him off at the wharf. I couldn't go home. I couldn't go to the mall in Destin because it would be closing by the time I arrived. And I needed to make the most of the Benz while I had it. My dad would come home to reclaim it the day after tomorrow and I'd be without wheels until further notice. Grounded, as surely as if I'd looked for invisible tape in his office.

I switched on the GPS and typed in *Seattle*.

The drive was long and dark and lonely and blank with no exit for miles on Interstate 10 toward Mobile. My body was dead tired but my brain was alert, energized by anger at everything Doug had said.

Was he a liar?

Thinking back, I couldn't put my finger on an actual lie he'd told me. Well, he'd fudged when he explained where he and Mike were going when we wrecked, but even then he'd constructed a lie as close to the truth as he could manage on the fly. He wasn't so much a liar as a withholder of pertinent information. For a talkative boy he could really keep his own counsel.

Except about Brandon, of course. Did I really know in my heart that Brandon was cheating on me with Stephanie Wetzel?

There certainly was evidence he was growing closer to Stephanie and pulling away from me. But when I asked my heart what it thought, my heart didn't respond. It didn't even speed up at the thought of him cheating on me. It raced when my mind wandered through the future, wondering who Doug would end up with if my fate with Brandon was sealed, as Doug had said. I couldn't *stand* the thought of Doug tossing back his head and laughing with another girl.

Had Doug and I used a condom?

Surely we had. As he'd told Officer Fox, he never did anything foolish. Of course, he'd said this facetiously. Fuck.

And this released a flood of questions about the details of what we'd done. Who made the first move? How did we end up going so far so fast? How exactly did my earring catch on his *zipper*, hello? Did I enjoy it? Did he? I could guess the answers to the last two questions by the way we'd acted when we wrecked. We'd definitely enjoyed it. But the rest . . . I had lost my memory. He would keep his forever. It wasn't fair.

Somewhere between Mobile and Hattiesburg, on a pitch-black stretch of highway, I realized the oysters had settled in my stomach and pumped salt and aphrodisiac into my veins until my mouth was on fire. I was rubbing my lips with my fingertips, driving in the wrong direction. And now I was two and a half hours from Doug.

IN THE DEAD OF NIGHT I eased the Benz back down Doug's drive, stopped it in the middle of the causeway, and killed the headlights. I'd feared the salty dogs would still be up and I'd be caught with no safe way out. But the pack had dispersed for the night.

I pressed the button for Doug's cell and listened to it ring. What if he didn't pick up? I would go crazy wondering whether he'd turned off his phone again or he was watching the screen, refusing to talk to me. Either way, if I didn't see him tonight, I would spontaneously combust, I knew it. I felt heavy from the pressure, desperate to get out from under it. At the same time, electricity zinged through me. My every thought zeroed in on the basement windows of the house, his room. I needed release from this. I couldn't go on this way.

"Zoey. Where are you?" Through the phone, his calm voice had that edge I remembered from the wreck. He thought I was in trouble.

It hadn't occurred to me that I would scare him when I called. For the first time I began to doubt this plan. The pressure and the electricity drove me forward. "I'm in your driveway."

"Give me two minutes." The phone clicked dead.

The basement windows glowed with light. Then went dark.

On the side of the house, a basement door that I hadn't seen before opened very slowly. He crutched out and pushed the door closed just as slowly behind him, without a *thunk* his dad would hear. He made his way toward me along the edge of the clearing, under the ancient trees. Then he stepped onto the causeway. Behind him in the distance, the ocean was black with whitecaps rolling slowly toward us. The sky was black, brightening to blue around the full white moon.

On the narrow strip of land, he rounded the car to reach the passenger side. He wore his swim team sweatshirt and gym shorts with the heathered gray waistband of his boxer briefs peeking out. Good. Easy off. He also wore glasses. I hadn't known he wore glasses at all. This was probably the secret behind the green eyes I'd fallen for: colored contacts. What a relief to know his beautiful eyes were fake.

He tried the door of the Benz. Locked. He pounded once on the door in frustration.

I unlocked it with the button on my door, then leaned over to open it for him. It wouldn't do for him to lose his balance and tumble off the causeway, into the surf.

The breeze and the roar of the ocean came in first. Then his crutches, narrowly missing my head. He tossed them over the headrests into the backseat. He smelled like toothpaste, exactly what I must have smelled like when he woke me up last Saturday morning and I thought he was Brandon.

He closed the door behind him and turned to me. Behind

his glasses, in the moonlight, I could see his eyes were the same green-blue as ever. They really were the color of the sea. "You rang?" he asked, dry and sober.

"Did we use a condom?"

"Is that all?" he asked, disgusted. He put his hand on the door to open it.

"It's important, Doug."

He sighed impatiently. "Of *course* it's important, which is why you had a freaking crate of condoms in the trunk of the Bug. Of *course* we used a condom. If that's all, I'll get back to my nightmares." He put his hand on the door again.

"That's not all," I said quickly. "I don't think my memory of that night is ever coming back."

"Do you want me to hit you on the head with a coconut? It works on *Gilligan's Island.*"

"I want you to reconstruct the night for me."

He looked at me over the rims of his glasses. That must be the origin of his hottest expression, chin down, lashes long. "You want to have sex again?"

"Yes."

"No." He turned, and this time he opened the door.

"Why not, if we did it before?" I called over the noise of the surf.

"Because you've been all Brandon, all week. You can't snap your fingers"—he held his hand out toward me and snapped—"and expect me to perform for you."

"You owe me," I said. "You've lied to me and manipulated me. This one time, you do what I tell you."

He paused for five seconds more with his hand on the open door. Then he slammed the door shut and leaned back against it, watching me. "Well?"

"Well, what?"

"Well, I didn't have sex by myself."

So *I* made the first move? I tried to visualize myself reaching out to him, like Coach told us to visualize ourselves winning swim heats. But Doug looked so distant, staring me down from across the car with his eyes sexy and his arms folded.

"Maybe you could set the stage," I suggested. "Was the moon bright like this?"

He shook his head. "It was raining hard. I got a little worried."

"Then why didn't we leave?"

"There wasn't a tornado watch. There probably should have been, but there wasn't. I thought it was safe. I was wrong." He sighed, and his voice softened. "Anyway, I wasn't exactly thinking straight. I was so full of you."

I slid across the seat toward him. He watched me. I stretched up to kiss his neck, just where the collar of his sweatshirt ended. I kissed my way up under his hair, toward parts of his neck I only saw when his hair was tucked under a swim cap in the pool. Then his chin where his stubble started. I felt him shudder, but he didn't touch me, and when I pulled away he was still staring at me, almost angrily.

"You did it before," I protested. "What's the difference?"

"It meant something before. Now it's all scientific. You're recovering data."

"You owe me." I slid my hand onto the front of his shorts.

His eyes widened. And in one motion he took off his glasses, tossed them onto the dash, and put his hands behind my head, drawing me closer. His mouth hit my mouth and opened me. His tongue swept inside me.

Doug was a great kisser. I knew this right away. And I wasn't surprised, because he *looked* like a great kisser. The girls on the swim team had talked about this before. We didn't want to mess with juvie, but we knew sooner or later whomever Doug finally hooked up with was going to get a mouthful.

Instead, I was the one who got his mouth. His lips were soft. His tongue was firm. His teeth were sneaky, nipping at me when I didn't expect it. We kissed for long minutes as our bodies slowly intertwined. My hand slipped between his shorts and the heathered boxer briefs. His hand shoved past my shorts and panties, onto my bare skin. Finally I was out of breath. I pulled a few inches away from him and gasped.

He wouldn't let me get away. He put his forehead to my forehead and chuckled. "That's exactly what you did before."

I rubbed the tip of my nose back and forth across his. "How did my earring get caught on your zipper?"

"Hm." He laughed. "I just said that to make you mad. We

didn't do anything like that. We wanted to save something for later. Your earring came out when I put my hands in your hair. Like this." He wove the fingers of both hands into my hair and held me firmly as he kissed me.

A long time later, his mouth had done everything it could possibly do to my mouth, twice. My hands were growing restless. I whispered against his lips, "Is this when we moved into the backseat?"

He breathed rapidly through his nose and blinked at me. He seemed to have a hard time focusing on me, but maybe that was because he was missing his glasses. "Yes, but—"

"But what?" I slid over the console into the backseat and opened the back door for him, holding out my hands to steady him as he leaned on the Benz and hopped from the front door to the back. As I pulled him inside I said, "This has got to be a lot more comfy than the backseat of the Bug."

"More roomy," he acknowledged as he closed the door. "But I didn't have a broken leg before. Equally awkward."

I pressed him backward until he lay on the seat and I lay on top of him. Not too different from the way we'd lain together in the back of the swim team van and the back of the police car, except this time I was in control. I kissed his mouth, his neck, and felt a new rush every time he moaned.

I tugged at his sweatshirt until he relented and helped me take it off him. I smoothed my hands across his lean chest and strong arms. I kissed from his neck down his sternum to the inny belly button I'd found so fascinating in the van. His belly button was mine for tonight. I dipped my tongue into it, licked the circumference and let my tongue trail down, just to get revenge for that joke about my earring getting caught in his zipper.

As my mouth reached the waistband of his shorts, he gasped, "Okay."

"Okay." I laughed, straightening so I could pull off my shirt. "Is this when you took off my bra?"

He squinted at me through the black hair in his eyes. "Yes, but—"

"Is this the same bra?"

He propped himself up on his elbows. "No, it was blue with white polka dots, and it had a blue bow right *there*." He poked me between the boobs. "So you still don't believe we did this?"

"I believe you." I'd had some lingering doubts, but I believed him now that he'd correctly identified the bra. "I still don't understand how I ended up in the car with you when I'd wanted to go parking with Brandon. But I understand completely how, once I was here, things snowballed and we went all the way. I've lived all my life in Florida and I have no experience with snow."

"Me neither." He lay back on the seat again, then reached up with both hands and framed my bra with his fingers. "Zoey, if we do this, what does it mean?"

"We *will* do this, and it means you owe me this memory."

He dropped his hands. "If it doesn't mean more than that, I don't want to do it."

I leaned forward until I was on all fours, face-to-face with him, hovering over him. "You *will* do it."

His eyes narrowed. I'd pushed him too far, telling him what to do. He shifted, feeling on the floor for his sweatshirt.

"Did I do this?" I asked quickly as I smoothed my hand inside his boxer briefs.

He said, "Mmmmmmmm," and then reached up with both hands again and pressed my head down until our lips met. We kissed so deeply that I hardly noticed when he unhooked my bra after all and unlooped it from my shoulders.

Eventually he slid lower on the seat and took my breast into his mouth. Every move my hand made on him, his mouth echoed on me, until I was buzzing with tension and eager to offer him everything.

We stayed just this way for long minutes, poised on the edge. I wanted to do more. I was afraid if I stopped what we were doing, I would lose it all. But after his tongue on my breast made me cry out, my fingers found a condom packet tucked into the seat. I'd let the gargantuan box of condoms lie on the floor of the car with a few packets scattered around it since I threw it there Tuesday, for the viewing pleasure of anyone who peeked into the Benz. Even my mother could have seen this Wednesday night if she'd had her faculties.

I'd never opened a condom packet before in my life. I sat up on Doug's hips and held the packet up to the light to tear it.

"Zoey."

"What. Am I doing it wrong?"

Breathing hard, he reached up with one hand and took the packet from me. "It's almost two thirty. You have an appointment to narrowly miss a deer and crash into Mike."

Coaxing had worked before, so I coaxed him again. I lay down on him, my bare breasts to his warm bare chest, skin to skin, such a strange sensation. I brushed his stubbly cheek with the back of my hand and ran my thumb across his soft lips, echoing caresses he'd given me during the week, which he must have given me Friday night but I hadn't understood until now. I whispered, "You owe me."

"I don't owe you, Zoey," he said sadly. "I only agreed to do this because I thought there would be more after tonight. But this is really all you wanted. I can't do it. I can't make it worse than it already is. I know you need this one night, to reconstruct your memory, and I care about you. But I care about me too, and I can't do this anymore." He sat up, swung his leg and his cast around to the floor, and handed me my bra and my shirt without looking at me.

I wanted to say something to keep him there with me, even if we didn't make love. More caressing, talking, anything. I *knew* I shouldn't have stopped. But he was right. His lies had ruined whatever there had been between us. I didn't want anything from him beyond tonight. And as badly as I wanted this one night, I wasn't willing to lie to him to get it. I, for one, was through with lying.

He ducked into his sweatshirt, picked up his crutches, and

paused with his hand on the door. "You have my cell phone number. I'll keep the same one when I go to college." He rolled his eyes. "*If* I go to college. I'll keep it wherever I go." He looked straight at me. "If you ever feel like doing what your mom did, call me."

I shuddered. "I won't."

"Please." It was the first time I'd ever heard Doug say this word. To anyone.

I shook my head. "I mean, I won't feel like that."

"If you do, call me. Promise."

I tried to picture feeling that way, and wondered whether I could really bring myself to call Doug if I did. But I couldn't imagine that feeling. Which was a good sign. I said, "I promise."

He put his hand on my knee and stroked there with his thumb. "I understand I can't have you. But I want to know you're in the world with me." Leaning forward on his crutches, he kissed me on the cheek. I got one last whiff of chlorine and the ocean. He made a slow, awkward exit from the car, during which he dropped his crutches twice and nearly fell off the causeway. I had plenty of time to call him back and stop him before he limped back to his house.

And then he was gone.

For the first time in my life, I was late for school. I dragged myself into the main office on four hours' of sleep with no parental excuse. I hoped the assistant principal didn't turn me in to Child Protective Services.

But by the time I interrupted Ms. Northam's lecture and stumbled down the aisle between the rows of desks in English, I'd forgotten all about that, and I didn't even notice whether everybody was staring at me. I focused on Doug. He might or might not be hungover. He'd had a long time to recover from his early night of drinking. But I knew he'd missed a pain pill.

Sure enough, his head was down, his face pressed into the open leaves of a battered hardback copy of *A Passage to India* on his desk (the rest of us had the school's pristine paperbacks). I'd intended to hand him his glasses, which he'd left on my dashboard last night, and use that as an excuse to talk to him and make sure he was okay.

But Keke had taken my seat behind him. Usually she sat across the room with Lila. It must be too hot for her over there today, with Lila so angry at her.

I dropped his glasses beside the book on his desk, then slipped into the desk across the aisle, behind Connor. Now I could see that Keke's hand was on Doug's back.

I resented how Keke had treated me yesterday, but jealousy and fear overrode that. I leaned across the aisle and whispered to her, "Is he okay?"

"Doug?" Ms. Northam prompted. She'd asked a question I hadn't heard. And she wasn't very good at identifying who caused disturbances at the back of the room.

Keke whispered to him, "Flat characters," as if she were the friend assigned to protect him and keep him out of trouble today. Which suddenly made me very, very angry.

"Round characters in *Aspects of the Novel*." He said it loudly enough for Ms. Northam to hear, but he said it to his desk without lifting his head from the book.

"That's correct," Ms. Northam said. She stepped to one side until she could see Doug. "Is your leg bothering you?"

"Yes ma'am," he told his desk. "My pill will kick in any second now."

"Well, go lie down in the nurse's office while you're waiting," Ms. Northam said.

Without being asked, Keke slipped his glasses and his books into his backpack and handed it to him. He picked up his crutches and slowly stood to his full height, towering over the class.

I whispered up at him, "Do you want me to go with you?"

He turned and gave me the most evil look with watery eyes. Keke turned from him to me and back to him.

"Aw, have woo been cwying?" Connor asked him. "Do woo need a tissue?"

Doug took a sudden step toward Connor. Connor fell backward out of his desk. An uneasy titter rose from the boys in the room.

Doug turned and limped up the aisle and out the door. Immediately there was a metallic crash like he'd fallen against the lockers. Keke half rose. Ms. Northam nodded at her. Before I could do anything to stop Keke or explain that *I* was the one who was supposed to help Doug, Keke disappeared after him.

He didn't need me.

16

Amid jabs of, "Skeered?" from other boys, Connor picked himself up off the floor and sat in his desk. I waited until Ms. Northam's lecture had absorbed the attention of the room again before I whispered over his shoulder, "Remember in tenth grade when Doug got suspended for starting a fight with Aaron Spears, I think, outside history class?"

Connor in front of me and Nate beside me both nodded.

"What set Doug off?"

"Aaron made a kung fu joke," Connor said. "Wait, that's not even Japanese. A karate joke."

Nate shook his head. "That was a completely different fight, last year with Jimmy Gillespie in back of Jamaica Joe's. When Doug got suspended, Aaron did his eyes like this." Nate placed his fingers at the corners of his eyes and slanted them up.

"That's right," Connor said. "On a positive note, if you ever want to get Doug suspended from school, just make a joke about Asians and stand there until he hits you."

"I feel heady with power," Nate said. He and Connor both said, "Bwa-ha-ha!" and rubbed their hands together like evildoers.

"Zoey!" Ms. Northam called with her hands on her hips. "Please move across the room where you won't disturb your classmates. I do hope we're not making this a daily occurrence."

No, the daily occurrence was thinking about anything in English except English. After flopping my book closed and schlepping across the room to the back corner desk, I renewed my effort to be a good girl and pay attention to the lecture. I truly did. All the same, my eyes kept drifting from Ms. Northam to the door, impatient for Keke to reappear.

She didn't come back to class until halfway through history. As she tiptoed to her desk across the room from me, she mouthed in my direction, *I have to talk to you.* I actually looked behind me to see who she was talking to, but I was sitting in a desk against the wall.

Well, that totally blew my concentration on the Boston Tea Party. She'd just spent the last half hour with Doug. Whatever she had to say must be about Doug, and about me. And whatever it was, good or bad, I was dying to hear it. I glanced at my watch five hundred times before the bell finally rang for break.

Lugging our backpacks, we walked toward calculus with our heads together conspiratorially. Which was very strange, because usually I walked fast to calculus to make sure I got across campus in time, and Keke ran toward calculus to get some energy out, checking the status of practical jokes she'd slipped into lockers along the way.

"I talked to Doug for a long time," she said.

I nodded, fighting down the butterflies in my stomach and

suppressing the urge to shake her to get the information out faster.

"I told him about that big fight we had yesterday. He got *really* mad at me. With that on top of his leg hurting, I swear I thought he was going to blow a gasket."

I laughed. "He doesn't know anything about cars," I said nonsensically.

"He said you always listen to me and put up with me," Keke said, "and the one time you really needed me, I turned on you. He made me feel like shit. So, I'm sorry." She stopped and held out her arms.

I stared at her for three full seconds before I realized she wanted to hug me. Then I stepped into her embrace. "It's okay."

"I just thought we were really good friends," she said in my ear. She pulled back to look at me. "I couldn't believe I had no idea something that big happened to you. People kept coming up to me asking how I could possibly not have known about your mother, like there was something *wrong* with me. It was embarrassing. But you went out of your way to hide it from me." She looked straight into my eyes, which she didn't do often either, waiting for an answer.

Slowly I said, "I've been kind of screwed up. Keke, I'm really sorry." I felt the butterflies rising with the tears as I said this. By the time I coughed out *sorry*, I was crying there in the hall with sophomores streaming around us, in and out of the driver's ed room. Keke's arms tightened around me, which made me cry harder. "See," I sobbed, "this is why I don't tell people."

"It's okay," Keke said, rubbing my back. And strangely, it was. Just as I'd seen myself retching over the public toilet in the swimming pool bathroom, I could see myself crying in the hall. I could hear what the sophomores would whisper to their friends later: "Zoey Commander lost it outside driver's ed. You know, that senior whose mom tried to kill herself and went ape shit at the last swim meet." But that was okay, because I was also that senior with friends. At least I had Keke.

Calculus was still a long distance away. We jogged through the halls as I wiped at my eyes with the backs of my hands, and I started to tell her everything that had happened with my mom. I told her more in snippets as we walked from calculus to biology, and at lunch we settled across from each other at the swimmers' table. I'd wanted to snag the end of the table away from the others so we could have a little privacy, but someone else had beaten us to it. Leaning across the table toward each other with their heads close together were Doug, looking like himself again (hot), and Lila.

Keke's eyes slid over to them, then back to me. She spoke softly (Keke was full of surprises today) so the junior girls sitting around us couldn't hear. "When *I* talked to Doug this morning, he also told me y'all had a huge fight last night. Your goal for the night was having a fight with everybody on the swim team?"

I cringed. "The one with Doug was special." I took a bite of salad.

"That's what he said. Are you going to try to get him back?"

I glanced over at him and swallowed. "Doug is hot."

Grinning, she nodded at me.

I said, "Doug is also manipulative and controlling."

She frowned. "He asked me to watch out for you today. I guess you could say that's manipulative and controlling. But you could also say he was worried about you and he cared about you. Any girl would kill to have a boy like that." I could hear the wistfulness in her voice. She and Lila must still be arguing about Lila going out with Mike. "A week ago, if you'd told me you were going to hook up with this criminal—"

"He's not." I sighed.

"—I would have laughed."

"You *did* laugh!"

"But after hearing the way he talks about you . . ." She shook her head. "Wow."

"I need to break up with Brandon first." I felt a flash of guilt that this was the first thought I'd had of Brandon all day. Automatically I pulled my cell phone from my backpack and turned it on to check for a text from him—or better yet, a message from my mother. Nothing from her, and no text from Brandon. I hadn't heard from him in two days, since I saw him Wednesday night at the meet.

Keke shifted closer across the table and talked even more quietly. "Funny you should say that. You know the swim team's having a party after the football game tonight. At least, we're supposed to be. I'm holding up *my* end. If Lila doesn't bring the hot dogs, that's not my problem. Anyway, Stephanie swears she's bringing Brandon as her date."

I sat up straight in surprise, then leaned over my salad again. "Does Brandon *know* he's Stephanie's date?"

"As his girlfriend," Keke said, "you should definitely ask him."

AT THE BEGINNING OF PRACTICE, I was standing in front of my locker and I'd just pulled off my shirt to change into my swimsuit when the door to the pool squeaked open a crack. "Ladies," Doug called.

Six girls screamed at once. I didn't. I only felt a little warm.

"The boy band has left the building," he called when the squeals died down. "Coach said don't change today because we're putting the dome on the pool. Zoey."

Six girls jerked their heads toward me.

I felt my face flush. As casually as I could manage, I called back, "Doug."

"Coach has lost the dome instructions again." The door to the pool squeaked shut.

I found the instructions in Coach's office where I'd filed them last year under *D* for *dome* and *duh*. When I took them outside, I saw Doug had used the word *we* loosely when he'd said, "*We're* putting the dome on the pool." He sat on the pool deck with his cast extended and his back against the door to the bathroom, guarding it against girls going in there to faint. He read *Howards End* as the rest of us unfolded the enormous plastic tent across the water, hooking it around the edges of the pool deck and tossing heavy cables across it. The rest of the boys and Coach argued about the best way to install the plastic corridor between the dome and the locker rooms. Doug stayed put, nose in his book. They installed it around him.

We'd been a little worried about the blower toward the end of last season. We came to school one day to find the dome sagging, half deflated. So I crouched inside the corner of the dome opposite Doug, making sure the loud engine worked. The dome hadn't filled completely yet and the ceiling was waist high, so I wasn't sure who was fighting her way through the plastic until Lila dropped beside me.

"I talked to Doug for a long time at lunch," she said.

"I noticed," I said, trying not to sound as jealous as I felt.

"I tried to convince him not to kill Mike so Mike will speak to me again. But Keke told Doug about that big fight we all had at the pool yesterday. He got really mad at me! You should have heard what he called Mike for throwing your clipboard in the pool!"

"Good!" I laughed. "Doug knows I was very attached to that clipboard."

"Mike fished it out with the net after you left, if you still want it."

"That's okay," I sighed. "I've moved on."

"Then Doug said you always listen to me and put up with

me, and the one time you really needed me, I wasn't there for you. He made me feel like shit. So, Zoey, I'm sorry." She scooted forward across the pool deck and hugged me.

"It's okay." As I hugged her back, I listened for titters above the drone of the blower. It must be a cruel joke, two twins apologizing to me, using almost the same words, after they found out my mother was insane. Kicking me when I was down. But the rest of the swim team paid us no attention. They held the plastic corridor in place above their heads. Below them on the floor, Doug read on. I pulled back and looked Lila in the eye. "Have you and Keke calibrated your watches today?"

"No, we're not speaking. Dad says we have to make up with each other by tomorrow morning or we're changing our brother's diapers for a month. Why?"

"Just wondering." Obviously I was doomed to live through everything twice, even now that I remembered both times.

She took my hand and squeezed it. "I thought you and I were really good friends. I couldn't believe something that big happened to you and I had no idea! People kept asking me how I could possibly not have known about your mom, like there was something *wrong* with me! I was so *embarrassed*! But you hid it from me on purpose."

Feeling the tingles of déjà vu, I waited for my tears to come.

Lila's eyes widened. She said, "Oh," and squeezed my hand again as she saw what was coming too.

"I've been kind of screwed up," I sobbed. "Lila, I'm really sorry."

She leaned forward to hug me again and murmured, "It's okay, it's okay," as I cried into her shoulder. After a while, when I could talk again, I told her about my mom. As I finished, she said with tears in her eyes, "I wish you'd told me."

"I wish I had too."

Screams pierced through the noise of the blower and echoed around the dome. We looked across the pool at the roof of the plastic corridor collapsing on the swim team. I decided I would give them five more minutes trying to figure it out for themselves, and then I would go do it for them.

And then I saw Doug watching me. He looked down at his book.

Lila saw it too. "Doug told me something else at lunch," she said. "That y'all had a huge fight last night. And then"—her eyebrows arched knowingly—"you did some other stuff. Some really *good* stuff. And then you argued some more."

I cringed. "That about sums it up."

"Well?" she demanded. "Are you going to try to get him back?"

I glanced over at him. Amid the commotion going on around him and over his head, he simply kept reading, then turned the page. "Doug is hot," I sighed. "He's also manipulative and controlling."

"You're nuts," Lila said. When I gaped at her, she went on, "No offense and all, but Doug is worried about you and he cares about you. He saved you from an exploding car!"

"It wasn't exploding. Doug just doesn't know anything about cars."

"Neither do I. It's perfect and dreamy!"

"Lila, that's exactly what you said about *Brandon* less than a week ago!"

"Oh!" She pointed at me. "I almost forgot. You're coming to the swim team party after the football game tonight, right? Stephanie Wetzel says she's bringing Brandon as her *date*! What is up with *that*?"

"I guess I need to come to the party and find out." And then, when I'd gotten that settled, I could have another talk with Doug.

A talk . . . or something else. I was touching my lips again, imagining what he would do to me, and how soon we'd do what we'd saved for later.

"Are you coming to the game?" Lila asked me.

I stretched and yawned. "No. I didn't get much sleep last night."

She winked at me.

"Yeah," I said. "And I need a little quality time to recenter before the party."

RECENTERING INVOLVED THE FOLLOWING STEPS: I took a four-hour nap. I repainted my fingernails. I chose my beach party clothes carefully, including my lucky blue bra with white polka dots and blue bow. I removed the large box of condoms from my dad's Mercedes. And I played sudoku to calm myself while planning what to say to Brandon.

He was so sweet and so clueless. I doubted he understood he was Stephanie's date to the party. Someone who didn't know him might look at the situation objectively, the fact that he hadn't tried to see me since the incident with my mom, and might judge that he just wasn't that into me. But Brandon and I were friends. We had this history. I was afraid he'd be very upset when I told him I wanted to break it off with him. My stomach twisted in knots at the thought, and I practiced my speech over and over.

When I drove the Benz to the beach, the parking lot was packed with junkers I recognized from school. I had to drive quite a way inland to grab an empty spot, and I found myself wondering whether this was exactly the way it had happened last Friday night. Another hurricane churned in the Gulf, and though it wouldn't hit us and we weren't expecting rain until tomorrow, wind tossed the black silhouettes of palms against the night sky. Along the wooden walkway across the dunes, it whipped the red warning flags straight out. It almost drowned the wail of a boy band on a radio at the beach.

Even in the moonlight, it was hard to pick faces out of the dozens laughing together in circles. But one of the first people I recognized was Brandon standing with a group of hulking football players, sipping from a plastic cup with his arm around Stephanie Wetzel's waist.

Keke stood in a group a few feet behind him. She saw me on the walkway and nodded frantically toward Brandon with Stephanie.

Lila was in the other direction, facing Mike and holding both his hands. When she saw me, she gestured to Brandon with exactly the same motion as Keke. I wished they would make up with each other so I could stop having every conversation with them twice.

Already in knots, my stomach pulled taut as I crossed the sand. I slipped between football players and touched Brandon's elbow on the side opposite Stephanie. "Hey, can we talk?"

"Zoey!" Brandon called, smiling, as if there were nothing wrong at all.

Stephanie looked over at me in outrage, then up at Brandon. She snatched his arm off her and flounced up the beach. The football players said, "Woooooo."

She definitely thought Brandon was her date.

"Sure, Zoey," Brandon said, talking to me but watching Stephanie go.

Even so, I didn't think he understood what was about to happen. We walked back to the stairs across the dunes and sat down. He lit a cigarette and cupped it in both hands to keep the rising wind from blowing the fire out.

"I wanted to—" we both started at once, then laughed.

"You first, baby," I said.

"Okay." He took a long drink of beer. "You know how you told me Saturday you didn't mind I was doing Stephanie?"

Still scanning the beach, I finally found who I'd been searching for all along. Doug was using the tip of one crutch to draw a picture in the sand for Stephanie and the junior swim team girls. As I watched him, I realized I'd misheard Brandon. I could have sworn Brandon had just told me he'd had sex with Stephanie Wetzel. "I'm sorry. What?"

"You know how you and Doug saw me and Stephanie doing it in the Buick last Friday night, and you were all upset? And then you came over to my house Saturday morning and told me you weren't mad and it was okay. Right?"

"Right!" I said, because if I'd said *What the hell are you talking about?*, he might not have told me the end of this story. *You know how . . . ?* always ended with a *well . . .*

"Well," he said, "Stephanie minds that I'm doing *you*."

She certainly did. I could tell from her steely glare, even in the darkness.

"Or, you know, that I did you the one time," he qualified. "That's why I told you the Buick needed work, so I could ride to school with Stephanie, and so I couldn't come to your house for the past week. I felt really bad about lying to you, Zoey. I tried to tell you at the swim meet Wednesday night. That's what I came to the swim meet for. But Doug was being a dick about it."

I nodded. "He didn't want you to break up with me right after my mom escaped from the insane asylum? He *is* a dick."

Brandon turned to stare at me like he was seeing me for the

first time. He was having a realization, a breakthrough! Good for him. I asked innocently, "What?"

"I never heard you cuss before," he said. "Anyway, you and I talked all summer about my girlfriends. You knew how I was, and you were cool about me doing Stephanie. Stephanie had a *cow* when I mentioned you. And I think I might be in love with her. That's never happened to me before. I really hoped you would understand."

"I do," I said brightly. "I'm in love with Doug."

Brandon took another sip. "Doug who?"

"Doug *Fox*!" I hadn't thought there was another Doug in our school.

"You *are?*"

I began to get a little annoyed that Brandon and I were not having the same conversation. "Yes. We've been together all week. We have some things to work out—"

Brandon talked right over me. "Doug told me you weren't together!"

I sighed in exasperation. "Why is Doug telling you *anything* about him and me?"

Brandon took a long drag of his cigarette, shielding it with his other hand so it wouldn't go out. "At the party last Friday, I was talking to some guys, I'd had a few beers, and I was kind of bragging about doing you. No offense, but that's just how guys talk. Nobody thought you'd give it up until you were through law school, so they were real impressed. Well, a few minutes later Doug Fox corners me and says it had nothing to do with me, so I shouldn't be bragging. *Anybody* could have gotten in your pants. He said you hated his guts and he'd *still* get in your pants in the space of two hours. All I had to do was let you catch me doing another girl. That's why I was with Stephanie in the first place."

I nodded. "And you said, 'Okay, Doug, see if you can have sex with my girlfriend. I'll go have sex with this other girl. That's fine.'"

"Well." He exhaled smoke. "I didn't think you and I were together. I mean, I know we were *together*, but we weren't really *together* together. We were just friends with bennies. And Doug Fox was up in my face, challenging me. What else could I do?"

I nodded again. It all made sense in the world of Brandon, a sunshiny plastic world very familiar to me because I had observed it all summer.

"The next morning when you weren't mad anymore about Stephanie and me, I thought, cool." He smiled a dreamy smile, then remembered he was in the midst of ruining my life. "But Doug had called me earlier Saturday morning and said y'all didn't get together after all, so I shouldn't say anything to anybody about it."

"You're telling me about it now," I pointed out, still not quite believing. Or believing, because it made so much sense, but wishing it weren't true.

"I would have warned you about him before, but you were both in that wreck. I figured he wouldn't be making any moves on you with a broken leg. But if he has . . . Zoey, you need to stay away from him. I've seen defensive backs with less of a temper than that guy. You know he's been to juvie."

"Doug Fox has no idea what a temper is." Out the corner of my eye, I saw Brandon's hand come up to catch me, but I was too fast. I leaped up from the stairs, stormed across the beach, and pushed past Stephanie Wetzel, dragging my feet across Doug's picture in the sand. "Two hours?" I screamed up at him. "You only needed two hours?"

He gaped at me for half a second, then looked over my head toward Brandon. "Motherfucker!" He crutched over to Brandon on the stairs.

I could have tried to stop Doug, but I just stepped out of his way.

"You *told* her?" Doug shouted at Brandon. "Man, you are stupider than I thought. Come on." He poked Brandon in the chest with the sandy tip of his crutch.

Some boys from the swim team crowded around. Every one of them had a hand on Doug, pulling a fistful of his T-shirt. But I just stood there watching it happen. Almost enjoying it.

"Scared?" Doug asked Brandon.

Brandon launched himself off the stairs at Doug. The swim team leaped out of the way. Brandon and Doug landed together on the beach. Doug's crutches went flying, and a cloud of sand billowed up. The rest of the swim team and the football team came running, crowding around. They pulled Brandon off Doug and handed Doug his crutches.

"Brandon, you ass," Ian said, "he's got a cast on."

"And he's on Percocet!" Gabriel said.

"That just makes it hurt less," Doug said, struggling to stand. Propping himself up on his crutches, he pointed at Brandon. "And I'm not waiting three weeks until I get this cast off to kick your ass. Come in the ocean with me where I can stand up."

The crowd parted for him. He limped into the ocean, nearly falling again when the tip of one crutch sank deep into the wet sand. He looked over his shoulder. "Coming, or are you still chicken?"

Brandon looked around at us. No one was stopping him. He waded after Doug into the tide. The rest of us gazed after them.

"You can tell neither of them is good at math," Nate offered. "The physics don't support this. The waves are too high. And if they get deep enough for Doug to stand without his crutches, they'll be too deep to punch each other with any force."

"My money's on Fox," said a football player. "That guy's nuts."

"Money?" Connor repeated.

The boys knelt on the beach and pulled out their wallets, discussing terms. When I looked out at the ocean again, Doug and Brandon had disappeared. Clouds had rolled in, covering the full moon. The black ocean and the black night were one.

"Zoey."

I looked beside me to see who dared disturb me observing my boyfriends clobber each other. Stephanie Wetzel. "Yes, Stephanie?" I asked. "Brandon was mine first, but you're welcome to him. So whatever you want to tell me, we really don't need to have that conversation."

She stepped closer and said breathlessly, "I can't stop Brandon. There's no way he'll stop now with the whole football team watching. You have to stop Doug."

"They both deserve whatever they get," I told her.

"You don't understand!" she shrieked. "I have a pool at my house. Wednesday night after your swim meet, Brandon came over."

"It's okay," I said. It wasn't okay. She and Brandon were cheaters. But I was a cheater too. Anyway, I was so furious at Doug that I didn't have much emotion left for Stephanie Wetzel. "Brandon told me you've been together."

"It's not okay! I found out Brandon can't swim."

I sucked in a breath. "Oh God." That's why Brandon had refused to take a promotion to lifeguard at Slide with Clyde. And that's why I couldn't see or hear him and Doug now. I pictured it all. The stormy surf had swept Brandon out over his head. Doug had tried to grab him, but his waterlogged cast weighed him down. They were already gone.

And I'd just said they deserved what they got.

I kicked off my shoes, wiggled out of my jeans, and shouted, "Brandon can't swim!" to anyone in hearing before I dashed into the black water.

17

I swam like demons were chasing me, like my boyfriend was drowning in front of me. When I reached the spot I thought they'd be, I tread water and shouted into the darkness, "Doug!"

"Zoey!" he shouted back, faintly over the roar of the ocean, way down the beach where the current had swept them.

I swam in that direction. Then I felt the current catch me too. It pushed me along too fast for comfort until suddenly, thankfully, I tripped over a warm body in the cold water and reached down to grab it.

Instead of grabbing me back, he shook my hand loose and struggled to the surface on his own. Doug panted, "Brandon can't swim. I've got him. Help me," and he was underwater again. There was no way he would let Brandon go, and there was no way I would let Doug go. We would all go down together. I took one last breath.

"Zoey, we'll get Brandon," Stephanie said, swimming past me. Another junior girl followed her, and they both dove under.

A wave crashed on top of me and pushed me down. In the blackness I put out my hands for Doug and felt only the sandy bottom where I didn't expect it. I didn't know up from down.

And then I felt him. Put my arms around him. Shoved off from the bottom as hard as I could and kicked until I ran out of breath, kept kicking past that threshold where I *had* to take a breath, kept kicking.

We hit the cold night air and both gasped.

"I'm okay," he heaved. "Get Brandon."

"We've got him," a girl shouted.

"I've got Doug," said Mike gliding beside me. "Zoey, just get to shore."

"We've got her," Keke and Lila said. One of them put her arm across my chest and said what lifeguards say. "Stop struggling and relax."

I didn't want to struggle and take them down with me, so I lay back in the water and let them tow me. I knew how to do this. I'd taken my turn being the victim in months of lifeguard training. I glided across the surface, the water cold but seeming warm compared with the colder air. I looked up at the sky and saw a universe of stars.

Closer to shore they handed me off. A boy's solid arm wrapped around me. I could tell from the shouts that Doug and Brandon were handed off too, a lifeguard relay.

My back raked across the sand, and the strong arm let me go. I flipped over and crawled the rest of the way up the beach to collapse in the frigid wind, one of a long line of parallel bodies. I allowed myself three deep breaths to recuperate, then sat up to look. "Brandon," I said, finding his bulk on the sand. I called, "Is Brandon okay?"

"He's okay," the junior girls called back, all four of them in unison.

Beside me, I touched Doug's soaked T-shirt stuck to his hard, flat stomach. "One," I said. There were seventeen people on the swim team, and I had to make sure we were all accounted for. "Two." I counted aloud to sixteen. "Where's seventeen? Who are we missing?" My heart beat frantically as I stood up and scanned the dark beach. "Oh God, where's number seventeen?"

"*You're* number seventeen," Doug said.

"Oh." I fell to my knees in the sand beside him. "I need another nap."

"I need another beer," Gabriel called. Boys cheered their agreement.

"I need another cast," Doug said. "And some crutches. My dad's going to kill me."

I put my hand on his stomach again. I was still mad at him. Seeing his life pass before my eyes hadn't changed that. But I felt better with my hand on his stomach. "I'll take you to the emergency room."

"I'll call my brother to take me," he said.

"I want to take you," I insisted.

"I'll get your dad's car all wet."

"Serves him right. That's what you get when you go out of town and give your daughter the keys to the Benz. Everyone knows seventeen-year-olds are irresponsible." I sat up and yelled down the line, "We could have died out there. The whole high school swim team plus one running back, gone. And you know what the people on the beach would have said? 'It all happened so fast.'"

Lila piped up, "It is *amazing* how quickly we can be stupid."

Mike snorted laughter, and Keke cackled, "Lila, I love you."

"You wouldn't say stuff like that to each other in public if you could see yourselves," said a football player walking over. "Did you *all* take your pants off? The swim team really knows how to throw a party."

Keke laughed. "You have no idea."

"THE LOVEBIRDS ARE BACK!" SAID A doctor in a long white coat over pink scrubs. She brushed my damp bangs aside. "How's the head?"

I glanced down at Doug filling out forms. He sat in a wheelchair with a blanket around his shoulders. We both looked like we'd half drowned in the ocean. It was a wonder the doctor recognized us. We must have made quite an impression last week. Of course, then we'd been soaked with rain, so we probably looked similar now.

Doug tried to say something to the doctor but coughed instead. All the way from the beach, he hadn't said a word. Now he coughed, and coughed, and finally hacked out, "Zoey still doesn't remember much about that night. Is that normal?"

"Oh, sure," the doctor said. "When I was in junior high, I was break dancing on roller skates one afternoon and you can imagine how *that* ended. I fell and hit my head. At least, that's what my friends told me later. They also told me I'd been shopping for new leg warmers earlier in the day. All I remember is sitting up in the middle of the roller-skating rink, screaming, 'Where are my leg warmers? These aren't my leg warmers!'"

Doug and I looked at each other. Doug raised one eyebrow.

"My memory of that afternoon never did come back," she said. "But twelve years later I graduated from medical school, so I must be okay."

"You could have told me that before!" I wailed at her. "It would have made me feel a lot less crazy."

"I *did* tell you that before." She grabbed a file from the counter and disappeared through a door into an examining room.

Doug scrawled something across his last form, set a soaked insurance card on top of it, and handed it all to the nurse. I wheeled him back through the double doors into the empty white waiting room that was way too familiar to me. I positioned him by a seat where I wouldn't be staring at those doors again, and I sat down next to him.

"I guess you don't want to hear why," he said softly.

With my eyes on the gray specks in the white tile floor, I said, "I'm here, aren't I?"

Doug talked in a monotone, staring at the blank white wall opposite us. "That Monday night after I saw you here,

I was so worried about you. I was afraid to call you because I didn't want to get my brother in trouble with your dad. I looked for you at the beach party. The next day I expected to hear this big hullabaloo at school. I thought the whole swim team would support you. I never heard a peep. But football and swimming dress out at the same time. I go in the locker room and there's Brandon Moore bragging about how he tapped your ass."

He held up his hands to shield his face like he thought I might slap him. When he saw I only glared at him, he slowly put his hands down.

"Brandon's words, not mine. You have a reputation for not putting out, so I knew something was wrong with you. I knew exactly what you'd done. I know that feeling. You have to do something. You have to change something radically, because you can't stay like you are for another second, or you're going to explode."

He was talking about running away to Seattle. I felt for his hand inside the blanket. It was ice cold.

He sighed. "But Zoey, the problem is that when you feel that way, your brain has already shut down. So whatever you do next to change your situation, it's bound to be stupid." He shook his head. "I tried all week to get you to call me. I tried to talk to you at the football game and screwed that up. And then, at the party, Brandon started talking smack about you again—"

"And you are so much better than him," I said, "because the

first words out of *your* mouth were, 'I'll bet you I can seduce Zoey Commander in the next two hours.'"

He turned to me for the first time, green eyes pleading. "I was trying to get you away from him, but I honestly could not have predicted we would do it. Still, if you were going to do it with *somebody*, I wanted it to be with me, because you could trust me." He laughed bitterly. "If it hadn't been for the wreck and everything that came after, that wouldn't sound the least bit ironic. I guess you don't want to hear that I've had a crush on you since seventh grade." He brought our hands out from under the blanket. His hand had been so cold and so still, I'd forgotten I was holding it. Now he placed my hand palm-up on his thigh and traced his finger to the tip of my perfectly polished pointer finger. "Or that I thought about you when I went to juvie. That I probably never had a chance with you long-term anyway, but now I'd sealed the deal." He traced his finger to the heel of my hand. "Those are explanations, but not excuses. Juvie is fond of that distinction." He traced his finger to the tip of my thumb. "Or that I couldn't stand to watch anything bad happen to you, because it was like it was happening to me too. Is that love?" His hand clasped my hand again and squeezed.

I swallowed. "It could be."

He kissed my hand. "Anyway, we shouldn't have done it. I shouldn't have let it go that far when I knew how vulnerable you were and I wasn't being completely honest with you. I realize that now, and I'm sorry." He squeezed my hand once more and let it go.

Suddenly the idea that this was the end of Doug and me seemed horribly wrong. No matter what path we'd followed to get here, now we sat side by side in the ER. Again. I whispered, "We shouldn't have done it so soon."

He kept staring at the opposite wall. But he went absolutely still. He'd stopped breathing.

Or was that me?

"I'd like to try again," I said. "Slower this time."

He turned to me. We shared a long look, and then he put his hand up to touch the corner of my mouth. I had the smallest lingering doubt that he was teasing me even now. And then he leaned forward to kiss me.

It was slow, all right, and very sexy, back to his thorough exploration of my mouth. In swim practice sometimes we took our pulses to see if we could keep our heart rates above a certain level for a long time. This kiss was as good training as any. While Doug was still in his cast, I would suggest we do this every day for his rehabilitation.

Someone bustled through the corridor. We kept kissing. Just as the double doors slid shut, the doctor called to us, "No PDA in the emergency room. I told you *that* before too."

I broke the kiss and blinked at Doug. "Did she?"

He nodded.

"Show me what we did."

He pulled my hands under his blanket. He was much warmer now. His lips found the most sensitive spot on my neck.

"I think a little of my memory of that night is coming back," I said, panting. "This seems so familiar. I remember being happy."

And that's when my phone rang. I pulled it out of my purse and looked at the screen blinking with the caller ID of the mental hospital, finally. I whispered, "My mom."

Probably it wasn't my mom. I couldn't get my hopes up. It was a psychiatrist calling to tell me my mom was worse, my mom was crazy, my mom was dead. The phone kept ringing. I took a deep breath and held it. Held on to this moment, not knowing who was calling or why.

Doug said, "Answer it or I will."

I exhaled and clicked the phone on. "Hello?"

"Zoey, are you okay?"

So she'd had another vision of my death. She was calling instead of visiting this time because hospital security had gotten wise to her. "I'm okay, Mom."

"I thought you were. What are you doing?"

My eyes wandered to Doug's lips. "I brought Doug Fox to the emergency room. He fell in the ocean and got his cast wet."

"Mmm-hmm," she said drily. "I know Doug Fox. I'll bet there's more to it than that." This was something she would normally say. This was something she would say if she were normal. But again, I didn't want to get my hopes up.

She went on, "Your father just called me all freaked out from the Los Angeles airport, coming back from Hawaii. He installed cameras at the house to watch you while he got married. In case this pseudoparenting scheme didn't contain you, his backup plan was to call his ex-wife in the insane asylum."

"Yeah," I acknowledged, "he was real keen on going, so I didn't point out this problem. I figured I could just stay out of trouble for a week. I almost made it."

"Mmm-hmm," she said again.

"But Mom, I swear, it didn't even cross my mind that I'd get in trouble for staying out late last night. I came home at exactly the same time I came home a couple of weeks ago, while Dad was still in town, and I didn't get in trouble then."

"Oh, you're not in trouble for coming in late." I could almost see her stroking her long blond hair away from her face with her manicured middle finger. "You're in trouble for going into your dad's office."

"I needed something," I grumbled.

She sighed. "This is totally up to you, Zoey. But if you want me to, I'll get custody of you again just as soon as I can. Okay?"

"Okay." I wanted desperately to move back in with her if she was normal. If.

"Just be prepared," she said. "When you do come back to live with me, you are *so grounded* for calling me the chicken that crossed the road."

I burst into laughter so big and good it hurt.

"What is it?" Doug asked, green eyes wide. He thought I'd finally lost it.

Between giggles I told him, "My mother is feeling more herself."

* * *

FIVE FRIDAYS LATER, I DROVE ALONG the beachfront road in Doug's Jeep, which I'd borrowed until he got his cast off. It had plastic sheeting for windows so I couldn't leave valuables in it and lock it. It was like driving a small pool dome. And it was lots of fun to drive. Not just the wind in my hair but whole-body wind. In short, the Jeep was quirky and high mainte-nance but worth the trouble. Like Doug.

Mom minded because the wind messed up her hair, but she put up with it. I was driving her back to her apartment after an hour of house-hunting and an early dinner at the Grilled Mermaid. Soon I'd pick up Doug for the football game, and afterward we were going out with Lila, Mike, Keke, and Keke's football player boyfriend she met at the beach— the one who had been so curious about our pants. It was a beautiful, warm October afternoon without a hurricane in sight, and so much weight had lifted from me lately that I felt a little giddy. I couldn't *wait* for tonight. I was just turn-ing onto the highway north toward town when blue lights flashed behind us.

"Did you run a stop sign?" Mom asked. "I mean, did you run *the* stop sign?"

I watched my rearview mirror until I recognized the police-man. "It's Cody. He's pulling me over to screw with me."

"Zoey!" Mom said in mock horror. "Can the language! Act sane or he'll drag us both back to the mental hospital. Good afternoon, Officer!" she sang past me through the opening that would be called a "window" in a normal car.

He nodded at her. "Counselor. I have orders from the chief to take you to the station. He needs to see you right away about that case. And Zoey, Doug wants you to meet him at the junkyard." He turned and sauntered toward his car.

"Oh, *that* case." Mom leaned over to kiss my forehead, then opened the passenger "door" and dropped to the ground in her wicked pumps we'd bought at the Destin mall last weekend. "Are you up for more house-hunting tomorrow afternoon?" she called back to me through the "window."

"Theoretically, but you'll have to drive. I'll bet this whole setup with Cody is an elaborate ploy for me to meet Doug and see him with his cast off. He was supposed to get it off this afternoon, depending on what the X-rays showed. And that means I'll give his Jeep back to him."

"Okay, then. I'll give you a call in the morning," she said without concern, as if she herself were part of the ploy. She walked along the shoulder, climbed into the passenger side of the police car, and applied more lipstick in Cody's rearview mirror. Yeah, I'd begun to have suspicions about her and the police chief. I would grill her about this tomorrow.

The country highway I'd driven down a million times looked like a postcard today with the trees turning yellow and red. In the flimsy Jeep I smelled asphalt and hay just as if I'd been walking along the shoulder. I negotiated the courthouse square in the center of town, turned off on another highway, and finally arrived at the junkyard. The Porsche had been moved in front of the office and released from its tarp to reveal the gaudy red sparkle paint in all its glory. As I parked, Doug got out of it and limped toward me across the sandy driveway with a big grin, without crutches.

"Look at you!" I exclaimed, springing from the Jeep to hug him.

He held out his bare leg for me to examine. "Look at me!"

"Does it walk okay?"

"It walks fine."

"More important, does it swim okay?"

"Coach is meeting me at the pool tomorrow morning to get me started."

"Wow, Coach is getting out of bed on Saturday morning? He must think a lot of your chances at a scholarship after all."

Doug gave me a smile and a small nod. Not like a diva. Like an athlete with confidence in his body.

"I want to come tomorrow morning," I said.

"I would love for you to come. You want to swim?"

"Yeah, I'll swim." Doug had been encouraging me to train harder and try out for the FSU swim team with him. He'd worked with me the last few weeks, and I'd actually qualified to compete at State. I wasn't doomed to come in sixth after all. Who knew?

"You brought me here to hand over the Jeep," I guessed,

tossing the keys up in the air and catching them. "Why here? Is there a ceremony for taking your cast off and getting to drive again? Is it like being saved from the junkyard?"

"No ceremony, but I do have something for you." He caught the keys the next time I tossed them, then gestured to the tacky Porsche. "Ta-da!"

"Ta-da," I echoed, not sure what he meant. "It's a car."

"It's *your* car," he said. "If you want it."

"*My* car? It's ugly."

"On a good day, with a recent wash and wax, your Bug looked like it had been partially digested."

"It's just . . ." I folded my arms. "I thought I would pick out my own car."

He nodded. "I thought you would too. When were you going to do that?"

I shrugged. "It just seems hopeless. There's still the whole thing I told you about. My dad won't let me buy anything I can afford."

"Yeah, but old Zoey would have fought a lot harder about that. Old Zoey would have a car by now." He raised one eyebrow at me.

I stared back at him. Why *didn't* I have a car by now? I couldn't see a way to solve the problem, so I'd pretended the problem wasn't there. Again.

"Truthfully?" he said. "Since your mom got out of the hospital, you've seemed manic on the surface, flatlining underneath." He passed his hand through the air, a flat horizon dividing sky and sea. Then he reached out to rub the back of my neck. "Are you tired?"

Was I? I was *so* glad my mom was back at work and in my life. I looked forward to moving back in with her. And with her support, I'd sat down with my dad while Ashley wasn't home and told him I did not want him insulting my mom in front of me anymore, I did not want to be watched by cameras, and I wanted an appointment with a shrink. Just to talk. I would see her for the first time next week.

Things were looking up, but it all took a lot of energy. When Doug pulled me toward him, I leaned my head against his chest. "Yeah, I'm tired."

His low voice vibrated through his chest and warmed me. "This thing with your mom. It's so much better now, but it's going to take a while for both of you to get over it. Do you want to talk about it?"

I took a deep breath and sighed. "I love you," I said into his chest.

"I love you too." He stroked one hand from the roots of my hair all the way to the ends. My scalp tingled.

"Can we talk about it later tonight?" I asked. "It's such a beautiful day." I couldn't see the beautiful day with my head against Doug's chest. I meant how the day felt, the sun warm on my shoulders.

"So accept this favor from me," Doug said. "I found a car for you. It's been sitting here since the junkyard owner's son went to college, like, a decade ago. It just needed one little repair, an air ... something."

I looked up at him. "Air intake?"

"Or something that pushed air out. It had something to do with air. Or water. Anyway, my brother's friend fixed it for you and checked all the hoses or whatever. The car's within your price range. And it has an air bag."

"Doug, that is so sweet." I squeezed his waist. "But you're doing the controlling thing again."

He held me away from him. "What's controlling about this?"

"For starters, you asked your brother to pull me over just now."

"Hm." He laughed. "Well, you don't have to buy this car. If you do buy it, you don't have to keep it forever. Just until you're not tired anymore and you feel like looking for another." He opened the driver's side door, ushered me in, and closed the door behind me.

As he rounded the car I took a few big whiffs, but I couldn't smell cigarette or pot or BO or a dead body in the trunk. Doug was right. I had a lot going on in my life, and he'd done me a favor. There was no reason for me not to buy this car, except that I hadn't been in command of every step in the process. I took another deep breath and exhaled slowly, letting go.

Doug crammed his tall frame into the passenger seat sooner than I expected. It would take a while for me to get used to him walking without crutches. The car filled with the scent of him, the scent of water. "I promise not to be controlling any-more, okay?" he asked. "Except I'll probably surprise you on your birthday. And maybe one other time per year, when you need a little boost." He nodded toward the key in the ignition. "Want to see how it drives?" He was so pleased with himself. His green eyes crinkled at the corners.

I grinned at him. "I want to see how it parks."

My heart raced as we watched each other from our sepa-rate sides of the car for one, two, three seconds.

Then we met in the middle.